Irene

Selected Writings of
Irene Paull

Midwest Villages & Voices
Minneapolis

The editors give special acknowledgment for assistance and support to: Michael Beckman, Steve Compton, John Crawford, Carl Davis, Rhoda Dizard, Alma Foley, Yank Levine, Toini Mackie, Bonnie Paull, Michael Paull, Gabrielle Rubinstein, Morris Schappes, Steve Trimble, June Ullom, the Minnesota Historical Society and Stanton Publication Services.

Irene Paull's work was previously published in the following publications: *Everybody's Studying Us: The Ironies of Aging in the Pepsi Generation, Every Woman Has a Story, Jewish Currents, Mainstream, Masses & Mainstream, The Midnight Sun: Stories and Poems on Old Age, Midwest Labor, Minnesota Labor, Minnesota Sings for Peace!, North Country Anvil, The People Together: A Century Speaks, 1858-1958, People's World, Poets of Today: A New American Anthology, Senior Power, The Timber Worker, Työmies Eteenpäin, We're the People,* and *The Worker.*

Photographs courtesy of Bonnie Paull and Gabrielle Rubinstein.

Permission to use Irene Paull's writings was granted by the estate of Irene Paull.

First edition
Library of Congress Catalog Card Number: 96-75442
ISBN 0-935697-07-1

Cover and section designs by Maria Mazzara
Manufactured in the United States of America

MIDWEST VILLAGES & VOICES
3220 Tenth Avenue South
Minneapolis, MN 55407

Editors

Gayla Ellis
Kevin FitzPatrick
Pat Kaluza
Linda Kelley
Meridel Le Sueur
Rachel Tilsen
Patricia Wilson

MIDWEST VILLAGES & VOICES

Many people contributed much time because of a belief that this was a worthwhile and vital book to publish. As a committee of editors, we selected which works to present and discussed how to bring a picture of Irene through her own words.

We have been publishing books for almost fifteen years, and every new book has its own unique excitement. Everything we do and experience is an expression of people's culture. We are all artists capable of sharing that culture beautifully in our own ways.

All books are the products of many hands and minds. Our everlasting appreciation for their work goes to the writer, the gatherers, the artists, the editors, the typesetters, the designers, the paper makers, the book binders, the printers, the distributors, the bookstores, and others. When you support small press publishers and independent bookstores, you keep alive people's culture in the midst of publishing corporations where books are commodities and the dollar is the bottom line.

We hope that whenever you pick up a book you think of all the workers and creators that made that volume for you.

Every generation has its struggles and its sufferings. No generation is ever a happy one. Enjoy each moment. It's from the despair and from the depths that we learn the most, not from the happy moments. Seek the truth. There's such a clean joy in truth, even when you're a victim of it. What will happen in the future belongs to the future. The moment depends on us.

IRENE PAULL

CONTENTS

Preface

PREFACE

The great energies, languages and nourishment of women are seized, hidden and violated by indifference and outright conspiracy in order to maintain the silence of women. It is a loss when the voices of women are muffled, lost or deliberately silenced.

Irene Paull is a voice of our time, of all the struggles, of the wars and depressions. Early she protested the violent, oppressed life of the Duluth harbor and the timber industry, the anti-Semitism, the exploitation of the immigrants in labor. She became a voice of the people, collecting the poems of lumberjacks.

A Jewish woman raised in a Ukrainian immigrant family and America, Irene wrote wonderful stories of a girl and her grandparents in the ghetto. She married a young labor lawyer, Hank Paull, and raised two children. She had such a wonderful face, her black flashing oriental eyes and her Semitic nose, stark around the Scandinavians of Duluth. Her colors were black and red. You could hear her laugh in a crowded room. Her ancient root spoke in her mode of writing.

Irene lived a life of struggle, from the *Sacco-Vanzetti* case to the defense of senior citizens editing their paper, from the Rosenberg executions to the march in Hiroshima. She went to Mississippi. She went to Cuba. Her magnificent notes, letters and reportage have never been collected and are even harder to find. The history of the Midwest and our radical women would be incomplete without a collection of her life's expression.

Neither of us would have survived without each other. We became close together in many ways: as writers, as women, as radicals and as humanists. In a way, we were very similar and yet different in our making a living, writing, trying to develop the woman in our own strong and deepest sense. I had a close, warm bond with her, working to develop as writers and as liberated women in the growing feminist movement.

The differences fed us. All of the time we both faced the terrible, deep self-immolation, female despair, abysmal loneliness. From the time you were born a female, you were impressed by your position—no choice of career, learning to be ladylike, meek, docile. Don't even try and be a writer. We were all struggling with our wounds in a new environment—the price of capitalism, the male day, volcanic explosion and possible death.

The independent strong woman was a bad woman, even in the radical press. Irene and I had a vision of the free new woman growing in her own pattern—a new crop, new protein, new communication, new connections, new conceptions—birthing out of terrible hunger and anger.

Her writing is often bitter. She hid a terrible anger and the guilt—reflecting the ancient struggle, not only of culture, but of the women in that culture.

All the silence and injury and humiliation. We tried to store up the courage thrust from our ancient woman roots. Out of the bloody earth wound, a new magnetic struggle was kept alive through the grief—new bloom exploding. What did she die of? I say she died of sexism, racism and capitalism.

This book strikes back at the silence, the social loss of her work being hidden, unpublished, unknown to us.

Oh, Irene, you roused and kept alive our feast! How fearful you were, how violent, the empty, the wound, the beating, like my mother over the prairie.

Oh, Irene, together we protected and fought for a woman's strength, to preserve the fierce female identity.

Irene gives us this rich, literary eloquence. Farewell, beloved woman.

MERIDEL LE SUEUR

k. School was dismissed. And everywhere this warm, hazy,
ternoon, while other boys were running for their baseball ba
eir catchers' mitts and the small ones were scrambling for
gs of marbles, boys were dragging their feet toward the inev
ebrew Sc   ed up bel
sk, chant   cient lang
he Hebre   ak old bu
helling of   and toba
  Debora   usty pave
laying th   h other i
ass, to h   ller at a
rtunate I   h me a fas
ll ya, Pat   , come on
  Such a   urs of fre
fore sup   embers o
hencumbe   ool playgr
o play ja   ould thin
uld be w   th pity or
 at least g   born a gir
f such on   gs warme
  Just th   d her that
orning he   hank God

t born a woman." She had called him a liar but he had threa
prove it. She didn't press the point. Three hours to play
  Resentfully she walked along, talking to her Maker, as w
stom. "Now, God,"   e personal way she a
dressed Him, but w   byance instead of the
urteous supplication   d such pleas as "Dear
ease help me with my arithmetic." "Do you think it's nice f
ys to say, 'Thank God, I wasn't born a woman'? What ki
ayer am I supposed to say? 'Thank you, God, I wasn't born
a cat or a snake'? Are boys your chosen sex, God, like Jev

SECTION ONE
DULUTH

To Die Among Strangers

"Dummy!" cried Uncle Lev, his face a grimace of anguish. "You haven't brought in a good load a' cattle in a month! What are you waiting for, the Messiah?"

Papa sat hunched over, silent, blinking his one blue and one brown eye, twisting his powerful head in that perpetual nervous twitch, like a patient horse warding off flies. The dimple in his right cheek where a bull had gored him deepened and looked like a hole in his leathery, sun-burnt face.

"Bad market," he muttered, blinking and twisting his head.

"Bad market!" cried Uncle Lev, looking as if he were about to cry. "So I suppose you told Gus Lindquist, 'Hold your cattle, Gus. Don't sell. Hold 'em for a better market.'"

Papa was silent and Uncle Dave hurled him a glance of withering scorn.

"He had lotta trouble," said Papa.

"Lotta trouble!" cried Uncle Lev, springing up and pacing the floor. "You hear that? Lotta trouble, he says. And what about us? All we got is trouble. We'll go bankrupt with a dummy like you buying our cattle. Look, I'm asking you, Moe, what in hell is business? Business is buy cheap and sell high. Get that? Dog eat dog. That's business. It's looking out for number one. You're looking out for Gus but who in hell is looking out for you?"

"Is that how Pa taught you to buy cattle, you goddam dummy?" growled Uncle Dave.

"Gus was a friend a' Pa's. He liked Pa," said Papa, almost under his breath.

"Don't go tellin' me Pa was a goddam fool like you!" shouted Uncle Dave. "You keep Pa out of it!"

"Shut up, Dave!" snapped Uncle Lev, and then to Papa, wearily, as if he were talking to a child, "Times have changed, Moe. You can't get that in your head but they've changed. When Pa first started buyin' cattle in Dakota, wild horses were still roaming over Montana. It's a tougher world now, Moe. That's what I'm trying to tell you. You can't afford to give the other guy a break or he'll break you. It's him or you. I try to knock this into your head but it's like talkin' sense to a horse."

Papa sensed that Uncle Lev had spent himself and it was safe to change the subject.

"So Debbie's startin' school tomorra, eh? Kinniegarten."

All eyes turned suddenly on me.

I had been watching this familiar scene in mute suffering. The fact that I did not understand it only deepened my depression as I contemplated tomorrow, the first day of school.

"For Chrissake!" cried Uncle Lev, his black eyes darting about like squirrels in his face, "Look at that kid, will you? Hey, everybody! Get a load a' that kid! Who gave her the spittoon haircut?"

"Her ma must a' put a chamber pot on her head an' cut around it," growled Uncle Dave in dour amusement. "Looks like she just come off the boat."

"Stand up and turn around!" cried Uncle Lev, his laughing eyes almost jumping out of his face.

I did not move. A tear was starting down my cheek.

His quickly changing face became contrite.

"Aw, I didn't mean that, kid. Come on, Debbie, that haircut ain't bad, ain't bad at all, is it, Dave, is it bad?" I saw him give Uncle Dave a threatening wink and Uncle Dave conceded grudgingly, "Naw, ain't bad."

"Looks different," clucked Uncle Lev. "Everybody should look a little different. No point everybody looking just like everybody else, eh, Dave? Here, have a stick of gum. Stop worrying. School ain't bad. I'm going to take you there myself tomorrow, take you right to the door, not a thing to worry about."

Papa tried to cheer me up.

"You know, kid, I used to go to that school myself—same school—bottom of the hill. Had me a little goat called Hymie. Used to follow me to school. Every day. Right through the door. Teacher'd say, 'Get that goat out'a here!' He used to wait for me out in the school yard but one day he got tired waitin' so you know what he done? He went an' butted in the glass door."

"Goat learned more than your Pa did," grimaced Uncle Lev good-naturedly, "only they both quit in the third grade."

4

Papa fell silent. I could almost hear the twitching of his eyes and the toss and twisting of his face.

Uncle Lev, I thought, torn by my love for him and my compassion for Papa, why do you call my father a dummy when he knows all he needs to know?

For all my five years I had lived *awf en barg* (on the hill) of this midwestern town, in a section dubbed "Little Jerusalem." It had been transplanted here from the old country and combined some of the spirit of the American frontier with the flavor and custom of a Ukrainian *shtetl*. We had two barns full of cattle, two horses, and the yard was always alive with matronly hens, arrogant roosters and a brood of little chickens peeping and scratching after them.

Sometimes I followed the cows to the pastures high above the town and sat while they grazed, looking out upon Lake Superior, stretching for endless miles to Canada. At other times I waited for the sound of cowbells and Uncle Dave in the summer twilight walking home the cows.

There was the synagogue and the familiar chanting and the bearded men going in and out. There was Shlaema's store where you could buy salt herring in barrels, kasha, salt crackers and penny candy. There was Lazar, the shoemaker, who also fixed harnesses for the horses. We were living in the house where Papa was born. Everything was loving and safe and familiar, and now they were sending me to school. It was only four blocks from my ghetto—at the bottom of the hill, but it was as foreign to me as if it had been located a hundred miles away.

I wanted to say to Papa, don't send me to school. You know all there is to know. You can teach me. I don't need to know any more. Just the clap-clap of the horse's hooves on the sunny country road above the town as we ride together in the black and red enameled buggy. The click of crickets in the fields of buttercup and clover and the tiny blue flowers that always grow on the hills. Below us the inland sea with the long boats trailing smoke. And your face not twitching so much—peaceful somehow, brown, and rocky, part of the earth and hills. You are so big and powerfully strong, yet you hold the reins gently in your sunburned hands.

I say, "Papa, let's stop awhile and let the horse rest," and you say, "Okay, kid, let 'im rest." I ask you questions like, "Papa, why do they call pigs 'pigs'?" And you answer, "Because they're piggish, that's why. You ask foolish questions." And then the buggy turning into Chris Westlund's farm, the smell of manure, the lowing of cattle, the chunking sounds of pigs feeding and the cluck of chickens. And Chris coming out of the barn wiping the milk off his hairy red arms. And Papa and Chris slapping each other on the back. "Well, how are ya, you ole coot, eh? Well, what do'ya know, you old son of a gun! Ain't seen ya in a dog's age. How's the world treatin' ya, eh? Well, ain't that fine. For Chrissake, ain't that fine!"

And gathering violets and wild iris in the swamps to the steady hum of Papa's and Chris Westlund's voices—why did I have to go to school? What more did I need to know?

I was crying bitterly now but Papa had no comfort to offer. He sat, blinking at me, with his one brown eye and one blue.

Baba, my grandmother, tried to come to my rescue.

"Why does she have to go so soon?" she asked. "Let her wait another year. She's only a baby. What is the big rush to send her there among the Gentiles?"

I looked hopefully at my grandmother but intercepted the flash of my mother's eyes. On this issue her mother-in-law was not going to have her way.

"She will go to school when all the others go," said Mama. "I would have given my right arm for the right to go to school. Without education a person can die of thirst on a sea of fresh water." And from Papa's silence and Mama's look I knew that school was inexorable. Nothing in the world could intervene for you. It was like death. When Grandpa died they put him in a box and carried him away and nobody, nothing could ever bring him back. Nobody, nothing could keep me out of school. Tomorrow would come and I would have to go.

And now it was tomorrow. Uncle Lev held me tightly by the hand as I plodded with him down the hills, my heart as heavy as my feet clad in clodhoppers from another era.

"Look, kid, you're gonna get an education. You should be happy. You're even going to college some day. That's what I wanted to do. Get the hell out'a this town. Be an engineer or something. Any goddam thing but cattle. Education is worth more than all the goddam cattle in the St. Paul stockyards and here you're cryin'." He held my hand so tight I winced.

There it was. The great brick building where I would begin my sentence. There was the school. Named after some man Uncle Lev admired called Benjamin Franklin.

Uncle Lev rushed me quickly up the steps and into the hall and left me there. Then he ran. I tried to run after him but he turned and waved me back.

I stood alone in the big strangely smelling hallway and looked around. There were children everywhere. They were chattering to each other. The mothers were kissing the youngest ones goodbye. But they looked different from me. The girls had pretty curls, most of them blond. And some had braids tied with bright ribbons. They wore short, stiffly starched dresses above their knees, half socks and patent leather slippers. I looked down at my heavy shoes and the thick black cotton stockings. My dress was of a heavy red and black plaid cotton reaching almost to my ankles. And my lank dark hair was bristling about my head in a spittoon haircut! I was different. It made me feel as if I were in the middle of the lake, drowning, and there was nobody to help because nobody even knew that I was there.

At this point a tall gaunt lady with white hair and thick glasses that made her eyes look like an owl's took me by the wrist and drew me into a big room. There were lots of little red chairs around low red tables. She sat down at the piano and played some kind of marching tune while a younger lady marched us around the tables until everyone of us had a place. We stood there until the old lady, fixing us with her great owl's eyes, gave us our first orientation.

"Now, if any of you want to go to the toilet," she said, "raise your hand. If you have to go number one, raise one finger. If you have to go number two, raise two fingers. Does everybody understand?"

The children answered, "Yes, teacher." My lips moved but I knew I wasn't uttering a sound.

"Now, sometimes you only think you have to go, but if you wait long enough, you find out you really don't have to go that bad. In fact, if you try hard enough, you can hold it until class is dismissed. I don't like my children jumping up every minute and running in and out. If you have to raise your hand, be pretty sure you really need to go. Understand?"

Again the class replied, "Yes, teacher," and again no word issued out of me.

The young teacher passed out paper and crayons and scissors. I touched them gingerly. I had never even seen colored crayons before. I watched the other children scribbling with them on the paper but I did not dare touch them. They were not mine.

I watched the children cutting little figures out of colored paper. Everybody seemed to know exactly what to do as if they had done it many times before but I didn't know. I played with chickens and followed the cows to pasture. I played with dolls made out of clothes pins. I played hopscotch in front of the synagogue, but I didn't know how to do what all these children seemed to know how to do.

The children were giggling and talking to each other but nobody talked to me. I sat frozen in the little red chair, gripped in a horrible anxiety. What if I had to go? What if I had to raise my hand?

I pictured myself raising my hand and the eyes of the old teacher fastened on me. I once saw an owl staring at a mouse just before it spread its wings and pounced on it. "If you really want to, you can hold it until class is dismissed," she would say and everybody would turn around and look at me and giggle.

I pictured all the kids looking at my outlandish clothes. I pictured them giggling to each other, "Spittoon haircut! Her mother must have put a chamber pot on her head and cut around it!" And with everybody tittering behind my back, I pictured myself walking out of the big room and down the hall and then not even knowing where to go!

And as I sat anxiously contemplating this eventuality, I was paralyzed by a slowly creeping horror—I had to go!

What could I do now? I tried to raise my hand but I couldn't lift it. It was like trying to scream in a dream. If I could only sit still like this until class was over everything would be okay—maybe. I would just sit tight like this and hold on. All around me as if from some great distance were the sounds of children chattering, cutting, scribbling. They sounded very far away like the voices of the doctor and nurse when they put a chloroform mask on my face the time I had my tonsils out.

And suddenly the voice of the old teacher struck me like a strap. "Everybody stand!"

We all stood.

"Push your chairs in!"

We pushed our chairs in.

"Oh, God, please help me raise my hand!" something in me was praying, but I couldn't raise it. And how could I hang on now, now that I was standing up. I shifted from one foot to the other. "Hang on! Hang on!" I was alone, all alone out on the vast lake, drowning, and there was no one to save me. They had sent me out of Little Jerusalem alone. They all loved me but they had sent me out to die of torment and humiliation—to die among strangers—if only the teacher wouldn't make us move.

But she was teaching us some strange jargon.

"I pledge allegiance to the flag…"

Now it was too late to raise my hand. They wouldn't even see my hand with everybody's hand stuck out like that. I couldn't stand it anymore. No, I couldn't hold on. I was going to go down—right in the middle of the lake. I was sinking.

The old teacher was back at the piano again and she was thundering, "Forward, march!"

My face was feverish and my hands clammy. I moved out of the little puddle by my chair. It was all over. The crime was done and now I must face the punishment, the execution.

The young teacher ordered us to sit cross-legged in a circle around her while she prepared to tell us a story.

Perhaps the morning would soon be over. Perhaps I would get away before I was discovered. If only the time would go fast and nobody would see the little puddle on the floor!

And then it happened!

The owl pounced! With a fierce, stern look the old teacher appeared, whispered something in the young teacher's ear and then took over.

"Children!" she said, fastening us with her huge bird's eyes, "I have something very serious and unpleasant to tell you. You know when you first came to school this morning, I told you about raising your hand if you have to go and one finger for number one? Do you remember?"

Again the chorus, "Yes, teacher." Again my tongue felt cleft to my mouth.

"Did any of you have any questions about it?"

"No, teacher."

"Well, I want you to know that one person in this class did not pay any attention to my instructions. That person piddled on the floor. Now I want that person to get up and come here to the front of the room. I want to know who that person was."

The children exchanged unhappy glances. I did not move a muscle of my face.

"Will that person come up here or will I have to find out for myself?" demanded the teacher.

Nobody moved.

"All right then," she snapped. It took me a while to realize the horror of what was happening. She was moving from one child to another feeling in each one's underpants. I watched her, fascinated, as she moved ever closer, as if I were watching preparations for my own hanging. And suddenly she was upon me, her claws about to clutch me, her eyes so huge they were ready to devour me.

"No!" I screamed.

Before she could lay her hands on me, I pushed her away with all my strength and tore through the open door. Up the hills I ran— away from these terrible strangers—back to the warmth of my family, my own people.

"Baba!" I screamed, "Mama!" It was Baba, my grandmother, who saw me first.

She clutched me in her arms. Her black eyes that always smoldered like live coals deep in their sockets caught fire and three thousand years of anger and hatred were blazing in them. "Oh," she cried, "a black year on them! What have they done to my child! Oh, may they roast in hell, the Gentiles and their schools and their teachers and all their works! May their schools burn down! May the cholera seize them! May the earth open and swallow them up and may they suffer a thousand years for all the suffering they have brought upon us!" She rocked me back and forth on her breast. To the music of Baba's curses my hysteria abated but I saw Mama looking down at me.

Her eyes were sorrowful, but unrelenting. From what one must do there is no escape. Tomorrow I would have to go back to school. And nobody could help me. Even Baba could not protect me from this fearful thing that every child must do. Nobody could know my suffering and nobody could share it with me. I was all alone in the world and tomorrow I would have to go—far from my ghetto—to die among strangers—but for this moment, for this precious moment at least, I was safe.

THE WRATH OF DEBORAH

School was dismissed. And everywhere this warm, hazy, spring afternoon, while other boys were running for their baseball bats and their catchers' mitts and the small ones were scrambling for their bags of marbles, boys were dragging their feet toward the inevitable Hebrew School. Another two hours of sitting cooped up behind a desk, chanting ancient prayers in a meaningless ancient language. The Hebrew School or *Heder* was housed in a dank old building smelling of decaying wood, old men and tobacco.

Deborah watched the boys shuffling along the dusty pavement, delaying the inevitable by stopping to wrestle each other in the grass, to hurl a pebble at a passing bird, or to holler at a more fortunate Irish lad running by with a baseball, "Pitch me a fast one, will ya, Pat? Just one, come on!"

Such a beautiful, balmy afternoon. Three hours of freedom before supper. Three hours to play with other members of her unencumbered sex. To turn handsprings on the school playground. To play jacks or hopscotch or jump rope. One would think she would be watching the boys' melancholy journey with pity or scorn or at least gloating over her own good fortune to be born a girl, free of such onerous responsibilities. But no such feelings warmed her breast.

"It's no fair," she was thinking with bitterness.

Just the other day Joel Nathanson had informed her that each morning he said a prayer in Hebrew that means, "Thank God I was not born a woman." She had called him a liar but he had threatened to prove it. She didn't press the point.

Resentfully she walked along, talking to her Maker, as was her custom. "Now, God," she chatted in the personal way she always addressed Him, but with a tone of annoyance instead of the usual courteous supplication that accompanied such pleas as "Dear God, please help me with my arithmetic." "Do you think it's nice for the boys to say, 'Thank God, I wasn't born a woman'? What kind of prayer am I supposed to say? 'Thank you, God, I wasn't born a dog or a cat or a snake'? Are boys your chosen sex, God, like Jews are your chosen people?"

She watched her own two brothers straggling after the other boys as they disappeared into the gloomy catacombs of the decaying building, and for some reason, perverse and incomprehensible even to herself, for she loved her brothers, she snarled, "Snotnoses!"

She strode into the kitchen and flung her books on the table and hoisted herself up on the sewing machine, watching Mama.

"It's no fair," she announced.

"Now what?" said Mama. It was really not a question.

"Why do you force the boys to go to *Heder* and you don't force me?"

"*Suffragetke!*"

"I want an answer!"

"So go to *Heder*, who's stopping you?"

"Does anyone force me? No!"

The back door creaked and Grandpa Posletsky came in carrying his basket of fish. Deborah ran to him and kissed his grizzled face.

"Grandpa, why doesn't Mama force me to go to *Heder* like she forces the boys? Why can't girls go to *Heder*? Why do they only force boys?"

"May you live a hundred and twenty years!" cried Grandpa, his bright eyes setting fire to the dry, yellow parchment of his face. "And why shouldn't you go to *Heder* if you want? Raisel, what kind of a business is this? A child famishes for want of learning—she faints for the bread of knowledge, and you give her a stone."

"Who's not letting her?" cried Mama. "If this little *suffragetke* of mine wants to be the only girl in the *Heder*, tell me who's stopping her? I say go, so she says that's not good enough. I have to force her. It's not bad enough that she wants to be one girl in a whole *Heder* full of boys, but she wants me to force her yet!"

"So if she has under one hair of her golden head more sense than those blockheads have in their whole skulls, you would deny her learning just because she is a girl?"

Mama carefully laid down the iron on the stove and leaned over the ironing board. She gave Grandpa a cold, penetrating look, so piercing, so full of irony, that his parched, yellow face withered under her eyes. Even his body seemed to shrivel as he retired into some secret corner of himself.

"That is strange talk coming from you, my dear father," she said. "Do you remember a little town of Peryaslov where I, a young girl, your daughter, a girl with just such a head of gold as you describe, pleaded with you, 'Father, dear father, please let me go to school. Teach me. Give me a chance to learn like you give my brothers. I thirst for learning. I am famished for knowledge.' And my father brushed me aside as you would brush a cockroach from a roll of noodles. 'Learn—you? What is there for you to learn? A woman's sense is as short as her hair is long. Learn to make *gefilte* fish. Learn to hem diapers! What more is there for a woman to learn!' " Mama picked up the iron again and set it down on the folded tablecloth with a heavy hand. " 'She faints for the bread of knowledge and you give her a stone.' How many stones did you give me, little father, when I fainted for bread?"

Grandpa did not answer for a long time. He sat shrivelled and still, as if he had fallen asleep. Then he said gently, "This is a new world, my daughter. In this new world a woman is as good as a man."

Deborah went to *Heder.*

The novelty of having a girl in the *Heder* soon wore off. She was placed in a class with students much younger than herself since she was just beginning, but with private lessons from Grandpa and diligent application, she moved quickly through the lower classes until she was in class with boys almost at her own age level. Yet *Heder* disturbed her.

It was not the taunts of the boys. She was not afraid of boys, having so many brothers and male cousins of her own. Ever since she could remember she had taken care of small boys—feeding them, diapering them, coaching them with their lessons and batting them on the ears. Boys were just other girls' gritty-faced brothers. A few taunts from them and she squelched them grandly with a commanding presence and a lofty contempt summarized in one sentence, "Wipe your nose!"

It was the way they taunted the teacher, Moishe.

He was a refugee from the pogroms of Kishenev.

In the evening when the elders of the family got together, Deborah would hoist herself on the sewing machine in the kitchen and listen as they described the pogroms from which all of them, in a sense, were refugees, but particularly Moishe. They said he had lost his whole family in the Kishenev pogrom, then wandered all over Europe, from relative to relative, and then managed to get to America just before the First World War.

Tears filled her throat when she thought of Moishe. Tall and lanky he was, with tremendous feet, like Ichabod Crane, and he had a long, melancholy face like a tormented horse. She had seen how an old horse looked with sad-eyed resignation when kids pelted him with stones, and that is how Moishe looked when the boys raised the devil in his class. They threw spitballs, rolled nuts and marbles down the aisles, pummelled each other, interrupted his lessons with catcalls and laughter. They meant no malice. It was just that they were trapped, and Moishe was their jailer.

Completely at a loss to maintain discipline, Moishe accepted his melancholy fate and conducted his class like one serving out a daily sentence. It was his bread and, to some, bread is not easily won. It was only when Deborah rose to recite that his face would lose for a moment that look of tortured resignation. "Go on," he would urge, encouragingly, in Yiddish, "go on…" and always he would conclude with the same words, shaking his head, "*Goldene kopp*!" (head of gold).

She was an oasis in which he slaked his thirst.

Sometimes he even smiled when she walked home with him after class, running to keep up with his long, awkward strides. He was not just Moishe to her. He was the symbol of her tormented people. He was the wandering Jew incarnate. But the more she identified herself with Moishe, the more she thought of the family he had left in bloody graves to wander restless and alone over Europe unable to find a bit of earth to call his native land, the more unbearable became the conduct of her colleagues.

Just last night she had fallen asleep daydreaming how she would have acted if she had been in Kishenev. How she would have gone into the village and taken from a Cossack the biggest white horse in the Ukraine. She would have mounted her steed like Joan of Arc and galloped up and down the Ukrainian ghettos summoning her men to battle, and they would all have mounted horses and flashing sabres like the Cossacks; they would have vanquished the enemy and Moishe's family would have been saved.

And thus she was dreaming on this particular day in October when the balmy sweetness of Indian summer drifted in from the open window with a maddening intoxication. Across the street in the open lot you could hear the boys bawling, "First base!" And the squeals of the little kids shooting marbles. The captives of the *Heder*, usually uncontrolled and undisciplined, were "stir crazy." The catcalls, the scraping feet, the general restlessness created such confusion that Moishe could hardly hear when someone got up to recite, but he plowed through patiently, quietly serving out his sentence, earning his bread by the sweat of his brow. Sometimes he threw an agonizing glance at the slowly moving hands of the big wall clock as if thinking aloud the core of his philosophy, "And this too shall pass away…"

It was Deborah who found his torment unbearable. Dreaming her dreams of liberation, she suddenly asked herself how she could sit there unperturbed and let her beloved friend, Moishe, the martyred symbol of her martyred people, be tormented by these monstrous boys without even coming to his defense. What kind of Joan of Arc was she to dream of saving Moishe's family from the pogromists of Kishenev and yet sit here in the United States of America, a free country, and let this den of lions tear him to pieces! "You're pumping out my blood," he remonstrated sadly and futilely as he tripped over an apple a boy was rolling down the aisle. "You're eating out my heart."

Deborah had as much as she could stand, and all of a sudden she leaped to her feet.

"Stop!" she cried.

Silence fell, with the suddenness of a thunderclap.

Thirty pairs of amazed eyes turned around to look at her. Beady little eyes. Crafty, restless little eyes. Studying her in stupefied silence.

"How can you have the heart," she cried, "to torture Moishe like this? Don't you know he's a poor immigrant and his whole family got murdered in Kishenev? So he can't understand English! Does that mean he isn't smart? He hasn't got a single relative in the world and here you are throwing spitballs and laughing and horsing around and trying to trip him with apples—I saw you, Jake, I saw you—and none of you are paying any attention—aren't you ashamed to treat a poor man like that? Aren't you?"

She stood there, fists clenched, consumed with her own fire. The silence was so profound that Moishe himself, standing in front of the class, his mouth open, his hands hanging down like shovels, was completely stunned and bewildered, as if he had been struck. He had not understood a word she had said.

And suddenly she realized the enormity of her accomplishment. Like the Gettysburg address. They said that after Lincoln made his Gettysburg address everybody was quiet— nobody said a word. Nobody even applauded. It was too deep. But they remembered forever. It went down in history. And she had accomplished such a miracle. She had made a second Gettysburg address.

Glowing in the tense and miraculous silence she had wrought, warm with tenderness now toward a recalcitrant male humanity that is nevertheless susceptible to noble sentiments when presented with proper passion, she was not prepared for what followed.

Thirty pairs of beady little eyes had been watching her like frogs charmed by a snake. Thirty bodies had been completely motionless, bewitched. And all of a sudden the spell was broken. Hell broke loose in the middle of bedlam. The room became speckled with a squall of catcalls, hoots, whistles, shouts, shrieks and raucous laughter. Boys wrestled each other because they couldn't wrestle her. But they pointed at her, laughing at the ridiculous sight of her, and wrestled again. Marbles rolled down the aisles and up the aisles and spitballs flew at Moishe. School was impossible.

And in the middle of this holocaust she saw Moishe. He was looking at her. Looking at her with tears in his mournful eyes. But not with tears of gratitude. He was looking at her like a man whose dearest friend has just delivered him a mortal blow. Such a look of abysmal reproach Caesar must have borne Brutus as he said in his deep, melancholy voice, "You too, Debbele—you too? I did not have enough to bear from these jackals who pump out my blood, who eat out my heart—but now you too have joined the camp of the enemy and have so little mercy upon me as to cause this infernal disturbance?"

And there she stood in the back of the classroom, stunned and defeated, alone with her blunted wrath. She was so dumb she did not even put up her arms to ward off the hail of flying spitballs. Somehow, she did not understand quite how, her foaming steed had been struck from under her and she was grounded—grounded upon a desolate island of martyrdom. Waves of injustice battered her lonely shores.

THE WAR AGAINST THE GENTILES

Across the street from our house was the Polish Catholic church, a great red brick structure crowned with a threatening cross of gilded wood. The house was on a corner lot, built on a hill above sloping lawns, and the whole property was surrounded by a steel picket fence and two steel gates. The time was the era shortly after the First World War when waves of post-war immigration carried to the new world like rotting bilge water all the bitter hatreds, prejudices and venoms of Tsarist Russia and Poland. The church faced our house, a solid citadel of ancient hatreds in a brand new city of the Middle West.

Every time Molly Lumpkin passed our house dragging her little brother by the hand, the gate was wide open, blocking the sidewalk. Molly would give it a fierce kick, and if the kick didn't do the trick, she would swing it shut with such violence that it hit our cement stairs with a resounding smack.

This enraged me.

"You kick that gate once more, Molly Lumpkin, and I'll come down there and personally tear your hair out."

"Says you," mocked Molly Lumpkin.

"Yeah, says I." I frowned threateningly, and Judy, my little sister, always my right-hand corporal, stuck her tongue out at Molly, "Yah, yah, yah."

"I'll get my brother Irving after you," warned Molly. "He'll tear your old gate off."

"I'll plaster you both with manure from my father's horse," I countered, warming to the subject. But by this time Molly Lumpkin had passed out of hearing and my threats fell on silence.

"Boy, how I hate that girl!" I summarized and my sister Judy cheerfully agreed.

But this was only a minor hatred in my troubled life. For the Polish Catholic church stood there always, facing me squarely: cold, menacing, wearing its great gold cross, the kind on which Christ died. And I dreaded the morning and evening mass. The church doors would be flung wide open and, with an insatiable curiosity bordering on the morbid, my little sister and I would strain our necks to peer into the inscrutable mysteries of Catholic ritual.

"Look at them," I would sneer, nudging Judy, "they're sprinkling themselves with holy water." But I would always feel a slight inner disturbance at the mysteries of a strange religion that utterly excluded me and all my kind.

There were two ordeals to pass through each day: morning and evening mass; the Polish boys on their way to church.

"Christ-killer!"

"Sheenies!"

"Hebes! Kikes! Dirty Jews!"

And those with a talent for mimicry had special tidbits like, "Izzy, you got fresh feesh today, no!"

And the inevitable shouting back, the screaming until your lungs were fit to burst, "I'm proud I'm a Jew! You hear that? Proud! Proud! Proud!"

"Why do they call us 'sheeny'?" I demanded of my mother.

"Don't worry about it," Mama said, " 'sheeny' means 'shiny' and 'shiny' means 'bright.' They just mean Jews are bright."

I withered my mother with my contempt.

"All right, so they don't mean that. Go tell them 'sticks and stones will break my bones, but names will never hurt me.' "

"That's not so. Names hurt me more than sticks and stones."

"So go do them something. What do you want from my life? It's their world."

"Why is it their world! We're God's chosen people."

"He shouldn't have done us such a favor. For my part we would have been better off if he hadn't chosen us."

"I don't like the way you talk about God," I frowned at Mama.

"Oh, go away, leave me alone, *tsadik*. You remind me of your grandmother."

Among the Polish boys who tormented us at morning and evening mass Anton Markovsky would steal by, sheepish and blushing, trying to appear unnoticed, not daring to look the enemy in the face.

Anton had a crush on me. He would always pick me for his dancing partner in school, hang around me at recess. Once he left a bunch of violets on my desk without a name or a note but I knew who had left them—and big, handsome, blond Anton did not leave me unmoved. I pretended indifference but when he was unaware I would summarize him with a glance and find him good. A tragic thought occurred perpetually to impale my love. "I can never marry a Polack." Still I could not still the fluttering of my heart as I waited for Anton to go to the blackboard just to catch the shy, sidelong glance he would give me as he passed my desk.

It was not that I hadn't been in love before. A year ago, at the age of ten, Hyman Gold, a husky Jewish boy, had been in love with me. I knew this because once as he was coming out of my grandmother's yard he hurled a big bunch of lilacs in my face so hard it knocked me down. Another time in the school yard at recess, with all the kids looking on, he had leaped on me from the back and sent me sprawling on my face, crying and scolding, while he ran away and the kids shouted, "Hymie loves Debbie, ha! ha! ha!"

I pretended to anger and indignation for my knee was bruised and my hand bleeding, but I was singing inside with jubilation. And many an evening, sitting on the sewing machine in the kitchen, I tried to broach the subject with my mother. I had wanted to say simply, "Mama, Hymie Gold and I are in love."

But I never had the courage. And now this much deeper, much more mature and disturbing love for Anton I could not even consider discussing with my mother. I would suffer its pain and poignancy in bitter silence. Such a love was treachery to my people, blasphemy to my God.

My mother was no help to me in the torment of morning and evening mass. She let me fight my own battles. What was special about them? Battles like mine were just part of being a Jew. So I would sit, thinking bitterly as the boys passed by. Thinking as I shouted back till I was hoarse, "Proud that I'm a Jew—proud! proud!"

And in full view of the enemy, when I saw my grandfather laboring up the hill carrying his basket of fish, as a supreme gesture of defiance, I would run to meet him, throw my arms around his wrinkled neck, kiss his yellow, bearded face, and walk up the hill with him, carrying his fish basket on my arm.

"You killed Christ!"

This was the unkindest cut of all. Suffering Christ. I had never dared to mention to anyone, not even to Mama, that I loved this Jew who had driven the money changers out of the Temple, yet whose face was so gentle. "Love thy neighbor as thyself," he had said. Perhaps some terrible plague would strike me down someday for loving this tender Jew called Jesus—could it really be that I had crucified him?

At night I would get down on my knees at the window of my room when Judy was asleep and stare at the golden cross that burned with a pale light in the northern moon. "God," I would whisper, "give me a sign, just give me a sign. If he was really your son and we killed him and you hate us and want us to burn in hell because we don't believe in him, give me a sign, make the cross catch on fire, do something—and I'll believe anything you want." My eyes would be riveted to the golden cross but God gave no sign and the cross remained cold and stolid in the moonlight.

The taunts of the boys increased in virulence and skill. It was as if all the hatred deflected temporarily by the war to the Germans had been redirected toward us.

Then one day they discovered their real power. I could withstand the insults directed against me and against my grandfather. But they discovered there was one insult I could not stand. As they passed they would sing in a chorus:

"Holy Moses, King of the Jews,
Bought his wife a pair of shoes.
When the shoes began to wear
Holy Moses began to swear..."

And then came the usual routine: "Fish peddlers! Hebes! Kikes! Christ-killers!"

And this was more than flesh could bear. I could endure all personal insults. But to attack the great Moses, the very foundation of my heritage—to ridicule and belittle him who had struck the whip from the hand of the taskmaster when we were slaves in the land of Egypt—to recite vile verses about him to whom God himself had spoken face to face and to whom he had given the law on the peak of Mt. Sinai—this was a crisis. It demanded action.

"Judy," I announced grimly, "we are going to organize a war against the Gentiles."

22

Judy nodded. It seemed like fun.

"We'll round up every Jewish kid in the neighborhood."

"Even Molly Lumpkin?"

"She's Jewish, isn't she?"

Judy caught her breath. This war was *really* serious.

No time was lost. In fifteen minutes I was at Molly's house, ringing the bell. She answered the door, dragging the inevitable little brother by the hand. Molly herself was aware that this was no ordinary crisis that brought her mortal enemy to her door.

Molly too had heard the new routine of "Holy Moses," but it was not that that had enraged her so much as the fact that they had hit her brother Sammy with a spitball. She looked interested.

"Be at my house tonight after supper and we'll figure it all out," I said. "You can be a major."

"What are you?"

"General."

Molly got cagey. "Is that bigger than major?"

"It's the biggest." Then tautly, "It was my idea, you know."

Molly pouted, then thought better of it.

"Okay," she said, "I'll bring my brother Sammy."

My little army was doomed to defeat and defeat it was. Judy had taken the lump on her head with her usual sweet stoicism but the other kids had run screaming to their mothers at the first counterattack. In fact I got a resounding scolding from aunts and uncles and angry Jewish neighbors. Why did I encourage five- and ten-year-olds to throw stones at the big Polacks who were twice and thrice their size? What did I want—to get the little kids killed? Why did I have to "start up with the *goyim*"? Weren't there enough pogroms going on in the old country, I had to start one here yet? They thought I had more sense, a big *moyd*, going on twelve, and usually so responsible with the children.

But Mama was hardest on me of all. Only she addressed me in the third person, directing her recriminations to my little sister as she pressed a cold knife against the blue welt on her forehead.

"Tell me," she demanded, "what did I do to deserve this? What kind of a holy flame burns in this child? On the eve of Yom Kippur she sets up an altar in the back yard and sacrifices a five-pound chicken. Why? Because it's the Day of Atonement and she is afraid

God is not on good terms with me because there are times when I give Him a piece of my mind. So God smells the chicken and His mouth waters. He licks His lip and says, 'Maybe this Raisel is not such a sinner after all. She burns a very good chicken.' My daughter, bless her, is doing me such a favor, putting me back in the good graces of God that one of these days I am going to clobber her good on both sides of her face.

"Then what does she do next? I look everywhere. I cannot find my rouge, my lipstick. I suspect something but how can I prove it? Sure enough I see the dog is coming out from under the house carrying my lipstick in his mouth. My *suffragetke* has buried them. This time she is guarding my morals. Only bad women use these things, she says, and anyway, I'm too old for such frivolities.

"Then I have a prophet too on my hands. God knows what they knock into her head at Sunday School—a black year on the rabbis, you should pardon the expression—but she goes around here with a 'Woe unto you for this,' and a 'Woe unto you for that,' as if I did not have enough woes already. Woe unto me, believe me, that I should have such a *tsadik* on my hands. I am a woman who has always had an open mind about such things, so the Lord punishes me by sending me his personal representative.

"Next, she wants I should adopt an orphan. 'It says in the Bible,' she says, 'we must protect the widow and the orphan.' May I be so bold as to ask why she is partial to orphans? Why not a widow or two? Maybe I could adopt myself a nice, plump little widow to complicate my problems?

"And now, now what does she do? Tell me. She organizes herself a little war against the Gentiles. She gets herself together a little army—all my enemies should have such armies—each soldier is big enough to promenade underneath the table, and she pits them against boys each one of them big as a teamster. And who gets hurt? The Polish boys? God forbid! No, you! *Shlimazel meine.* Always you are the lucky one. You are the one who gets the lump on your head. And do you cry even? God forbid! You must show your general, this *tsadik*, this *suffragetke*, how brave you are. How you are willing even to die for this Joan of Arc, the devil take her! War against the Gentiles! You hear that? For five thousand years they have pumped out our blood, but this *meshugene* of mine—she is going to put an end to it!"

I listened cheerfully as Mama poured on my head a stream of colorful invective. How well I understood Mama's curses! I remembered the time I was playing with Auntie Tanya in Baba Kerner's shed. Auntie should have known better. She was five years older than I but she tried to pull my beads away from me and I threw them at her and said, "Here, take them and choke yourself!" Auntie Tanya ran into the house and pretty soon the whole family knew what I had said and all bedlam broke loose.

"Her mother!" they cried. "That is what she teaches them!"

"Oh, mother of mine, God have mercy on us," Baba cried, wringing her hands, "that I should live to have such a daughter-in-law! A thousand plagues on her! Look what she teaches a Jewish child!"

I was trembling with fear and shame at the holocaust I had brought down on the head of my poor mother. How could I explain that Mama meant no violence? How many times had she cried, "A black death should seize you! May you be overcome with cholera! A black year to all my children! May the earth open and swallow you whole! May you go to the depths of hell! You are pumping out my blood! You are eating out my heart. Woe to the day I ever bore you!" She said these words in Yiddish, and in Yiddish this was not violence. This was just a tired mother crying aloud her frustration and exhaustion. I took no offense. I saw her standing over the washtub in the hot kitchen, the sweat pouring from her face, the house a turmoil, bread baking in the wood stove, the *gefilte* fish still unmade for the Sabbath, two cases of over-ripe fruit to be canned by sundown—and if she cried out, "A thousand deaths to you!" this was not violence. This was only my beloved mother crying aloud.

So I listened cheerfully as Mama cursed me. I knew it was not really me she was cursing as she pressed the cold knife to Judy's forehead. I knew she was crying out from every wound every pogromist had ever laid upon a Jew's flesh. And I was thinking, "They were just too big for us, but wait, I'll think of something." I did.

The sword had failed, but the pen was still at my disposal. I could write. Didn't the whole *shul* cry at the speech I wrote and recited at the Hanuka festival that ended up, "Next year in

Jerusalem!" Writing wasn't just to write. You wrote for a reason. And I had a reason.

For hours I scribbled away, entranced with the possibilities taking shape under my pen. Then, chuckling and laughing with delight I lined up all that remained of my local cohorts, Judy, Molly, a few miscellaneous cousins of varying stages of immaturity, and taught them the lines of what would be our secret weapon.

I lined the children up on the top of the slope on which the house stood. They were safely protected by the steel picket fence and the two steel gates and the stairs and slopes leading to the house. This time we had no plans to meet the enemy head on. We would remain standing on the slopes and, if necessary, duck swiftly into the house. We waited for evening mass. The boys came into view. Before the taunts could begin, we began to chant in a dreamy monotone:

"Jehoshophat Polski, the Polish priest, bought his wife a cake of yeast—" and there followed a ditty salted with what, to a child's mind, is the ultimate in vulgarity and mortal insult, having to do with a priest feeding his congregation bread kneaded with his feet and sprinkled with holy water, naively unaware that even the implication that the priest had a wife was an insult incredible beyond words.

The boys' mouths fell open as they passed. Speechless, they stopped to listen to the words, as if they believed the skies might crack open and thunder down fire at this blasphemous horror.

Seeing Anton sneaking by, head down, in the heat of battle I thought heartlessly, "You too! You too! You're one of them! Suffer because I hate you too!"

Even in that very first skirmish I could already savor the taste of victory. Too startled to shout back at the strange little chanting army, the boys hastened their steps to church. Relentlessly our voices pursued them and we were there again when mass was over. Our chanting voices, now raised in triumph, began again the blasphemous assault:

"Jehoshophat Polski, the Polish priest—."

To my wild delight, as the days wore on, I noted the boys were beginning to take a roundabout way of getting to church. They would go around the block and come into the church through a side door. Even if one of them was caught going alone to church by the regular route, he was not spared the horrible, taunting chorus:

"Jehoshophat Polski, the Polish priest—"

"You see," I summarized, when my little army sat with me watching the boys sneaking around to mass through the side door, "this will teach you the pen is mightier than the sword."

But life is terrible in its complexity. Nothing is ever neatly settled. Even a twelve-year-old knows that. It was shortly after this historic triumph that I approached Mama. The enemy defeated, my thoughts returned repeatedly to Anton, who was now wearing his first suit with long pants. His sidelong glances and blushes put me sorely in need of spiritual assistance. I wanted desperately to discuss these feelings with Mama. Had it been a Jewish boy, perhaps I could have discussed them. Or even an Irish or Swedish boy would not have been so difficult, though practically impossible. But a Polack—a mortal and irreconcilable foe—this was only between me and God.

"Mama," I said, "why don't you teach me a prayer?"

"What prayer?"

"Any prayer. All the Gentile kids kneel down and pray and they say prayers like 'Now I lay me down to sleep.' But I don't know any prayers. Not a one. I have to make up my own prayers. So all I have is conversations. I don't think that's nice—conversations. What if God doesn't like that?"

"My *tsadik* again."

"Stop calling me 'tsadik.' "

"So what's wrong with that? *Tsadik* means 'religious.' So you're religious—so you're a *tsadik*. What are you getting mad about?"

"You don't get along very well with God, do you, Mama?"

"I don't know, to tell you the truth. We've never had any conversations. He minds his business and I mind mine."

"Teach me a prayer."

"All right then. I'll teach. Say it after me. *Sh'ma Yisroel Adonoi Elohenu Adonoi Ehod.* 'Hear, O Israel, the Lord our God, the Lord, is One.' "

"Well?"

"Well what?"

"What else?"

"That's all."

"That's a prayer?"

"Sure that's a prayer. That's a good prayer."

"That sure is some prayer, that's all I can say."

"Stop shnorking!" cried Mama, "I am teaching you the greatest prayer in the whole world and you shnork. Do you know what this prayer is? To this little prayer your people were slaughtered, burned, tortured, beaten, boiled in oil. In the Spanish Inquisition they said, 'Eat pork or we'll break your bones. We'll tear you to pieces.' But they didn't eat pork and their bones were broken on wheels like sticks of wood. They were burned in fires but they died with this prayer on their lips. Now for my part they could have eaten pork and lived. I'm not a *tsadik* like you. To me it is all a superstition this business you don't eat pork and everything else for my part—but that's not the point. The point is they were willing to die for a principle, something they believed in. And it is something great to believe in too, because it means if there is only one God then all people are brothers. That's why they died with this last cry, *"Sh'ma Yisroel!"*—all down the centuries. Yes, this is a brave thing—to die for a principle. This is not something to shnork at. This is no 'Now I lay me down to sleep.' This is *really* a *prayer!*"

I trembled as Mama spoke. I saw my people burning. I saw them broken on wheels. I saw them dangling from the gallows. And I heard them crying their great prayer into the echoing abyss of centuries—*"Sh'ma Yisroel!"*—that there is but one God, one father—and therefore all men are brothers. Oh, I thought, Lord! Let me die for a principle someday myself. Let me be among the silenced great—my dead but ever living forebears. Let me be among those who can suffer to the ultimate extreme to stop the suffering of the world. Let me too die someday, if need be, crying *"Sh'ma Yisroel!"*

I dropped to my knees that night by the window looking out over the tops of the apple trees at the gilded cross on the spire of the Catholic church. And suddenly in an ecstasy of joy, a thought was born.

If there is only one God in all the world, and all men are brothers, then the Gentiles are our brothers too! I caught my breath. Even the Polacks!

I peered into the darkness of the fir trees. Oh what a world-shaking discovery! How it could change my life!

"God," I said confidentially, "maybe someday they'll realize that we're brothers and they won't hate us any more. Maybe someday there won't be any differences between anybody and everybody will get along. Isn't that so, God?"

God made no audible reply.

I dropped my head to the window sill. I was thinking of Anton. The beauty of him in his brand new suit. And the long pants. He was almost as big as a full-sized man. None of the Jewish boys was as big as Anton. The way that hunk of blond hair was always falling over one eye and the way he tossed his head to get it out of his face. And his shyness. And the way he held my hand when we danced "Coming Through the Rye." And how I wanted to press his hand and smile at him, but I didn't. I was remembering him sneaking past me with his head down as I stood at the top of the slope hurling vulgar insults at his priest.

"I wouldn't have done it to Anton, God," I apologized, "but you see, there was no other way. They were insulting Moses."

Suddenly with a surge of love I turned toward my Maker.

"God, dearest, will you please make it come out so everybody realizes that we're brothers by the time I grow up so I can marry Anton Markovsky?"

DULUTH "KASRILEVKA"

Who would have supposed that there could have been transplanted shortly after the turn of the century, in the nordic Duluth, Minnesota, a little colony of Sholem Aleichem's people from Kasrilevka? Zayda (Grandpa) Pozletsky used to say with pride, "I knew Sholem Aleichem, the great writer. He was my friend, my own brother. His Kasrilevka is only a false name for our village of Peryaslov in the Ukraine, and we are truly the 'little people of Kasrilevka.'"

I lived the first five years of my life in a divided world. One was the transplanted village of Peryaslov, and one was the sweet green of my native land. I liked to sit on the very top hills in Duluth, like the pastures above "Little Jerusalem," where Baba Kramer's cattle grazed in the clover, watching the long black ore boats move across the unsalted sea—"By the shore of Gitche Gumee, by the shining Big-Sea-Water."

We were "Jews without money." The aristocratic German Jews had their temple in the stylish section and looked down their noses at the newcomers on the high hill *(oif 'n barg)*, called "Little Jerusalem," a motley ghetto. Mama sewed buttons in an overall factory. Her brother, Eli, worked in a shop on Michigan Street as a glass cutter. Her sister Malle's husband was a carpenter, such a perfectionist no one could hire him by the hour. Her sister Dinha's husband carried stoves and sofas on his broad back for a furniture store. He was the family socialist, cursed and despised by my father's relatives who, as cattle buyers and earlier immigrants, looked down on him. But my mother's family shielded him— "What is so terrible about a socialist? Is he robbing them, that they curse him? What is so evil that the rich could part with some of their fat cattle so the poor could eat meat on Friday night?"

But in this poor ghetto everyone was tolerated, cared for. Mishka, the liar, Schmelke, the drunkard, Fishel, the *shlimazel* [an unlucky one]. "So what can we do?" they would shrug. "Fishel is a *shlimazel* and can never make a living, but after all he's our *shlimazel*—the Gentiles wouldn't have him for a gift." So they cared for him and his family.

Baba and Zayda Kramer were among the Jewish pioneers, bringing over the rest who had lived in the same cold, rocky, muddy little Ukrainian town. Their house was a center for immigrants coming and going, and they all swore at Mishka, the liar, who had told them the streets of Duluth were paved with gold. They had found the streets the same as in Peryaslov, a muddy blubber they had to throw planks across in the spring. In the Ukraine there was cold and rock and mud, and here there was cold and rock and mud. If children ran after them hollering "Greenhorn!", in the old country the *muzhiks* [peasants] spat *"Zhid."* So they drew their shoulders deeper into the collars of their sheepskin coats and turned hurt into laughter.

When the family gathered in the kitchen in the evening, there was talk and laughter and crunching of sunflower seeds. Mama would sing in her warm voice a song about a little cousin who had come to the new world, her cheeks blooming like red apples, her feet tingling with the dance. She went into a sweat shop and the apples faded from her cheeks and her feet no longer yearned for dancing, and she sang to herself to the purr of the machine, "Woe unto me that I ever accepted the gift of Columbus." Only Zayda Pozletsky would brook no criticism of the new world. He hopped about on his spry old legs, chuckling over America as if it were his personal discovery. The slightest criticism of it he took as a personal affront. He gloated to the new immigrants, "Well, when did you ever see such a thing as this in the old country?" Whether it was autumn's first apple or a Lake Superior herring, or such an abstract thing as freedom, he would demand a comparison. "Well, did you ever see a thing like this in the old country?"

Like a queen, Baba Kramer handed out her largesse in the big house to all the pioneers, the exiles coming and going to North Dakota or coming back. And when a friend asked, "Tell me, Pesha, who is that strange man with the red beard who is sipping your borscht with such gusto?"—she would turn her majestic head toward the unknown guest, shrug, "Who knows? Let him eat." But Baba's wrath was like a flame from Mount Sinai. Who would dare use a milk towel on a meat dish, or sneak a caramel on Passover, or write his name on the Sabbath? God himself would be in her wrath, cold, fierce and jealous from Mt. Zion.

She had many friends among the Polish immigrants who lived one hill above "Little Jerusalem." The Poles, full of the official anti-Semitism of the old world, brought this poison with them to America. But they were people. Could Pesha Kramer turn from her door a toil-eroded woman who asked her, "Could you spare a few eggs from your chickens? My youngest is sick with consumption and she must have eggs and my hens are not laying." Could she refuse to come when a young Polish mother came to the door of this tall, strong woman with the high piled white hair and asked, "Will you come and help me, please? You have had many children. My baby is whooping and I do not know what to do." She gave to these arch enemies of hers, these Poles, as if they, too, were Jewish immigrants. As individuals she spoke of them lovingly, but in general she hated the Gentiles with a hatred terrible to behold.

She would come into a room and if she did not like the smell of it she would turn her head away in disgust and cry, *"Feh, es shtinct Goy"* (it stinks Gentile). She would warn her children, "You know how cold it is out there upon the lake in December? If ever any child of mine were to tell me that he was going to marry a Gentile, I would go down to that lake with a hatchet. I would chop a hole in the ice, and in that hole I would drown myself." But the memory of pogroms and ghettos beyond the pale was not the heritage of her children. Even as she said these words, her eyes burning deep and black in their sockets like the threatening eyes of the ancient prophets, her son Lev lowered his eyes with an anguished frown. He was already bitterly in love with one of the Polish girls who lived just above the hill.

Once a year the children got together and bought Baba Pozletsky, my humbler grandmother, a new dress of lavender poplin or purple satin. For Yom Kippur, the Day of Atonement. This was Baba's big day, for she was the only old woman in the community who could read. Downstairs, the men rocked back and forth on their heels, wrapped in their long prayer shawls, praying aloud in a fantastic babble of voices. Upstairs, separated oriental fashion, were the women, and the center of attention was Baba. The old women sat around a big table headed by Baba. She alone could read the Hebrew, so Baba chanted and gave the cues. She had an extraordinarily big nose, red and purple veined, and she always carried a man's handkerchief. For Yom Kippur it was a particularly large and white man's handkerchief. When she came to a tragic section in the reading, like the burning of the Temple, she would whisk out the handkerchief from her pocket, bury her large nose in it, and this was the signal for a general burst of wailing and a flood of tears. Just as suddenly she would swish it under her nose, the handkerchief would disappear, and as abruptly as a closed faucet the wailing would stop and the tears cease—until she arrived at the next tragic incident of Jewish history.

I looked forward to sunset on this day of fasting and mourning. For each year at sunset an old patriarch (the *shammos* [sexton]) of the synagogue, with a beard as long and as white as the beard of Moses, would come to the open door of the synagogue, wrapped in a long prayer shawl. Facing the eastern hills, he would blow a long blast on his ram's horn, and then another—and I would forget for a moment that I was in the world of my birth. I was the dreaming daughter of Abraham—lifting my eyes unto the hills beyond the desert of Haran.

And there were happier holidays—like Sim'has Torah. The white bearded old men would open the Ark that bore the Torahs in their beautifully colored velvet wraps, embroidered with the star of David. Cradling the scrolls in their arms like children, they would dance around in a circle, chanting their joy as proud possessors of the law of Moses and of Abraham. Children like me were borne in the arms of our smiling fathers and allowed to bend down and kiss the Torahs the old men carried, or at least to touch the smooth velvet with our fingers. "Long life to you, my little one!" an old man would nod. "A hundred and twenty years may you live, daughter of Judah!" Most of the old men were intoxicated with joy, but some added a few *schnapps* under their belts, and one year Schmelke, the drunkard, tried to climb one of the polished pillars of the synagogue to the women's balcony.

Though mine was a divided world, I learned with shock at school that it was necessary to establish stringent quotas to stem the tide of certain "undesirable" stocks immigrating to our shores. I remember the mixture of feeling with which I bore this avalanche of knowledge. First a feeling of shame and revulsion that I was the issue of such "undesirable stock." And then a rush of love and loyalty came over me for the little people of my old and familiar world. Nobody could convince me that Baba Kramer, who moved like a white swan and fed every hungry stranger, was an undesirable immigrant. Or humble Baba Pozletsky, crying her people's sorrows into the big, man's handkerchief, or Zayda Pozletsky, who hopped about on his spry old legs and sang hosannas to the new world—or Mama with her gypsy eyes and her fiery talk of women's freedom—or Papa, who looked like a weatherbeaten Yankee farmer and had a heart as big as Baba's house—or Uncle Nathan, the socialist, or even lovable Mishka, the liar, Schmelke, the drunkard, or poor Fishel, the *shlimazel*. They were my people!

Again I remember Sim'has Torah and the old men dancing before the Holy Ark with the Torahs clasped in their arms like children—a holiday celebrating the law—the moral law plucked by an ancient people out of the jungles of barbarism, commanding "Thou shalt not kill!"

No school, no teacher, however glib, could turn me against the prophets who shaped me:

> *"Is this not the fast that I have chosen?*
> *To undo the bonds of the yoke*
> *And to let the oppressed go free...*
> *Some day there shall be a highway and a road, which shall be*
>   *called the way of Holiness—*
> *Men shall come singing and sorrow and sighing shall*
>   *fade away.*
> *For behold! There shall be a new heaven and a new earth, and*
>   *former things shall not be remembered...*
> *Men shall build houses and inhabit them, and they shall plant*
>   *vineyards and eat the fruit of them.*
> *They shall not build and another inhabit; they shall not plant*
>   *and another eat.*
> *For as the days of a tree shall be the days of the people, and men*
>   *shall enjoy the work of their hands..."*

Oh, no, not shame, not shame, not shame, but pride in such a heritage—we the people of Minnesota's little Kasrilevka—we were worthy children of America!

SECTION TWO
WE'RE THE PEOPLE

So I Visited a Transient Camp

A steel trust newspaper is intended to deceive workers, not to make them comfortable, so if I read the paper every morning with a sourpuss and a craving for a dash of Alka-Seltzer, it's nothing unusual. But the other morning the paper had more than the usual effect of raising the acidity of my blood. I felt my temperature rise and a prickly sensation from head to foot. A little editorial called "Service" at the bottom of the page was responsible. It started innocently: "Those poor fellows in the transient relief camp at Grand Marais certainly deserve sympathy…or something" and proceeded with snarling sarcasm: "If news reports are correct, they don't even have anyone to bring in their wood and water for them. They have to make their own beds. They have to wait on themselves, but according to the story, they don't even have to do that now"—no doubt just a quaint little commentary on the front page story the night before, "Jacks Demand Maid Service"—but the physical discomfort was now so unbearable I sprang up from my desk and barged into the union office. "Say, Frank," I cried, "how far is it to Grand Marais?"

"This bunkhouse is too crowded. Let's go in one of 'em that has single bunks." The boys gathered around me in the transient camp at Grover Conzet. Even the two old jacks who were whittling away at a handmade violin looked up and smiled. At my request one of the old jacks drew his bow across the strings and brought forth a few sweet strains of Scandinavian music. They pushed a little table toward me and laid my notebook on it and, beside it, a large round rock. "That's just for protection," a jack laughed. "You sure got a lot of nerve coming up here with all us wild men. Ain't you 'scared of us? Don't you believe the papers? We're not men—we're wild animals." We all laughed and one jack shook his head slowly. "When you get poor and old and hopeless, you even get ugly so people are afraid of you, yes?"

I took the clipping from my purse and passed it around. The murmurs of resentment became chuckles of amusement and before long the whole bunkhouse was shaking with laughter. "Now, what do you think of that?" One grinned, "We never thought of that before, did we boys? Service! Now that's an idea. We ought to demand that the state furnish us with little tea wagons. The idea of us having to get out of bed to eat! Now ain't that terrible?"

But kidding aside...

"You see, this is what happened," the boys explained. "It was on Lincoln's birthday. He freed the slaves, and we decided to celebrate by freeing ourselves. This fellow Morgan, our superintendent, he thought he was a little Hitler and he had us locked up here in a concentration camp. 'When the bell rings at eight o'clock,' he says, 'you all go out to work for six hours!' That's the law that he made. Now listen, sister, nobody that knows the jacks will believe that we're lazy and that we don't want to work. We wanted to chop all the wood that was needed for the camp, and more, do all the chores, keep the floors scrubbed, keep the whole camp up to snuff, but this six-hour rule...

"We knew this six-hour rule to keep us working even when there wasn't any work to do was just to make Morgan feel like a real boss. We sent a committee to see him and told him if we got to work in the open six hours we got to have clothes. Our clothes are falling to pieces. One old jack was working in a pair of cotton socks and pieces of burlap wrapped around his feet. His orders were, 'Clothes or no clothes, out on the road!' A fellow who was working in the kitchen came to him and said, 'I need a change of clothes, I'm lousy.' Morgan answered, 'Well, if you're lousy, I don't want you in the kitchen. Get out on the road!' For four hundred men we have no way of washing—only two tin barrels over a fire outside. Morgan ordered that none of us can wash until the six hours' work is done, then after work two hundred of us would start crowding around one barrel. Mostly we washed in the snow banks. A fellow who tried to wash before the time set by Morgan was chased back.

"One jack was sick and the first aid men said to take him right to a hospital but he laid around for three days until Koivunen happened to be in camp and drove him back to town with him.

"He used to refer to us as 'sons of bitches.' A committee went to him and complained about the liquor that was being sneaked into camp through the office. But he was so damned drunk himself that he couldn't stand up, he had to sit on the end of the table. We could tell when the chef was drunk because there was vinegar in the sauce.

"Well, one day we had a mass meeting. That was on Lincoln's birthday. We went in an orderly fashion to the office and we said, 'Morgan, we don't like the way you're running things, we want you to go,' and Morgan went. And that's the story. We've got a new super now and we think he's going to be okay. And without any bells ringing, we all go to work, and do all our chores and keep the camp one hundred percent. We're men, not slaves. We don't want no concentration camps."

The bell rang for supper and the boys invited me in. As we left the cook shack, the boys grinned, "How did you like the supper, Calamity?" I shook my head. "The spaghetti was too salty and the tea was too bitter." "Say, what do you think this is," one of them laughed, "the Grand Hotel?"

"There's only one thing I'd like to know." I turned to an old-timer. "How do people wash with tin cans outside?"

Their laughter rang through the woods as they led me to the two tin barrels suspended over a fire. "A fine lumberjack she is, eh, boys!" they roared. "A fine lumberjack!"

Only my good friend Gus, the "Michigan Stiff," wasn't laughing. "What do you think of it, Calamity," he said, with an odd little gesture of helplessness. "A transient camp for strong men—and tin cans to wash with—in the richest country in the world…"

I can still see him walking slowly back to the bunkhouse, shaking his head, "In the richest country in the world…" I can still hear the words of Jim McDonald as he drove me back to town, with the moonlight gleaming on the North Shore's icy cliffs, "Beautiful, this country, isn't it? Transient camps—funny, eh? And we're the guys who built this land. We opened up this country, cut it right through the wilderness."

EIGHT BUCKS AND ONE MEAL

Sunday afternoon is reserved for arguments at my house. It always follows somewhat the same pattern. At about two p.m. my dad arrives to see the kids. He bounds up the stairs, big and burly and bursting with rugged individualism, and booms in a voice overwhelming with good nature, "Where's my little goats?" At this the kids scurry for cover and I have to urge the oldest, "Go on, kiss your grandpa. What's the matter with you. Go on, kiss your grandpa." And when she pouts I have to remind her again how when I was a little girl her age, I had to kiss two grandpas, six aunts, eight uncles and great uncles and all except the aunts had whiskers. "Yes," she whines, "but he bites!" And then I have to admonish my dad, "For heaven's sake, Pop, kiss the kids but don't devour them!" And following the usual Sunday afternoon pattern he looks the kid over with a puzzled expression, shakes his head, "Spunky little tyke," he says, "who does she take after?" And that's that for the preliminaries.

Then my dad sits down and says, "Turn off the radio." Which I do. "Radios are just a lot of noise," he says, to which I agree. He pauses for just a moment and then he asks, "Well, how's the boys?" And I say, "Fine." My dad pops back, "What's fine about them? Jimmy ain't got a job yet, has he?" "No," I reply, "but he's looking. He's trying real hard." "Humph!" says Dad. "It's unions, that's what. If those kids didn't have unions on the brain all the time they'd both be sitting pretty." He turns to me confidentially, "Now look here, nanny goat, I'm not sayin' nothin'. You're old enough to think what you want an' I ain't buttin' into your business but you had no right to spoil the kids. You spoiled 'em." With that he sits back with an air of having settled the question and I begin to tattoo a little tune on the table with impatient fingers.

But he is not through with me yet. "You gave 'em all those notions about unions. Billy had a fair job. He could have worked himself up, but what does he do? He helps 'em start a union and he gets canned. My goodness, some fathers really have a pleasure out of their boys. Take Herbie Kynes—there's a boy for you. Got himself a little business, worked himself up, now he rides around in a nice car, and it's really a pleasure for his old dad."

"Yes, Pop," I sigh, "Henry Ford was a poor boy. Worked himself up. Now he's got a couple of billion and he rides around in a nice car and it's really a pleasure for his old dad, I'll bet."

My father blinks at me with a puzzled look. "Nanny goat," he grins, "sometimes I'm going to get darn good and mad at you."

At this I generally laugh and tousle his hair and it relieves the tension for the time being.

Then he starts again. "If it wasn't for unions everything would be all right. It's just a racket. All they do is collect dues from the poor working people. The working people mean well, sure. But they got these unions racketeering them. And I got to have kids that all they think about is unions. Why did Bill have to start a union? It was a fair job he had. He could have worked himself up."

"It was a very good job, Pop—fifteen bucks a week for twelve to fourteen hours' hard labor. That was what you call a honey of a job."

"I don't know why it is. Some boys their age got good jobs, work themselves up, but I don't get any pleasure from my boys."

"Well, Pop, there's about eleven million people unemployed, got no jobs, walk the streets every day from early morning to late at night, will probably never work themselves up, and their fathers probably don't get much pleasure out of them either."

"When I was a boy..." my dad shakes his head.

"When you were a boy, there were plenty of jobs for all. All you needed was a little guts and a little ambition. When your dad came over here, America was a young country with a frontier yet to conquer. Folks were still staking out homesteads. When you were a boy, the Republican party was still the liberal party of Lincoln who freed the slaves."

"Don't start politics. I'm a Republican so I'm a Republican. Never mind politics. What do you hear from Jimmy? What's he doin' in New York? When's he gonna get a job?"

"I'll read you his letter..." My father listens attentively as I read:

"Dear Sis, boy, are things tough or are they tough? But I'm not licked. Don't think I'm licked. Boy, I'm wearing the bottoms off my shoes but I'm trying. I start out early in the morning and I pound the sidewalks all day long. I'm bound to find something looking this way. Funny, all this war business but it doesn't seem to do any good as far as finding jobs go. I just started working on a job but it's awful tough. Eight bucks a week dishwashing in a restaurant, ten and one-half hours and one meal. The kid who worked here before me, he quit. He worked here a week but he couldn't take it. He came from Scranton, Pennsylvania. He says to me, 'I came here from Scranton to work because my dad worked there in a mine and he got killed. Plenty of 'em get killed in those mines so I decided to come to New York to work. I figured if I come here I'd live longer.' Then he cries, the poor kid. Honest. He cries. 'I'm going back to Scranton,' he says, 'I figure now I'll live longer there.' "

My dad interrupts angrily. "Eight bucks a week! What's the matter with that town! I thought they had unions in New York! I thought everybody had to join a union in that town!"

"Why Papa," I said drily, "I thought you were against unions—"

"Sure I am. I'm dead against 'em, but that's a fine kind of a town where they work a poor kid eleven hours a day for eight bucks a week. It's a disgrace!"

And so ends another Sunday afternoon...

To One Who Died for Us

Can't think of anything today, Casper. Ever since I heard that you were one of our American boys who went down with that ship that Mussolini bombed—down to the bottom of the Mediterranean—can't think of anything but the ache in my heart and the last words you said to me before you left, "Goodbye, sister, carry on!"

Somehow or other, you had a "hunch" you weren't coming back, you had a hunch the fascist killers would get you. I remember how you sat in the office of *Midwest Labor* and looked at your watch. "In twelve hours," you said, "I'll be gone."

I met you during the Minnesota strike last year. You were in charge of strike headquarters at Grover Conzet, the transient camp that Governor Benson gave the strikers on the North Shore. You were excited about the place. "It's got electric lights," you said, "and a washing machine and we wash all our clothes every day, and everything is clean and swell. We got good food. Christ, I hate to leave the place and go back to the lousy camps!"

A clean transient camp was a luxury to you, Casper, you and the rest of the lumberjacks who had spent a lifetime "following the woods" from one rotten camp to another. The woods was your only home. You went on strike, you and the rest of the boys, because you felt you were getting a rotten deal, and you won because you stuck it out. You had nothing to lose.

You were going to Spain when they got you—you were going to Spain to stop fascism before it could spread to the rest of the world. You knew what fascism did to the workers of Germany and Italy. You knew how it smashed the trade unions, stopped the workers' press, slashed wages, kicked the working class in the face with an iron-spiked boot. You knew that Ford and Hearst and Morgan and Girdler and the rest of America's iron-fisted bosses who hire thugs and spies to murder the workers and smash their unions are American fascists and, if Mussolini and Hitler get away with it in Spain, what's to stop the fascists from trying to get away with it in America? You went with the advance guard to stop fascism before it could spread to the country that you loved. You went bravely, right into the camp of the enemy, and you knew that you weren't coming back....

Can't think of anything today, Casper. Can't think of anything but how you said, "Goodbye, sister, carry on!" You, Casper, symbolize the struggle of the working class for a better life, you symbolize the courage of the working class who are ready to die to make a better life for their working brothers!

We'll carry on, Casper! We won't forget. We won't forget our brothers who were massacred by Republic Steel on the streets of Chicago, we won't forget our brothers who were beaten to death in Newberry, Michigan, by the stooges of the lumber barons. We won't forget that you and hundreds like you lie at the bottom of the Mediterranean and in the fields of Spain because you challenged Mussolini's right to murder our Spanish brothers and sisters.

Give us the courage to fight, and if we die, let it be the dignity of dying to make a decent world, without misery, poverty and war, a world free from the dictatorship of iron and money, a democracy of the human race!

Goodbye, Casper Anderson, fighting lumberjack, who went down for the working class! Goodbye, brother, we shall not fail you!

AND SO LET FREEDOM RING
Newspaper Guild Strike of '38

The sun is breaking through the clouds of a chilly Monday morning. We are marching two by two in a picket line almost a block long: newspaper men, lumberjacks, sailors, school teachers, steel workers, chemical workers, Coolerator men. Men are marching with their wives, mothers with their sons. A tall lumberjack towers above the crowd carrying a sign, "Don't scab." A crowd is gathering across the street, near the City Hall, behind the sacks of grass seed piled along the banks like barricades. They watch our picket line in neutral silence. The police swagger by them, their riot sticks swinging at their sides. It is a quarter to seven.

We watch the loudspeaker on the roof of the newspaper building connected with wires to City Hall. We watch "Safety" Commissioner Culbertson's police lining up in formation, the sun flashing on their tin hats. "Someday we will take the City Council out of the Wolvin Building and put it back in the City Hall," a striker says. The Wolvin Building is the office of the Steel Trust. It is ten minutes to seven.

Over one hundred police are lined up on the street, facing us, guns in their hands. Their faces are flushed with an inner excitement. They watch us like beasts watching their prey.

My country tis of thee
Sweet land of liberty
Of thee I sing…

Our voices ring out against the hills. Among those hills most of us were born. We can see the sun flashing on the roofs of our homes and the spires of our churches. We see the sun flashing on the tin hats of Culbertson's police. It is almost seven.

Land where our fathers died
Land of the pilgrim's pride…

"In the name of the law I order you to disperse—"

A deep and ominous voice spreads over the streets. It is the loudspeaker. The police lift their guns. We keep on singing. The voice is reading the law. Throughout the history of our country ominous voices have read laws to our people, interpreting them to protect not human life, but lifeless property. "In the name of the law I order you to disperse or take the consequences—"

O'er every mountain side
Let freedom ring!

It is seven o'clock. A signal. Looking straight into our faces, the police cock their guns. There are shots. Clouds of tear gas rise into the streets. Fine shot grazes our flesh. Fire singes our clothes—coats and suits not yet paid for. We stop singing. Bewildered, we stand for a fraction of a second facing our assailants. We cannot believe what is happening. Now the riot sticks are coming down on our heads and shoulders. An old man falls and the police beat him as he lies on the ground. We begin to run, the tears streaming down our faces and the gas in our lungs, but they follow us, beating us with their clubs. On the edge of the crowd towards Fourth Avenue West, well-dressed gentlemen with eyes like steel laugh as we run and choke. Laugh at the tears coming down our faces and the clubs coming down on our heads.

And now the gas has cleared and we sit here in strike headquarters, some of us are quiet. We are thinking of the oddness of being chased like that through the streets of our own town. It was odd seeing you running through the streets like that—Carl, Gladys, Glenn, Herman, Helen, Ilmar, Ed—seems like such a short time ago since we sat in our seats over there where the big clock marks the time in the high school tower.

You sat in front of me, Carl, remember? You were editor of the high school paper and I was your assistant and we read romantic stories in our newswriting class about the newspaper business. Stories like "Deadline." Remember?

We learned a lot of things in school, didn't we, Carl? We learned about the sanctity of our laws, about the glorious history of our country, about the revolutionary birth of our nation. We learned to take our hats off when we sing "America." You didn't learn, did you, Carl, that America is a lot of things: that America is the workers who gave thousands of lives to win the famous American standard of living and the eight-hour day, that millions of workers still risk their lives to preserve that standard. And that America is the corporations, cold as the steel of their guns.

Who would have thought, Glenn, when your kid brother tagged after you on the baseball field and you had to quit the game to look after the kid, that some day you would have to watch an officer of the law break a club over his head for having the bravery to join his fellow workers in a struggle for a little better standard of living? Who would have dreamed that you'd be clubbed into unconsciousness for rushing to save your father from a policeman's murderous blows? Gladys with the curly hair, Gladys who knows all the dance steps and the popular songs, you didn't know that someday you would sing "Solidarity Forever" with rough lumberjacks and sailors. You didn't even know that you belonged to the working class.

But now we all know where we belong. We march down the picket line together, white-collar workers and men in overalls. And we know what we never learned in school, and we sing "America" because we love our country as we never loved our country before, because we know that it is the likes of us who built it, we the workers of this land. That it is we who built its American standard of living and it is we who will preserve it. That it is we who sewed the stars and stripes of democracy into our flag, and it is we who will protect that democracy from the growing fascism of corporations. We will stand our ground like millions of workers before us, and in the face of the tear gas and shot guns of Big Business, we will hurl against our native hills, "LET FREEDOM RING!"

SHE WHO DIED WITHOUT LIVING

I read a news item today about a brilliant young student who killed himself in a homemade electric chair because he couldn't find a job to enable him to continue in his studies. It was a little item sandwiched in between a story of terrible carnage on the battlefields of Spain and the picture of dead bodies being dragged from the bombed ruins of a Chinese village. Everywhere headlines of war and violence and death struck out in fierce black type, and the little item about a boy who did not want to live seemed crushed between them.

Last Sunday I stood beside a grave of fresh-turned earth. The leaves were just turning yellow with September, and over the silent field a fresh breeze murmured through the tall grass. Part of myself lay buried in that grave—you, my little sister, hardly turned twenty-five. If they should ask me how you died, I should say that you died of frustration. You had the twentieth century blues. You were mangled in body and soul beneath the ruthlessly moving wheels of a mad and changing world. Too bad that you were lost and could not find your way in a world of chaos and brutality! Too bad that you did not live to learn that never in the history of the world has a generation had a greater destiny to fulfill!

A little while ago I said goodbye to "G"—we three were children together. With bated breath we used to map the great uncharted worlds that we were born to conquer. "G" went to Spain. He went to fight in the Abraham Lincoln Brigade with the workers of Spain. He wrote, "I've got to go to Spain. They're fighting out my own future on those battlefields. Fascism means death to everything good and human and decent. Fascism means death to everything worth living for. For the whole purpose of fascism is to forge new chains to bind us workers to our slavery. If fascism draws its black curtain over Spain, how long before the whole world will be shrouded in darkness? The world in terrible agony is giving birth to a new and better world. Can I sit by while that new world is strangled in its mother's womb? I am not sorry that I was born into the chaos of the twentieth century. No. I am glad that I can be one of the youth to see that fascism shall not pass."

If "G" dies on that battlefield, he will die living. For it is fulfillment to die for life. But you, poor kid! You who die without hope, in an agony of desolation—there is not a spring breeze that will not moan your sterile passing. There is not a summer rain that will not weep upon your needless grave.

The ones we love are like lighted candles in our being. When one goes out, it leaves a part of us in darkness. I have a duty to perform, grappling with the darkness where once you used to be—a duty to you and to all youth like you born into a world of poverty and depression and war, a world which seems to have no present and no future. I have a monument to build to your memory…a better society where youth can blossom to its rich fulfillment.

Goodbye, little sister! Thousands of crushed and broken youth lie like you in their needless graves, youth who had no present, and saw no future. But millions of us have set our teeth against the wind. The working class is moving toward a happier world where its beloved children will not be gnarled and twisted and broken, but will grow straight as the young trees straining towards the sun.

SPRING SONG—IN OCCUPIED EUROPE

The water bursts the ice and rushes by
The earth gives birth and life is pressing through
We stand and stretch our arms into the sky
And feel that we can almost touch the blue
We fill our lungs, but only breathe a sigh
Against the crushing weight upon our chests
Like birds who lift their broken wings to fly
But only find them limp against their breasts
Whose swollen throats are full, but cannot sing,
Why not, oh Mother Earth?
This is our spring!

This is our spring! Oh stay! For when you go
Spring shall not come again for us…we know
Springtime comes only once in every year
What if our joy is strangled by our fear?
What if we lift our faces to the sky
Only to see the bombers roaring by?
What if the rumblings of the cannon sound
Louder than water bursting from the ground?
What if the earth's once sweet and steaming breath
Reeks of the stench and rotten smell of death?
What of all that! Don't say our spring is lost!
Even if hunger plucks us 'til we stand
Bleak as the trees in a November frost!
What if we swell our throats but cannot sing?
This is our spring!

Oh Mother Earth, tonight the stars are bright
We feel your warm breath steaming from the ground
The water at our feet is sparkling white
The very silence has a living sound
This is no night to give us up to death
Lying alive against your massive breast

Feeling the throb and panting of your breath.
We who would climb and climbing touch the sky!
We who could run and leap…and leaping, fly!
We who would laugh and rock the world in mirth!
We who could stretch our arms and hug the earth
Clasping against our hearts each living thing
Oh Mother Earth! We want to sing! To sing!
This is our spring!

Give us our spring, you fascist foes of life!
Give us our spring, sowers of pain and death!
What if we die by those bright guns you wear!
What if we stifle in your poisoned breath!
Hunger's a dangerous weapon that we bear
And we shall turn it on you like a knife!

Makers of war, beware! For we shall come!
We'll come like green blades bursting from the earth!
Come like a raging hurricane in motion!
We'll come like life impatient for its birth
Come like the tide out of an angry ocean!
We'll come like hosts of eagles taking wing!
We'll come like wind across an arid plain
We'll come like winter in a jungle rain
Torrents of youth! And you shall hear us sing
Give us our spring!

THREE LITTLE GIRLS WENT SKATING

It was the night of the Joe Louis fight. Three little girls sat at the supper table, talking, giggling, eagerly planning their evening together. One was pretty, talented Janet Winfield, a Negro schoolgirl. The other two were her white classmates. The mother of one of the white girls smiled to herself as she served the supper. She smiled at the gayety, the bubbling laughter, the bright-eyed youth of three light-hearted girls.

They were going to finish their supper, then practice some dance steps together—for Janet knew every intricate dance step ever invented—then they would listen to the fight, then they would all go down to the Duluth Curling Rink for indoor skating and then they would go home and all spend the night together.

The evening proceeded just as the happy girls planned. Supper was over, dancing was over, Joe Louis won the fight, and they were on their way to the curling rink. The girls admired Janet's skating outfit, and she admired theirs. They made a pretty, graceful picture, swinging, arms locked, down the street. And prettiest of all was Janet.

They bought their tickets and hurried along to get their skates. Janet lagged a little behind the girls and they had already gotten their skates when Janet caught up, presented the ticket for her skates, gave her size, waved to her friends, who waved back.

She did not notice the dull look on the attendant's face, nor did she comprehend when he handed her ticket back to her.

"I want my skates…" she smiled, and told him the size again. Perhaps he hadn't understood.

He held the ticket out to her.

"But my skates…" the little girl persisted.

The man shook his head. "That's my orders. You get your money back if you present your ticket at the office."

She felt her blood get hot, so hot, her skin seemed to burn as if it were on fire. Then she got cold, as if she had a chill. Tears sprang into her eyes and blinded her.

"Janet—hurry!" her girl friends called to her.

She didn't answer. She hardly heard them. She stumbled toward the door.

Learning what had happened, her friends came running from the skating rink. They could not adequately express their indignation. They talked. They scolded. They chattered to cover the embarrassment, the shame that they felt. For somebody, something had set up a false, artificial barrier between them, a barrier that had no right to be there. They felt responsible for it somehow.

"We'll bring our skates back and we'll go away from here too," the girls declared.

"No!" Janet turned away from them. "No, please—please, don't. You go back and skate...please. I'll go on to a movie."

The girls protested but Janet was already out of the door and hurrying down the street. The girls looked after her. The gayety had gone out of their evening. They felt heavy-hearted, resentful at this ugly thing that tore the three of them apart, that threw up artificial barriers where once there were none. They felt sick inside. They didn't feel like skating.

About a month ago I went to the funeral of a Negro woman who was loved by everyone who knew her. Reverend Dunnington, a white minister, was asked to preach a sermon. And he said something like this:

He said: "You people in life are troubled by the color line. But when you get to Heaven, you will be happy, for in Heaven there is no color line, no inequality. In Heaven there is no injustice. There they do not ask you what is the color of your skin, only what is the color of your soul. Heaven is such a wonderful place that, if we only knew how wonderful it was, we'd fill our pockets full of rocks and go down and jump into Lake Superior to get there sooner. But fortunately, we do not know these things. But it makes it easier to endure the injustices and inequalities of this earth to know that we are all going bye and bye to a place where there is no injustice, no inequality, no color line."

But Jesus devoted his life and work to banish such injustice from the Earth. It was for the brotherhood of man *on Earth* that he preached, for equality *on Earth* that he labored, and it was for this that he was crucified. It was to banish inequality, injustice and color lines from *the Earth* that he cried to the unjust and the arrogant, "I bring not peace, but a sword!"

Little Janet Winfield, hurrying from the curling rink, hurt and humiliated, and her white classmates looking after her, just as hurt and humiliated, ask themselves, why must there be this inequality, here, on Earth, in America, the land of liberty and democracy? Why must there be injustice and discrimination in a country watered by the blood of hundreds of thousands of brave Americans who died to make it free? The answer is, there must not!

The appeasers of our country are taking their cue from Hitler. To prevent the unity of all our people against the fascist menace, they turn race against race, nationality against nationality. This is the method of fascism. Fascism is born and bred in the rank swamp of prejudice. It perverts science, morality, religion to create a monstrous philosophy based on racial superiority and the theory that the people are born to be ruled by sadistic supermen—like Hitler. Any man, any organization, any group whatsoever who injects into the bloodstream of America this poison of discrimination and race prejudice is helping to disrupt the unity of the American people that has pledged itself with the liberty loving peoples of all nations to wipe fascism off the earth.

"Why Did They Treat Us So?"

A little aching band of lumberjacks straggled wearily into the town of Munising, Michigan, on a Friday afternoon. Many of them were covered with blood. Some carried wounded buddies. Some had their packsacks on their backs. All were footsore from many long miles of walking. Wounded in body and soul, they lay down upon the cold bare floor of strike headquarters and nursed their wounds.

We arrived in Munising at midnight in answer to the union's call for help. The headquarters was a one-room, dingy building. A dim light was burning, and sprawled grotesquely on the floor were the dozens of injured men. We went from man to man and all of them told us the same story, the story of the massacre that morning at Newberry, cold little company town, dominated by the two black smokestacks of the Newberry Lumber and Chemical Company and the Newberry Charcoal and Iron Company, facing each other grimly across the public highway.

They had slung their packsacks on their backs and started out early that morning for the Newberry plant. They were going on a peaceful mission, to ask the Newberry sawmill workers to join the union.

"They didn't give us a chance to talk or nothin'. The minute we got into the yard, the siren on a fire engine started to blow and kept on blowing and the factory whistles blew and right away men started to flock into the yard.

"They were running out of parked cars and trucks. They had lead pipes and clubs and loaded hoses and axes. They surrounded us, they didn't give us a chance to talk. They chased us in cars and on foot, beating us like cattle. When they got tired of running, they got into a car and a fresh crew started after us, beating us on the head and back, and when we fell, they kept on beating us. And they tried to run over us with their cars. A big red-faced man with a white shirt and sleeves rolled up—he looked like a prosperous businessman—he was standing on the fender of his car and beating an old lumberjack over the head with a loaded hose, right and left, right and left, and somebody in the car yelled, 'Keep it up, old man, you're doing fine!'

"There were women too and they were giggling. There's an insane asylum near Newberry but it seems like all the good citizens were in that insane asylum and all the crazy people were let loose.

"They chased us for three miles, us running on foot. They left us on the edge of town and went away, then they came back twice while we were layin' on the ground and resting, to beat us some more.

"We walked twenty miles to the next town, carrying our wounded buddies. Some of our boys just laid down in the brush. I don't know what happened to them. And I guess some boys just went to parts unknown. We called up the state police at Seney and asked them to help us take the wounded men to hospitals but they said they wouldn't. It wasn't their business.

"We had two union cars but they smashed them up. They had plenty of liquor and were well piped up...we saw jugs in the cars.

"The sheriff and deputies and town officials and businessmen led the mob. Beers, the superintendent of the company, said, 'Let's go down and tear down the Finn Hall!' They smashed everything in the Finn Hall the Finns had lent us for strike headquarters. They hacked the new piano to pieces and while they hacked it someone said, 'It's "The Internationale"—how do you like it?'

"Sister, why did they have to treat us like that? We were only strikin' to live like men instead of in slop like pigs. They wouldn't put their pigs where they put us in them camps—men on top of each other in double bunks with hay to sleep on crawlin' with bedbugs and lice. Blankets that never were washed and knotted with haywire to keep them from fallin' apart. No bathhouse of any kind. In some camps no water to drink even—just yellow water from a ditch that makes you vomit. Nothing in your pocket at the end of the month. Gee'z, that ain't no way to treat an American!"

They told their story gently, without excitement, more hurt than angry, more stunned than indignant. We tiptoed softly past the injured men, into the darkness of the company town, where hostile eyes followed us to our hotel.

BALLAD OF A LUMBERJACK

We told 'em the blankets were crummy
And they said that we like 'em that way.
We told 'em that skunks couldn't smell like our bunks,
But they said that our bunks were okay.

We told 'em we wanted a pillow
And a mattress and maybe a sheet.
And they said where's your guts? Goin' soft? Are you nuts?
That hay on your bunks is a treat.

We told 'em we wanted some water
And a tub into which it could squirt.
And they said why wash clothes? Wanna smell like a rose?
Why, it's healthy to wallow in dirt!

We said that we wanted some windows,
And we wanted a little more space,
'Cause, we said, it was punk sleepin' two in a bunk
With a guy snorin' booze in your face.

We said that we wanted some money.
We hadn't enough to get by.
A month in the wood with ten bucks to the good…
But they promised us pie in the sky.

But one day we all got together,
And we put the old boys on the spot.
We laid the axe down and we tramped into town,
And we left their old timber to rot.

The bosses they crawled on their bellies,
And they wept that they couldn't get by.
So we melted with pity and passed out a kitty
To buy the boys pie in the sky.

MURDERED ON A PICKET LINE

What is that moving down the dusty street
That black mass swelling in the August heat
That marching sound of twenty thousand feet?

Manhattan, we are coming with your son
The sweet, the brave, the little smiling one,
Who said, "My hunger's yours, and yours is mine…"
He died today…upon our picket line.

Manhattan, how he loved you, you his mother!
"All of her sons," he said, "I call them 'brother.'
How many anguished evenings I have lain
Under the burden of Manhattan's pain,
Feeling the sticky sweat upon her hair,
Hearing her gasping for a breath of air.
In sultry, crowded tenements compressed,
I've heard her children whimper on her breast,
I've seen her beggars groveling in the street.
I've heard her jobless pass, with leaden feet.
And yet how many nights I've seen her wear
The stars all tangled in her dusty hair,
And when the moon slides softly into space
How white and lovely seems her hardened face!"

Manhattan, we are bringing back your son…
The sweet, the brave, the little smiling one.
We bring him back to you, exploited mother.
"All of her sons," he said, "I call them 'brother,'
My hunger, it is theirs, and theirs is mine…"
He died today upon our picket line.

We heard our brother scream and gasp for breath
They drove the knife that stabbed your son to death.
They drove the knife who every single day

Measure the hours that grind our lives away.
Measure the hours and pay the paltry sums
That doom us to the everlasting slums.

Manhattan, we are coming with your son,
Ten thousand strong, and yet we march as one,
A single whole, and every one a part,
The ocean is not pounding like our heart
The thunder is not rolling like our wrath
The morning sun is blazing in our path.

How long can greed and ugliness survive
How long can violence and murder thrive
When boys like these can say, "Your hunger's mine…"
And die like this upon a picket line!

Manhattan, we are coming with your son,
The sweet, the brave, the little smiling one.
He is not dead; such beauty does not pass,
He's bone and sinew of the working class.
He is our own…humanity's to cherish
He is not dead…such beauty does not perish.
We'll see him smile in children's happy faces,
That dawn he died to bring…oh, when it comes…
We'll hear him laugh in cool, majestic places
Where once there sprawled the city's ugly slums.

HE HIT MAXIE BELOW THE BELT

Tony was mopping up after the last late customer and watching Zizzie Crocker slop coffee all over the gleaming counter. Zizzie was talking excitedly as usual, rolling his banjo eyes and shifting a hunk of doughnut from one cheek to the other. Tony yawned. "Two pounds less 'n an elephant, she weighs, dis dame," Zizzie was saying for the sixteenth time when the door opened and Maxie came in. Maxie was pale. He took off his hat and wiped the sweat from his forehead.

"I smacked him right in the mouth," he said shortly, "right in the puss. Smack. Like that."

The doughnut stopped short on the way to Zizzie's left cheek and his eyes popped. "Who?" he said.

"He's a big shot," Maxie went on. "A lawyer. Sure. He's a educated dope. He should know somethin'. Hangin' schoolin' on him is like hangin' earrings on a pig. His brain's in the gutter."

"Sure," said Zizzie, who always agreed amiably with everybody.

"It's like this," Maxie sat down on the counter and plunked his hat back on his head, "I goes into Benny's for a beer an' I'm on my way out, so I sees him standin' there, playin' the pinball machine. I says, 'Hi,' an' that's all. He done some work for me once—a little lease or somethin'. He says, 'Hey, Maxie, come 'ere. I ain't seen you for a dog's age,' he says. So we gets to talkin'.

"So he starts right off runnin' down the Jews. Low down ignorant stuff he pulls. Ku Klux stuff. Right out 'a Hitler's mouth. I'm gettin' mad, see? I'm gettin' hot. 'Look here, Mister,' I says, 'Did you hear that German fellah talk at the big Shrine meetin' the other night? The hall was jammed. This German says, "Don't be suckers for that stuff," he says, "don't be suckers. First Hitler gives the Jews the works, then he starts polishin' off everybody else." Don't go for that Hitler line, Mister,' I says. 'It ain't American,' I says. 'If it hooks you, you're a sucker.'

"Then he starts given' me the old international banker line, see? An' I says, 'You're a lawyer, you're supposed to know somethin', Mister. Why don't you find out a few facts before you shoot your trap off? *Fortune* magazine run some statistics showin' less'n one percent of all the bankers in the U.S. is Jews, see? Where do you get that 'banker' line? An' when you talk big dough, talk dough, not peanuts. Who's got the dough in this town, these Jewish guys that own a few scrap iron yards and corner stores, or the birds who own the factories, the steel mills, the iron ore, the banks, the grain elevators, the ships, the bus companies, the railroads, the Minnesota Power & Light, the telephone company? Yeah, who owns the big dough in the U.S.—J. P. Morgan, Henry Ford, Vanderbilt, Rockefeller, Girdler, Dupont, Knudson an' the rest a' the four hundred. That's talking dough, not peanuts. An' when you talk about New York Jews,' I says, 'just remember there's more Jewish workin' men there than any other nationality. Needle trades, truck drivers, bus drivers, building trades workers, fur workers—an' they're good union men too,' I says.

"He says, 'Look here, Maxie, get it straight. I don't mean you. Some a' my best friends are Jews!' he says. 'You're a white Jew. It's them damned black Jews gets my goat,' he says.

"That's when I clipped 'im, Tony. Right in the kisser. Whack. Like that. An educated dope but I lets 'im have it. Right in the teeth.

" 'Don't give me none a' that black an' white stuff,' I says, 'get me? Black's good as white in this here country, see? It's a guy's guts, not his color, that makes him a man or a rat, and I don't like your guts.' Y'know, Tony, I'm so mad I'm shakin'. 'An' don't give me none a' that phony baloney, that best friend stuff, get it? Don't grease me,' I says. 'You wanna give me an honest right hook, go ahead, but don't grease me. What d'ya mean,' I says, 'I'm a good Jew? Who am I? Maxie, that's all. You're not talkin' to Einstein or somebody. Just Maxie, a punchy ex-pug, that's me. So don't grease me.' "

"Gee!" breathed Zizzie.

"Give 'em a straight from a' shoulder, Moosalinis!" Tony spat.

"When I was a kid the little Hitlers called me 'Christ killer'! Me, Maxie. Easy-goin' guy. Never hurt a fly. Heart as big as a house. Used to come home all banged up, my clothes torn. Ma'd cry, 'Don't fight, Maxie,' she'd say. 'Don't fight. It don't pay. Just be a good boy. That's all, just be a good boy.'

"Well, I been a good boy. They called me the gamest little

fighter west a' Chicago. An' every cent I made in the ring I sent home to Ma an' the kids. The boys—they all like Maxie. I never hit a guy below the belt, an' I don't aim to take it below the belt, see—not even from an educated pig, get it? I'm an American an' I'm fightin' them little Hitlers back, eh, Tony?"

"Like to give 'em little Moosalinis good ponch too. I get letter from my sister in the old cauntry. No got spaghett'—no got bread. Moosalini he kill 'em off all a' young boys. Ah what's a' da' use. I talk, I get mad. I get mad, my heart pomps. Doctor say my heart in a' bad shape. How's about hot cup a' coffee, Maxie, eh? Cool 'a you off."

Heil, Lindbergh!

Are you scrapping with your wife?
Do your in-laws give you strife?
Are the bill collectors sore?
Is your job a bloomin' bore?
Does your husband tend to guzzle?
Can't you solve that crossword puzzle?
Here's the cure-all for the blues…
Go out gunning for the Jews.
Is your trouble halitosis?
Flat feet, B.O. or thrombosis?
Pink tooth brush or indigestion
Constipation or congestion?
Is your diet your main topic?
Is your sight a bit myopic?
Have you got that tired feeling?
Has your sunburn started peeling?
Are you bilious and dejected?
Do you need your teeth inspected?
Here's the formula to use…
Go out gunning for the Jews.
Have you got a skin infection?
Did you lose the last election?
Are your bunions feeling tender?
Did your spouse go on a bender?
Are you losing on the horses?
Did you eat too many courses?
Did your stock go down two notches?
Has your skin got yellow blotches?
Did you blow another fuse?
Sure, you guessed it. It's the Jews.
Don't you like the county sheriff?
Do you want a higher tariff?
Has the country a depression
Or is it a mild recession?

Did your party take a beating?
Do you retch when overeating?
Do your muscles kind a' sag?
Do you need a punching bag?
Don't you like the foreign news?
Heil, Lindbergh! It's the Jews!

LETTER TO MY GRANDFATHER

Dear Grandpa: This is not really a letter to you who have been dead for twenty years. It is a letter to what you stand for. Today I walked up to the Federal Building and watched them fingerprint and register the foreign born. I watched them standing in line, waiting—bewildered, anxious, and hurt. Women with babies in their arms, old men, old women, middle-aged women, a Catholic nun, timber workers, farmers, and if they were alien to America one could not see it on their homespun faces for they were the stuff that America is made of.

I watched them lift the large, work-worn hand of a Scandinavian farmer and take the print of his fingers, one by one. If he were alien to America, one could not see it. For he seemed like any one of the millions of Scandinavian farmers who settled the prairies of the Middle West. I looked at his blue eyes and the sunburned furrows in his face and then I turned away, sick and ashamed. "Oh, Grandpa," I thought, "what are they doing to your America!"

I remember you, Grandpa, with your little parched, yellow face and your dry hands—your body seemed so old. Yet your hair was thick and black, and your dark eyes were bright and alive, like the eyes of a boy. I remember you had two weaknesses—candy and reading matter. Your body still craving the sweets denied to a poverty-stricken childhood, no licorice, gumdrops or lollypops were safe from your bright, prying eyes. Nor was any package inviolate that was wrapped in a newspaper or a magazine. I remember my mother's mingled amusement and irritation when she came into the kitchen one morning and slipped on a fish sprawled naked on the floor while you leaned over the table where it had been, completely oblivious, reading the smelly newspaper it had been wrapped in.

You would lure me into the living room and sit me down and try to teach me history and languages and shake your head sadly when I preferred to run out and play. "In the old world girls did not have to know anything," you would sigh. "Your mother wanted to learn but I would not teach her. We used to say 'A woman's hair is long but her sense is short.' But that was in the old world. This is a new world, my granddaughter. Here a woman must know as much as a man for things are different here. This is the new world."

You loved this country. You hopped about on your spry old legs, chuckling over it as if it were some personal discovery of yours. The slightest criticism of it you took as a personal affront. You gloated over the new immigrants, "Well, were things like this in the old country?" "Well, when did you ever see such a thing as this in the old country?" Whether it was autumn's first apple, or a Lake Superior herring, or such an abstract thing as freedom, you would demand a comparison, "Well, did you ever see a thing like this in the old world?"

This is a new world! Oh, Grandpa, will I ever forget sitting at a shiny, newly varnished desk in the sixth grade schoolroom with thirty or so other children, remembering your stories of the old brutal world from which you came, of Czarist Cossacks riding through the village with gleaming swords and big teeth flashing in coarse laughter, striking terror in a hundred hearts. Of my grandmother standing in the market place selling bits of fish and meat to eke out a miserable living, clothed in rags, her feet wrapped in gunny sacks against the bitter cold, and a charcoal fire in a pail at her feet to keep her warm. The taunts of intolerance. The pressing stone of oppression. The secret police. The terror.

Will I ever forget singing "America the Beautiful" in that little sixth grade classroom looking out upon the green hills, sliding down to the lake where the ships moved free and graceful across the ice blue water, with the full-hearted gratitude of a child who has seen her grandfather's face when he breathed, "This is the new world!"

And if the teacher was sometimes startled at the passion of a dark-eyed child when she recited, "Breathes there the man with soul so dead who never to himself hath said 'this is my own, my native land!' " she could not know what passion for liberty a child could learn from a grandfather who was an immigrant!

Grandpa, watching them fingerprint those common people in the Federal Building today, I could almost see your little parched, yellow face. I could see you yielding your fingers heavily, one by one, your dark eyes asking in hurt and helpless bewilderment, "But this is the new world!"

JAILED FOR HER THOUGHTS

Oklahoma is the "Okie" state. The state made famous by the popular novel, *The Grapes of Wrath*. The state where thousands of pioneer farmers scratch a dry existence out of the dust-swept plains, or are crowded off the land by the big tractors to become migrant wanderers. Travelers hate the sight of Oklahoma's poverty. It's disturbing. But Oklahoma is not all poverty. There are millionaires in Oklahoma. They coin their millions out of the black gold in the heart of Oklahoma's earth. Oil. Rockefeller loves Oklahoma's oil, but he hates its "Okies."

A few weeks ago a young woman was sentenced to ten years in prison in Oklahoma. Pretty, studious, thirty-two, born and raised in New England, Mrs. Ina Wood was thrown into a cell with prostitutes, pending her trial. She had committed no crime. She merely believed that the rich oil of Oklahoma should not be the property of a few corporations while Oklahoma's millions eke out a bare existence in anguished poverty. She believed that the oil, the coal, the cotton, the rich resources of America should belong to the people as a whole to be developed for use and not for profit. Mrs. Wood is not charged with writing about these opinions of hers, nor is she accused of trying to convince others through speeches. Nor is she accused of distributing leaflets on this subject. She is accused of being a member of the Communist Party because of books expounding these ideas found in her home, and such membership is a crime in Oklahoma. In the United States of America, a young American-born woman of pioneer parents is going to serve ten years for "dangerous thoughts."

In the dawn of recorded history, there was a man named Jesus. He believed in the brotherhood of man. He preached "Love thy neighbor as thyself," and in a burst of wrath drove the money changers out of the temple. The rich and powerful of his day said his thoughts were "dangerous." They crucified him.

In the dark ages there was a scientist named Galileo. He said he believed the earth moved on its axis. The established gentlemen of his time said the earth was motionless. They said to believe the earth moved was heresy, "dangerous thoughts." They forced him to recant or be tortured to death. He dropped on his knees before his executioners and recanted, but as he rose to his feet he mumbled under his breath, "But the earth does move."

In the year 1941 was a man named Hitler. He said to believe in the brotherhood of man, in labor unionism, in equality, in liberty was "dangerous." And he filled the concentration camps to over-flowing with trade unionists, liberals, Communists, Socialists, ministers who took the gospel too seriously, Catholics, Jews...and blood flowed in the streets. In America great and small made speeches thanking all the powers that be that we Americans live in a free land where a man is entitled to his own thoughts.

History itself is the only arbiter of "dangerous thoughts" and to whom they are dangerous. For the world does move. Men's thoughts change as the times change. You can no more freeze the thoughts of mankind than you can stop the earth from moving on its axis, than you can freeze a lovely face into eternal youth. To try to do this is not only to make a mockery of democracy, it is to stop the movement of progress and to whip up a fierce tide of reaction. Who should have the right to determine that another man's thoughts are "dangerous"? To the Taxpayers League, the resentment of the W.P.A. [Works Progress Administration] workers against the W.P.A. cuts is a "dangerous thought." To the National Bankers Association, the anger of the farmers against mortgage foreclosure is a "dangerous thought." To the National Association of Manufacturers, the speculation of workers as to how they can make their paychecks keep pace with the cost of living without striking is a "dangerous thought." You need not even ask yourselves what will happen to democracy if Americans are allowed to be prosecuted as criminals for "dangerous thoughts." You need only to see what happened to Germany.

MY FRIEND YOU'RE SLIPPING

_____, you're a swell guy. Your clean, honest, loyal devotion to progressive politics has become part of the tradition of the Minnesota labor movement. I like you. You're my friend. But, pal, you're slipping.

You know what's the matter? You've gotten a little tired. It's a big job and you've worked hard at it, and now you're tired. But you have no right to be tired. What if every fighter in the labor movement were to get tired tomorrow and just fan out. What if the sun would get tired and not rise tomorrow. Boy, what a world!

The last time I saw you, you got my goat. I didn't like your line of argument. In fact, if I didn't like you so well, if I didn't know your tremendous contribution in the past to the progressive movement, if I didn't know that your heart is in the right place, your arguments would have made me sore. They ran something like this: The labor movement is full of racketeers. A good many of the A.F.L. [American Federation of Labor] labor leaders, and some of the C.I.O. [Congress of Industrial Organizations] labor leaders, are really misleaders of labor. Therefore the greatest menace to the country is the organized labor movement because it can be used as a force for evil in the hands of dangerous and dishonest men. The workers never learn. Their memories are short. What hope is there to ever teach them when they misunderstand the people who are willing to sacrifice their time, their money, their energy, yes, often even their lives, in the interests of the working people? When will they believe the lies of the misleaders and turn on their own benefactors? What hope is there?

In the first place, you know better than to make that first argument. Furthermore, you don't mean it. Everything you have done in the past to contribute to the building and strengthening of organized labor proves you don't mean it, but that's loose talk. It doesn't do anybody any good. It's downright irresponsible.

Of course it's obvious even to an amateur, if the leaders of labor are bad, the only way to get them out is by building the organized labor movement, educating the rank and file, giving the movement a stream of new fighting blood, daily, hourly. Without the organized labor movement, you could give the axe to Mr. Henry Ford, Mr. J. P. Morgan, Mr. Dupont, and Mr. Rockefeller, and say, Okay, boys, hack us to pieces.

Now this argument about the workers never learning, it's hopeless, etc., etc. I am always amazed that we have accomplished so much when you consider that twenty-four hours a day, the radio, the press, the educators, the forums are at work in the interests of the big business groups that own and control them, forging public opinion, paralyzing the class consciousness of the working people, steeping them in big business propaganda, guiding them away from the path of their own best interests. And still, despite all this, the C.I.O. was born, a movement that in the space of five short years has organized five million workers, has rallied to its fighting slogans millions more, has educated, enlightened, given hope and direction to the American labor movement. The last year has seen accomplished a gargantuan task that until now people thought could not be done. The hundred thousand workers in the Kingdom of Henry Ford have been organized, despite the most elaborate labor Gestapo ever conceived and conducted by a monopoly capitalist anywhere. Despite the wails that workers won't stick together, all this has been done and more. In the deep lynch South, a wonderful start has been made in uniting white and black workers and farmers in their common struggles against the southern landlords and mill owners. Of course the workers will stick together when they realize their common interests. Anyone who doesn't believe that has no business in the labor movement.

As to the workers not appreciating our efforts in their behalf, you know, the trouble with most of us middle-classers, we can't seem to feel that we're flesh and blood of the labor movement that we work for and with. "They" don't appreciate. "They" don't learn. As long as we can speak in these terms, we have not identified ourselves with the workers. We are on the outside. "We're doing the boys a favor. They should appreciate that fact." We get sore at their mistakes. We refer to them as "their mistakes." As a matter of fact, when a person becomes flesh and blood of the labor movement, he never speaks of "their" mistakes. It never occurs to him to think in those terms. The mistakes of the workers are also his mistakes.

They are "our" mistakes. "They" as a pronoun means only those on the other side of the fence. He not only talks like this. He thinks and feels in those terms.

As to appreciation…when you do something for yourself or your family, when you save yourself from a great calamity, or insure your family's future, you do not expect appreciation. It's natural to do things for yourself and family. When a person throws in his fortunes with the labor movement, with all that is good and progressive, he is serving himself, his family, his future, his conscience. It is he who should be grateful. Grateful to the labor movement and the working class for giving him the opportunity to find himself as a man. Grateful to the labor movement which is the backbone of the fight against fascism that would destroy us all as civilized human beings. A person who doesn't react in this way isn't hitting on all fours. He needs a repair job. Yes, pal, he's slipping.

Sittin' on a Rail

Sittin' on a rail, broiling in the sun
Sittin' on a rail when the timber work is done.
Can see the trains come rollin' in, the ships go out the bay
And get a whiff of perfume from the match mills in
    Cloquet.
Can hear the fruit trucks rumblin' by, can see the county jail
The whole damn town goes rushin' past me…
Sittin' on a rail.

The good old Zenith City…she's a pretty ritzy joint,
There's playgrounds from the boulevard to Minnesota Point
There's playgrounds in the west of town and playgrounds in
    the east,
But there isn't any playground for the lonely timber beast.

Sittin' on a rail when a fellow wants to talk
No place else to chin awhile unless you wanna walk
Or drop into a tavern for a beer, and still another
Until a fellow is so stiff he wouldn't know his mother
It's "Welcome, Mr. Lumberjack!" when you got a lump
    a' kale
But a lumberjack without a stake…
He's sittin' on a rail.

I know this bloomin' city…I know it up and down
For every lousy cent I earned, I blew it in this town.
I know this country from the lake way back there to
    the mines
I knew it when the Chippewas built wigwams in the pines
The streets that cross it up and down, I cut them through
    the brush
I cut them with an axe and saw, through snow banks and
    through slush.

It's pretty now from end to end, with parks on hill and dale
But it isn't very pretty here…
Sittin' on a rail.

I curse the bloomin' bowery, it's dingy and it's rowdy
But where else would I know a soul who'd even tell me
    "howdy"
Some folks got a little yard…something that they own…
But there isn't any moss that grows
On a rollin' stone.

Sittin' on a rail in the lazy Sunday heat
Isn't hardly anybody walkin' down the street
Tennis courts and golf and boating, everybody's busy
Cars are whizzin' by so fast, makes a fellow dizzy
Isn't any place to go…
Life is pretty stale
When you're just a timber beast…
Sittin' on a rail.

A Baby Born in a Sausage Truck

Snow still clung to the icy Wisconsin roads as the sausage truck rolled cautiously to town. It was a raw April night in 1935. The truck stopped before the hospital in the little lumber town of Laona. The hospital was owned by the Connor family. So were the bank and the stores and the hotel and the light plant and the long black miles of virgin timber. In fact, the fifteen hundred wage slaves who made up the population of Laona bitterly referred to themselves as "subjects of the Kingdom of Connor."

A lantern threw a dim light over the open truck where a blanket was thrown hastily over the bottom covered with particles of dust and dirt. On the blanket a woman was groaning in agony. Dudley, the sausage maker, parked the truck in front of the hospital and jumped off. "You take care of her, Joe," he shouted up to the woman's husband, "I'll go in and show 'em this requisition you got for relief and we'll have her inside in a jiffy."

He burst into the hospital and slapped the relief slip on the desk. "Mrs. Kalata out there is havin' a baby...it's on the way now...we gotta get 'er in right away. We can't waste a minute..."

The head nurse looked up coldly. "We're not taking in relief cases anymore."

The sausage maker didn't comprehend. "Lady, she's havin' a baby...out there in my truck...call the doctors...hurry up...tell 'em it's important...quick..."

"I have my orders," the nurse replied.

Desperately the man appealed for help. The nurses were hard as steel. The doctor refused to come. The sweat standing on his forehead, Dudley returned to the sausage truck to tell Joe the bad news. The baby was being born. Seeing Joe standing over Rose with the lantern, helpless and terrified, he ran back to the hospital.

"Please, lady," he begged the nurse, "if you can't take her in, come on out and help her out there...me and Joe we don't know nothin'..."

She turned a cold shoulder. When he returned to the truck Joe had cut the baby free with a jackknife used an hour before for cutting tar paper for the roof. There were no bandages, not even a piece of string. Joe took off his sock and unravelled it, and tied the baby's navel with a piece of soiled yarn. Then the truck rolled on, leaving a trail of blood.

Almost dead from loss of blood, she tossed for three weeks in a fever from infection. When she was well enough to talk they told her how Connor had her blood washed off the streets. "He can wash my blood off the streets of Laona," Rose Kalata smiled wryly, "but he can never wash the blood off the Kingdom of Connor."

JUSTICE IN CONNOR'S KINGDOM

It is midnight and the courtroom in the little Wisconsin town of Crandon is still packed with workers, their wives and children. They are even lined up against the walls. They follow each word intensely. This is their trial. Above the judge's desk on the cream-colored wall are inscribed the immortal words, "Justice Is To Give To Every Man His Own."

Most of these workers are from Laona, the Kingdom of Connor. The kingdom is torn by inner strife for the slaves have rebelled. To prevent the C.I.O. [Congress of Industrial Organizations] from bringing economic freedom to his company-controlled town, Connor became the over-zealous host of the American Federation of Labor. He stuck union buttons on all his straw bosses, made them union officials, made one of his bond holders organizer of the A.F.L. and signed a closed shop contract with the A.F.L. slashing wages and lengthening hours. To save their jobs the C.I.O. men struck. To force the unwilling A.F.L. workers to break their fellow workers' picket line, Connor brought vigilantes, made them "deputies." They swung their brickbats and their lead pipes. Yesterday one man died.

Uneasy is the head that wears a crown. Still afraid of the rebellion of his slaves, Connor arrested whole batches of C.I.O. men and threw them into jail. Tonight five are being tried for "interfering with laborers going to work."

All the defendants but one are old employees of Connor. They have served the king eight years, ten years, twelve years, but Horne, the prosecuting attorney, says they are "agitators coming in here and taking the bread out of our children's mouths."

A witness testifies that the vigilantes were going to "drive the C.I.O. out of town because they're a bunch a' foreigners from Minnesota and Michigan." It's a small world!

One by one the prosecutor calls his witnesses. Some of them are Connor's straw bosses, dutiful flunkies of Connor. "God how they lie!" murmur the workers in the courtroom. "How can they have the brass to get up there and lie like that!" Some of the witnesses are browbeaten, misled slaves of Connor's. Men who have worked too hard and too long to question what it is all about. One of these witnesses is a barnman.

"How many hours a day do you work?" the union attorney questions him gently.

"Nine or ten hours a day," the barnman answers.

"How many days a week do you work?"

"Seven days a week."

"Didn't you know that the reason the C.I.O. was organized and the men struck was precisely to put a stop to such conditions as this—where a man like you is compelled to slave nine and ten hours a day for seven days a week? Didn't you know that your C.I.O. brothers were fighting on the picket line to raise the wages and better the conditions of all the employees of Connor?"

"I object!" shouts the prosecutor. "That is unfair cross-examination!"

"That's all," shrugs the attorney for the defense.

The witnesses for the defense take the stand. One is Darlie Patton, a "Kentuck," president of the C.I.O. union. He looks the prosecutor square in the face. His reddish hair stands up in a bristle from his forehead, like a boy's. His suit seems too short for his long arms and legs, and when he smiles, he smiles like a child and his white teeth flash.

Bill Bradley, an A.F.L. man, stooging for Connor, beat his way through the picket line, striking everyone in his way. He was the only Connor stooge the sheriff arrested. Darlie Patton testified that he went to the judge and asked him to release Bill Bradley and not to impose any fine upon him.

"Do you mean to tell me," shouts Horne, "that you went and asked the judge to release Bill Bradley, an A.F.L. man?"

"Ya-as, I did," Darlie answers with his Kentucky drawl.

"Why did you do a thing like that?"

"I says to th' judge, I says, 'I wants you to release Bill 'cause he's jest a po' workin' man an' he's got a family an' he can't afford to pay no fine, an' anyway Bill's always been m' friend.' "

The prosecutor looks nonplussed. "Is that the only reason you asked him to release Bradley?"

"That's enough reason. I didn't figger Bill could afford to pay no fine."

"Bradley was fighting you on the picket line. Do you mean to say you deliberately asked for his release and that was the only reason?"

"Wa-all…he didn't kill nobody."

"You thought he was breaking the law. Do you mean you'd swear to it that that was the only reason?"

The attorney for the defense springs up from his chair. "Here is a man who sits before you and gives you one of the finest answers I have ever heard in any court—an answer so warm with generosity towards his fellow man that you are not capable of comprehending it. In fact, you do not want to comprehend it. You know it is too good an answer!"

"I beg you, members of this jury, to find these men guilty. These agitators were committing a great crime against their fellow men! They were robbing them of their legal right to work!" Horne, red in the face, shouts to the hand-picked jury. "Why, you have heard the witnesses testify that the pickets called them 'Scabs.' Scabs! Think of that! Why the worst thing a man can do is to call his fellow man a scab!"

The attorney for the defense leans his tall figure over the jury box. "Mr. Horne says the worst thing a man can do is to call his fellow man a scab." He wheels suddenly facing the prosecution's witnesses. "No. I say the worst thing a man can do is to be a scab! A scab keeps his fellow man down, holds him in a condition of slavery and prevents him from bettering his conditions and the conditions of his brothers. But we do not say that all these men are scabs. Many of them are honest, hard-working people. Darlie Patton believes that. That is why he went to the judge and asked him to release his friend, Bill Bradley. The milk of human kindness was not gone from his heart. He realized that the workers, when they would understand, would join him and his brothers on the picket line. He is an honest, straightforward working man who scratched below the surface, who realizes the forces that motivate many of the fellows who do not understand the class struggle, who understands the fears and the sorrows and the difficulties of his misled brothers, who knows that to keep the workers divided is of benefit to only one man, the employer himself. Darlie understands these things. He knows that when Bill Bradley understands these things he will not fight his fellow workers on the picket line. That is why there is no hard feeling in the heart of Darlie Patton for Bill Bradley. Only compassion. Do you see any of the witnesses for the prosecution asking the judge to release their fellow workers? No. Because the sinister force of the Connor Lumber Company, seeking tremendous wealth at the expense of these men, women and children, yes, the black heart of Connor is the directing force seeking to send these men to jail. That is why you don't find any compassion, any generosity such as was displayed by Darlie Patton."

It is almost three a.m. when the sheriff's jury returns with the verdict—guilty!

"Guilty of disrespect to the crown," a worker says dryly.

"Look!" A woman points to the immortal words inscribed on the cream-colored wall, "Justice is to give to every man his own."

The tall "Kentuck" beside her reads the words slowly. "Connor will get his justice yet," he says, and leaves the courtroom with a smile.

A Leader Who Went Haywire

If they had told me a year ago last winter that Fred Lequier, then president of the Timber Workers [Union], would ever go haywire, I would have said, "Go sit on a tack."

I remember the first time I came to strike headquarters shortly after the first strike, Fred, and you were there in your lumberjacks' clothes. I watched your quick, energetic movements. I watched you hold the men spell-bound with your fiery speeches, and I said, "What luck for the jacks. Now they have a real leader."

Do you remember, Fred, who led the jacks to the Labor Temple when you heard that the A.F.L. [American Federation of Labor] phony, Andrew Leaf, was selling out our strike behind closed doors, and brave old Double Breasted Joe burst in, shouting, "Who'sa sell'a strike? Who'sa buy'a strike? Who'sa low-down snake who'd sell out a poor working man?" It was you, Fred.

Do you remember who it was who overheard Andrew Leaf disposing of our strike with Bill Hutcheson over long-distance telephone in the Spalding Hotel? Who it was, who, burning with excitement, rushed to strike headquarters and shouted, "Boys, are we going to let Bill Hutcheson and his sell-out gang break our strike?" It was you, Fred.

Yes, Fred, it's hard to forget it was you who mounted a bench and shouted to the boys, "Boys, if I ever do a thing to harm the lumberjacks, I hope you'll throw me right into that lake!" It's hard to forget because I heard you, Fred. Could I have believed the day would come when you would be one of Bill Hutcheson's sneaky little chore boys?

I was with you throughout the strike in Minnesota. I was with you when you shouted encouragement to the jacks in Marenisco. I remember how you used to shake your head and laugh, "It's no use, Calamity, old girl. Until you learn how to spit snoose you'll never be a lumberjack." I remember how you lifted my kid on a chair and said, "Come on, Little Calamity, make a speech for the jacks," how she clenched her little fists and lisped,

"I'm just a tiny little girl
But I have joined the fray
And I will fight for what is right
Until I'm old and grey."

You cocked your head on one side and roared, "You're rich, Calamity. Damned if you don't get richer every day." But behind your laughter you really believed then, as passionately as I, that you've got to teach a kid right from the cradle the only thing in life worth living for. Didn't you, Fred?

About two months ago I met you on Superior Street. You had been suspended from the union for putting whiskey and women before the interests of your union, for forgetting that union funds are the hard earned savings of the lumberjacks. The union gave you chance after chance to redeem yourself because everyone believed that you had just hit a detour and were riding rough, but one day you would find the highway and ride straight again.

"What would you say, Calamity," you asked me, "if I were to come down the street sporting a big A.F.L. button?"

"I guess you know what I'd think," I said.

"And if I went A.F.L. I would fight just as hard against you as I fought for you too."

"That's not strange," I said, "when folks go rotten they generally go the whole hog."

You grew a little thoughtful. "Well, even if I go A.F.L., I'll fight the old bureaucrats and phonies of the A.F.L. just the same as I always did."

I shook my head slowly. "No you won't, Fred," I said, "you won't bite the hand that's feeding you."

Funny, isn't it, Fred, when you're going up, the sky's the limit. But when you're going down, funny how quick you hit the ground.

You seemed to think, Fred, that because you had a hand in building the union, it was yours to build or break. You didn't know that the union is bigger than yourself, that there's not a human being on this earth so big that he's bigger than the working class. When you're with the progressive tide of the labor movement, you may be swept to the front, but bigger men than you, Fred, have been drowned bucking that tide.

So you're trying to build a dual union, Fred. So you're trying to sneak the jacks back into Bill Hutcheson's union that you helped to deliver them from. So you're trying to get the jacks to cheat on themselves, get them fighting each other, and finally leave their union pinned at the boss's feet with a knife in its back. But you can't do it, Fred. You who could desert your union for a slug of liquor and a night's carousal can't stage a comeback with the lumberjacks. Why? Because the lumberjack is the real McCoy. Honest and clean and straight. Yes, Fred, you were the man who told me so.

I Checked and Double-Checked

It's awful. I believe everybody. And my mother always used to warn me direly, "You never can tell." And here I am way past the age of discretion. In fact, for the past six months I've been paying my oldest kid a penny apiece for every gray hair she can pull out of my head at the first tweak, and still I believe everybody.

Now here's a case in point. The other morning I was sitting at the table trying to eat breakfast and give the morning paper a quick once-over in between diapers, for I have it scientifically estimated that, after changing the baby's diaper for the twentieth time, I have just exactly enough time to down a cup of boiled-over coffee in three gulps and one-half before the baby is ready for his twenty-first change. And what do you think I saw? An exquisite picture of our congressman, Mr. Pittenger, and something or other about his being a friend of labor. I took a gulp of coffee and it tasted even worse than usual. The cream had curdled.

"How I have underestimated this man!" I whispered huskily, and I was going to lean dramatically against the piano but I had forgotten to take up the hem of my house coat and I tripped. Besides I leaned against the broom by mistake because the broom was leaning against the piano. I walked upstairs muttering to myself. "All this time I thought Bill Pittenger was an arch enemy of labor. I thought he voted wrong on every issue of benefit to the people.

"I done him wrong," I moaned. "Find me my shorthand notebook!" I called downstairs. "Sharpen me a pencil! Get me my hat! It's in the baby's playpen! Find me my purse. The last I saw of it the dog had dragged it under the studio couch. I'm on my way!"

I kissed the kids goodbye and flourishing my pencil like a sword, I cried, "Goodbye. I won't be home for lunch. I may not be back for supper and if I should not be home before dark, don't forget to put the dog out." And with that I swept out of the house and grabbed a bus.

Reaching the public library, I seized the Congressional Record, flipped my notebook to a clean page, and prepared to take down the speeches of the great man of the people whom I had so cruelly underestimated. Somewhere in this record this champion of the poor and oppressed must have opposed the vicious Woodrum Amendments. Somewhere must be an impassioned speech against crippling the Wage-Hour Bill. Somewhere his voice must have rung out against destroying the union scale in W.P.A. [Works Progress Administration]. How he must have pleaded for a housing bill! To think that this champion would have the courage to leave the reactionary fold of his own party and demand with the fervor of a Patrick Henry and the brilliance of Webster that Congress increase old age pensions! I checked page by page. I began to get tired. My eyes gave out. My head got heavy, and still no speeches.

"Something is wrong with these records," I said grimly. In the course of another hour three librarians were scampering madly about, treading on each other's toes, dropping books. They begged for mercy. "Something is wrong with these records," I insisted. "I have looked through the whole record and Mr. Pittenger never let a peep out of him and that's impossible." They exchanged glances as if to say, "Should we throw her out in one piece or should we quarter her and tar and feather the pieces?" Suddenly a cry of victory rose from one of the exhausted girls. "I've found something!" she cried. We all dashed forward. It was something Mr. Pittenger had said about grasshoppers when nobody was listening. "Will one of you girls please lend me an aspirin?" I asked weakly.

I went home a disillusioned woman and went listlessly through my mail. And glory of glories! Among my communications was a copy of the Congressional Record "not printed at government expense" dated August 5th. It was the "extended remarks" of Mr. Pittenger on work relief written for the benefit of his constituents but not spoken on the floor of Congress where such remarks might make his reactionary colleagues kind of sore. And in these extended remarks Pittenger said it was a shame not to do something for the people because he sure was for the people in a big way and it was a shame for Congress to go home before doing something for the people whom he, Pittenger, was for one hundred percent. So I sat down in a rocking chair and just rocked. Something was screwy somewhere and it wasn't me. I'm sure of that 'cause I checked and double-checked.

To a Young Girl Graduate

I heard you last Friday night at the Duluth Armory deliver the Farewell Address to the Class of 1941 of Central High School. You were a stranger to me. I had never seen your face before, but you looked very sweet in your cap and gown, and by your words of youth's high hope and courage, I knew you. Yes, I have known you all my life.

You said people feel sorry for you young boys and girls graduating into a world of war, of turmoil, of change. And you asked, but why should they feel sorry for you? This world in its terrible state is a challenge to youth, and the greater the challenge, the more glorious the victory!

You asked, why should the world be in such a state? The machine age has created all the conditions for full, happy and creative living. Why then this frustration, this agony, this despair? It is greed, you declared, greed that is responsible for the plight of a world, the kind of greed that hacked away our forests and laid bare a green and lovely land for profit. We must not say, "What of the world…enough that I am safe and comfortable!" It is greed that presents the challenge to the Class of '41! Yes, little girl, how right you are!

And to the six hundred boys and girls like you, the Board of Education brought an old man from the deep South to deliver the class address. This old man talked vaguely of democracy and American ideals and, mouthing these precious concepts, he launched into slanderous, vulgar jokes against the Negro people. And I blushed for this hollow old man, for Superintendent Eelkema, and for the Board of Education who brought him there to give you guidance, for revealing their inner bankruptcy before the clean, youthful eyes of you six hundred boys and girls, Negro and White. For it is precisely this that is a challenge to the Class of '41—this anti-democratic, un-American spirit of an old man who dares to speak to you of democracy and Americanism. Greed and hypocrisy are indeed inseparable companions.

But you, little girl, you were probably born in the city of

Duluth. Every day of your life you awake to a wide expanse of water breaking in white caps on the rocky shores, or spread still and blue as a painting upon a lifeless canvas. To high and jagged cliffs where sea gulls swoop with mournful cries and nest their young almost in the heart of a city. To hills as high as mountains. To open fields. To beauty so perfect you can never take it for granted, but wake each morning to embrace it as if it were yours for the first time. Yes, it is a beautiful country.

Of course it is a challenge to a girl like you that in this lovely land, the richest in the world, with natural abundance and technical perfection to make every American happy and prosperous, there are fifty-two million hungry people, there are starving sharecroppers and feudal landlords, there is the poll tax, the lyncher, the vigilante. There are little children in crowded slums who have never seen lilacs in blossom, who have never run with bare feet upon green, sun-baked fields.

There are the people of *The Grapes of Wrath,* wandering homeless and disinherited, in the land that once said, "Give me your poor, your tired, your homeless, longing to breathe free, the huddled masses of your teeming shores..."

There are many who will smile at your idealism, many who have lived longer than you. They will pat you knowingly on the shoulder and say with kindly indulgence, "Dream your dreams for awhile. Youth is rebellious. But when you are a little older, like me, you'll settle down and get wise. You'll know it's not worthwhile to try to change the world."

I too am older than you. It is sixteen years since I left the classrooms of Central High School. I too have done a lot of living in sixteen years, and I tell you, "Little girl, take up the challenge!" If you take up that challenge, you will never be smug. You will never be safe. You will never be comfortable. But you will never stifle in a small, crowded, overheated little niche of the world, breathing over and over the air that you exhale.

Your roof will be the sky, your floor, the earth, and your range as wide as America. You will ask yourself, "Am I my brother's keeper?" and every time that the answer is "Yes," you will win a victory, a victory over your own self, and a hard won victory it may be.

You shall say to the hungry and the disinherited as Ruth said to

Naomi, "Where thou goest, there I go also; thy people shall be my people, and thy God, my God," and you shall go with them into the bleakest corners of America and build light in the darkness, and every victory of your brother over poverty, hypocrisy and greed will be your victory. You will expect no gratitude, for you will get none. But your recompense will be the greatest recompense that comes to any human being—the confidence in your own integrity. You will never grow old. If your body lives to be a hundred, within its aged shell you shall always be as young as you are today. Yes, take up the challenge! The challenge of the Class of '41!

WORKER'S PAPER

When I was just a babe in arms
My mother used to boost my charms.
"Oh, boy," she'd say, "this kid is cute
I'll bet he's going to be a beaut…"
When I was big enough to tussle
My pa he used to feel my muscle.
"Gee whiz," he'd say, "this kid is good.
He'll lick the whole darn neighborhood."
Since then I've worked the country over
And sure I've never been in clover.
I've sailed the ships and laid the roads.
I've cut the trees and lugged the loads.
But no one ever sang my praises
Especially when I asked for raises.
Nope, no one ever stopped to say,
"Say, Mr. Worker, you're okay."
The papers didn't raise my hopes.
"Those workin' stiffs they sure are dopes."
But one day all us boys went walkin'
And let the union do our talkin'…
A union paper comes each week.
"My gosh," it says, "Man, you're too meek!
Why don't you get out there and fight?
Afraid you haven't got the right?
Go on, go on, get out and hustle!
Look at your chest! Look at your muscle!
Together you'd outfox the fox.
You're stronger than Paul Bunyan's ox!"
And say, you know, I'm feelin' good
Like when I licked the neighborhood…
As one good worker to another
I feel like when I had a mother.

re very blue and sunny in your face. "So long," you said,
te with Hitler and Mussolini somewhere in Spain. Gotta
Quiet John Erkilla, stump farmer and lumberjack, who h
organize the Timber Union and win the strike. Quiet John
ved demo   ay to die
honored,   per, whos
rds were   rs in your
cause yo   back and
ver did. I   it even re
e Spanish   i is dead.
And yo   ay throug
ng depres   uncles' ca
thes, ind   penny in
cket. We   m? You w
ddle ther   lp right
cket line   ow to fig
ok for g   en fascis
ashed, I   ether, and
ughter we   d. But th
laughte   of this
om, "Star   are not v

The future is a green and happy land, but it was not mea
o long in the jungle to enter the Land of Canaan. We
shed through the muck of fascism, we've been splashed wit
od of our brothers. We have looked upon so much perversi
manity that   carcely feel p
rror. We wh   as seen men
ap and lamps   seen human b
rocessed" in murder factories, we are the heavy-hearted
nnot enter the Land of Canaan, where hearts will be ligh
ughter young and there will be no memory of man's te
humanity to man. We stand at the gates of the future, sure

SECTION THREE
LOVE AND SORROW

MAMA'S BOY

Mama sat rocking to and fro in the stuffy little front room, looking out of the window. Two dead geraniums drooped on their wilted stalks in the compacted earth of the clay pots on the fire escape. Mama had not watered them. A fly trapped on the smooth surface of the window pane buzzed wildly. Mama ignored it.

Papa touched her shoulder lightly.

"Try to lie down a little, Mama."

"I've tried already," she said, and kept on rocking.

"Today you have not tried. I will turn on the electric fan. I will put it so it will not blow right on your face. I will pull down the shades. Sunday is a quiet afternoon. Maybe you could sleep."

She turned her emptied face to him. He wanted to cry out. Her eyes looked as if they were bleeding purplish black into her flesh.

She tried to smile.

"You go lie down, Papa. It is no use for me. I cannot sleep."

She wanted to reach out and touch his hand but she did not have the strength.

He paused and reached out timidly for the bundle of letters that lay inert in Mama's lap.

"Maybe I'll take them, Mama. What is the use? Why should you read them? It only makes you feel worse. Let me put them away."

She shook her head.

He turned away.

What could he say to Mama? What could he do for her? Did he not feel the sorrow of losing his children, two sons, first one and then the other? The first in a war he was not even asked to fight? Who can describe the suffering of a father bereft of his sons? But even so it was nothing compared to the anguish of a mother. Such an anguish he could not even hope to share.

Besides his children he had work. A shop, such as it was. He earned a living, which took thought, absorbing a part of him, even against his will. There were things to think about. Even other worries to distract him. People came in. He talked. Something happened in the street and he laughed despite himself.

But Mama was bereft of everything. Her children were her work, her thought, her worry, her distraction.

With a shudder of pain he thought of the bundle of letters in her lap. Her letters from Paul, her letters from Max, Paul's letters from Max. He should have burned them—at least hidden them away so they wouldn't be lying in her lap right now. Cursing his negligence, he shuffled slowly to his room.

Mama made a helpless gesture to his retreating back. She wanted to talk to him, to explain to him why she couldn't sleep. But when she opened her mouth to speak, no words came. It was like crying out in a dream. You think you are screaming but no one about you hears a sound. If the words would come she could explain to him that she was afraid to sleep. Sleep carried her into such a world of horror that she fought to delay it, and when it came against her will, she awoke from it drained.

It was Paul, her youngest.

There is such a difference between sons and sons. One son seems to be a man from the very first. Even while he is nursing he looks at you in such a way you are almost embarrassed with him. And the other still has the dew of babyhood on him even when you have to stand on tiptoe to kiss him.

The day she brought Max, her oldest, to school, there was nothing to make her heart ache.

"Do you want to see my top?" he said right away to the first boy he saw and, when she turned away from the teacher to say "Goodbye, Maxie," he was so busy playing he didn't even hear her go. But Paulie clung to her and cried, "Don't go, Mama!" She had to push him away and run. She ran all the way home remembering how he stumbled a little when she pushed him, looking at her with startled and reproachful eyes as big as chestnuts, and she cried until it was time to go back to school and bring him home.

When he was six they had gone to visit a relative in the country. Hours passed in gossip, when suddenly she realized her Paulie was not around. A search began for him. For hours they scoured the surrounding hills and forest but he could not be found. She was running hysterically across an abandoned farm and calling his name when she heard a cry of "Mama!" so faint she thought she imagined it.

"Paulie!" she shouted, running in all directions, and the cry of "Mama!" came to her ever more urgently from under the earth.

She tumbled at last upon an abandoned well. There at the bottom of the well was Paulie.

"Mama!" he screamed to her, holding up his arms.

"Paulie, are you hurt?"

"Yes!" he cried.

She restrained an impulse to leap into the well. She leaned over to comfort him. "I'm going for help, Paulie. I'll be back."

"Don't go, Mama!"

She turned away. She heard him crying after her as she left him in the pit alone. The sound of his voice crying to her got fainter as she ran stumbling across the open field. Running she knew she would never forget the cry of "Mama!" as long as she lived.

The telegram came only a month ago. From the War Department. Paulie was killed in action.

What action? How? Was he killed at once? Or did he lie for hours in agony calling her name? Did he die in anger? Or did he die in fright?

Why is the War Department so merciless in its brevity? Didn't they understand she had to know or she would never be able to sleep again? For every time she fell asleep she saw herself running across a no-man's-land of barbed wire and dead men following a cry of "Mama!" from under the earth. And every time she found him he was at the bottom of a gouged-out canyon running with red streams as if a great wound had been blown in the earth and left it disemboweled and bleeding.

She bent over the fearsome pit in which her Paulie seemed lost and miles away and with the sudden weird closeup of dreams she saw that his face was running blood. "I'm going for help, Paulie!" "Don't go, Mama!" His voice echoed against the canyon walls and followed her across the fields. She was screaming for help knowing there was no help. There were only the helpless dead and the gouged out, wounded belly of the earth so deep and her son so wounded nothing could ever save him. Still she ran, seeking. And the terrible cry of "Mama!" grew fainter and fainter from under the earth until she awoke, sweating and sick.

Why did she never dream such dreams of Max, her first born?

It wasn't that Paulie was dearer to her. She loved both her sons.

She remembered when they were children—the time Paulie had come in crying.

"He called me 'Christ Killer,' Mama. He took a stick and hit me. I never killed Christ, Mama."

"Oh, a black year on them!" she had cried, seizing a knife and pressing the cool blade against the blue welt on his head. "A thousand curses on them and their Christ. How many more centuries will they torment us in his name! May the cholera take them! God in heaven, what have we done to you that you will not let our children walk safe in your world!"

But Max, who was twelve, rushed in between them.

"Why didn't you hit him back?" he demanded, gripping his brother by the shoulder and shaking him. "Why did you just stand there like a dummy and let him hit you?"

Mama lunged at him.

"You want they should kill him!" she shrieked. "You want they should give him like they gave you—six stitches in your head?"

"I gave them some stitches too. Don't you forget that, Mama."

"You gave them. Hero! That makes me feel good. Fine. You gave them. I'm telling you, leave Paulie alone with your advice. He's only a baby. He isn't getting into any fights. And you're not getting into any more fights either, you hear me, Max?"

"Oh sure. I'm gonna let them call me names, beat up on me. Eh, Mama? Well, here's one guy who isn't gonna be shoved around!"

"Oh Max, Max!" she shivered at the fierceness in him. "What will become of you, Max, in this bitter world!"

She remembered the time Fritz Kuhn and the Bund were goose-stepping on the streets of New York. And Max got wind of the fact that one of the Bund gang was drilling neighborhood boys with rifles in the empty lot behind the McFarland garage.

"In our neighborhood, Mama, do you know that?" Max cried. "Taking the kids and turning them into Nazis!"

"What can we do?" Mama had shuddered. "Maxie, keep out of it. Don't get into trouble!"

"Mama!" he had cried, "we *are* in trouble! Can't you understand that? Have you forgotten the swastika they painted on our door?"

"Go to the police, Maxie. Let them handle it. That's their

business. That's why we pay taxes."

"Sure it's their business," Max had sneered, "except that the cops on this beat are Nazis too. You think they don't know about the drilling? 'That's why we pay taxes.' Oh Mama, that's rich!"

"Go to the chief then. Go to the mayor. Don't mix in."

"Don't mix in. Don't mix in. Boy, Mama, if you only knew how mad it gets me when I hear that old don't-mix-in business. We've gone everywhere. Chief. Mayor. Nobody is stopping them."

She knew what they were going to do. And Max was in the hospital for two weeks after that battle. There was no more drilling behind McFarland's garage. The pitched battle had brought the Bundists unfavorable publicity. But her Maxie was so terribly beaten she couldn't recognize his face.

That was why she shook with fear the time she came upon them suddenly—Max and Paulie whispering together.

"What are you whispering?" she demanded, for she knew that there was a demonstration scheduled at the waterfront when the Nazi ship *Grossland* was due to arrive in the New York harbor.

Paulie was shamefaced, Max defiant.

"You're taking Paulie with you to the ship, is that it, Max?"

"I'm not taking him, Mama. He wants to go," said Max.

"He wants to go. A lot he knows what he wants! It's you who puts in his head what he wants. But I know what I want. I want you to leave Paulie alone, Max. It's enough one like you! He's not like you—a tough! He can't turn a picket sign into a club and hit them back!"

"Why can't he, Mama?" Max asked softly.

"Why can't he!" Mama's face was distorted, her eyes wild. "He can't because I say he can't. That's why. He can't because I don't want him marching in your parades. I don't want him on your picket lines! I don't want him going where the fascists, may they burn in hell, can hurt him. That's why he can't!"

"You'd rather wait until they come and get him, eh, Mama?" Max asked her.

"They won't come. This is America."

"Where did I get this scar on my head, Mama? Germany?"

"You go into a pen with a bull you get gored. Who asked you to go? Didn't I tell you, let them holler. Let them parade. Let them drill. They will get nowhere here! But what are my words to you? With you I am nothing. A stupid old-country mother with no respect. What you do to yourself I cannot help. But you will not do this to Paulie. With one son at least I have some influence!"

With this she tore in between them and pushed them apart.

"Paulie, go away from him, do you hear!" she cried. "Go practice your piano! Don't listen to him! With him you will always be walking into fires!"

"You're bringing him up to be a coward."

"Better a live coward than a dead hero."

"And is it better to be a dead coward than a dead hero?"

"Dead is dead. There is no difference. Hero or coward. Dead is dead."

"There is a difference!" Max took a step toward her. There was such a cry in his voice, such a fire in his eyes, that involuntarily she shrank from him.

"Mama, don't you ever tell Paul there is no difference!"

"Leave Paulie alone!" she muttered darkly.

And then came the day Max told her he was going to Spain.

Silently, stubbornly, but his eyes deep with pain and compassion for her, he had let her drive the battering ram of her grief and rage against him. Again and again, with all her strength, until exhaustion defeated her.

"Well, it's done. It's done," she had at last acknowledged bitterly. "Nothing I can say will move you. My tears cannot melt you. You are made of stone. If there is a war it is time enough to go when they come for you, but my son cannot wait. He runs into fires. What is this Spain to me? Tell me, what is this Spain? To this Spain that is nothing to me I must sacrifice my son, my eldest, my own flesh? It is done."

"Mama," he had said gently, touching her shoulder.

She recoiled from his touch.

"You ask what is Spain to you. Is Hitler nothing to you?"

She did not answer him.

"Everyday I read how our people are jailed, are humiliated, are murdered. I read and vomit. There is something obscene about such a fate. Are we sheep or pigs? Is this a fate for men? Must men accept it? You say death is death. You are wrong, Mama. There are ways of death like there are ways of life."

Mama bristled.

"You call them sheep. What do you want of them. What can you do when a gun is over you?"

"I don't know, Mama. But there is no gun over me—yet. No one will ever get the chance to drive me like a sheep to slaughter."

And he had gone. He had gone with his faded laundry case stuffed with a shirt, socks, a sweater, a razor and a toothbrush, smiling and looking like a young man starting out for a new semester in college.

And she knew how he died. He had died with his own hot fire protecting him. He had never called, "Mama!"

"What have I done to you, Paulie!" she groaned silently, only her hands, gripping the bundle in her lap, betraying her despair.

Seeking something to distract herself, she looked down at her hands. With a sudden sharp gesture she tore the ribbon from the letters and they drifted loosely in her lap. Not knowing herself what she was searching for, she began to reread the letters from her sons. And she read the letters from Max to Paul. Letters from the front in Spain. Factual letters. Letters briefly describing past battles. Letters interpreting current events. These she skimmed without interest and was going to put them aside when she caught the word "Mama." Her hands trembled as she turned back to the paragraphs she had skimmed.

"Look, I appreciate how much you want to come and join me here, Paul, but take it easy, eh? I've got a feeling this is only the beginning. There will be plenty of fronts to fight on and a guy with your guts will be needed. I'll never forget how you scrambled up that pole like a greased monkey and brought down that Nazi flag before anyone knew what was happening. Know something? That was one of the big moments of my life when somebody said, 'Who's that kid?' I said, 'That's my brother.' But do me a favor. Stick it out for now, will you, kid? Don't hurt Mama. She's had all she can take for now."

Mama read and reread the paragraph, trying to fix in her mind a new image of her sons. She rocked slowly, back and forth, back and forth, with a slow, inexorable rhythm, thinking. Until, exhausted, her head dropped against the soft back of the rocker and she fell into troubled sleep. Relentlessly her dreams advanced upon her. But this time it was another kind of dream.

An army of skeletons was fighting fascists. They poured out of the concentration camps and the gas chambers and some crawled out of the ovens charred and half of their naked bones burned away. They carried no weapons, only their outstretched claws in a gesture both supplicating and vengeful. The skeletons of countless children clattered along beside them. And as this strange army loped weirdly into the field of battle, the hand grenades of the fascists exploded among them and shattered each oncoming vanguard into dust.

She felt herself rooting for this ghostly army, weeping for them, screaming as each advancing legion exploded in splinters.

And suddenly, with a gasp of recognition, she saw that two of the skeleton children were dressed in snow suits. Red snow suits with blue piping and peaked hats. On the top of each peak was a silver bell.

"Paulie! she screamed. "Max!"

The little figures ran. And the tiny bells jingled among the flying splinters the way they used to jingle when she took her boys to play in the snow at Central Park.

"Help! My children! Save them!"

She started to run with the skeletons, not knowing why or where, right into the fire of the enemy. "No one will help," she was thinking as she ran. "God has forsaken us. We are lost."

And suddenly she heard a crack of countering fire. Yells. Cries. From so many throats at once the sound seemed to move forward like incoming tide. She stopped and stepped backward and saw the field coming to life with a mass of living soldiers. They were running swiftly, surely, their clumping boots raising a dust upon the earth.

Speechless with gratitude, she flung out her arms to them.

The armies lunged forward, their fire exploding. And as they moved she saw that one soldier was leading. At the head of the thickly massed columns he ran. In a squall of bullets. He ran like a man on fire.

She heard herself shouting, "Run, soldier!"

He turned to wave his armies on and in that moment, in an agony of joy, she saw that the leader was Max!

"Max!" she cried. "Run, Max! God is with you!"

But as he tore past her, he turned his burning eyes her way and gave her a swift and fleeting glance.

And she saw that the leader was not Max.

The avenging soldier was her Paulie!

Mama's head rolled back against the rocking chair. A sigh, heavy as a sob, broke from her chest, relieving her. She relaxed. Her breathing came deeply and evenly as she slept.

It was dusk when she awoke with a start. Papa was sitting in the chair opposite her, watching her with tired and anxious eyes.

"I slept!" she cried.

Papa nodded. "Thank God! It seemed like you were resting for the first time since that day."

"Yes, Papa. I was resting for the first time."

"Good. Good. Ach, that is very good."

Mama smiled. She reached over and, with a tender hand, she touched his face.

SONG OF THE WARSAW GHETTO

Remember us!
We are your brethren of another April
Salute us!
We were your soldiers
Exult for us!
We are the ones who cheated their abattoirs
Our ashes never dusted the cabbages of Auschwitz
We hurled our bodies like bullets
Made them gag on our blood
Choked them on our defiance
Know us!
We are the granite in your bones
The stuff of your survival
We light the catacombs
Of your doubt
And your darkness
Forever.

AT THE GATES OF THE FUTURE

It is over, brothers. The long nightmare of fascism in Europe is over. The reign of Hitler and Mussolini forever is closed.

As I write these words I watch the wind rustling over the great blue plains of Lake Superior and I wonder why I am not wild with happiness and rejoicing. The fight against fascism has dominated my every thought for the past ten years. Yet how can I sit so calmly at this hour watching the wind bend the giant willows to the water, and the seagulls moaning over the jagged rocks? Calm? I think today I feel as the Italian people must have felt when they kicked the lifeless carcass of Mussolini and spat upon it. Not wild rejoicing. Not happiness. Just grim, pitiless satisfaction for justice done.

Today in the sunny quiet of this room I share in solitude the triumph of this hour with the memories of beloved friends who hated fascism unto death.

You, Tony Puglisi—fiery Tony, who shook your fist in the faces of all fascists and cursed them in Italian and rich, broken English. Gentle Tony, with eyes like ripe olives. "I am working man," you said. "Many long years I work hard labor. In my country sun a' shine all a' time. Sea is blue. People poor but they laugh. Sing. Mussolini come. Make people poorer. Kill. Murder. No more singing. No more laugh. But some a' day gonna smash this a' fascism. Some day this a' gonna be nice world. All people gonna live together, be brothers. Sun a' shine. Children laugh. Then you can say some time, 'This is world Tony Puglisi dream of. This is world Tony Puglisi fight for.' "

Then humbly, with the wistful apology of the foreigner whose spirit is imprisoned in a strange language, you begged me, "Write this for me, my friend. But don't write like Tony talk. Write it like Tony feel. Give it a sound like music." Tony, my friend, Mussolini is dead.

I share this day of triumph with you, Reino Tantala, farm organizer. With you, Casper Anderson and John Erkilla, lumberjacks.

I remember, Reino, the bright summer day when you walked away with your knapsack flung across your shoulder as if you were going for a jaunt into the country. You were smiling and your eyes were very blue and sunny in your face. "So long," you said, "got a date with Hitler and Mussolini somewhere in Spain. Gotta mow 'em down before they decide to head this way."

Quiet John Erkilla, stump farmer and lumberjack, who helped to organize the Timber Union and win the strike. Quiet John, who loved democracy so much you calmly set out one day to die for it, unhonored, in a foreign land. And Casper, lanky Casper, whose last words were, "So long, sister, carry on!" You had tears in your eyes because you knew somehow that you'd never come back and you never did. Mussolini blasted your ship to bits before it even reached the Spanish coast. Now, Casper and John, Mussolini is dead.

And you, Stan, my brother, who shuffled your way through the long depression, living in cheap hotels, wearing your uncles' cast-off clothes, indifferent to the fact that you never had a penny in your pocket. Were there leaflets to get out blasting fascism? You would peddle them. Wrongs to be righted? You would help right them. Picket lines to tramp, workers to organize, Jim Crow to fight? I took for granted you'd be there beside us. When fascism is smashed, I thought, we would share our joy together, and our laughter would be as light as it was in our childhood. But there is no laughter, no rejoicing. I whisper to the silence of this empty room, "Stanley, my brother, Hitler is dead."

No, we are not wild with rejoicing. The future is a green and happy land, but it was not meant for our generation who wandered too long in the jungle to enter the Land of Canaan. We have sloshed through the muck of fascism, we've been splashed with the blood of our brothers. We have looked upon so much perversion of humanity that our emotions are jaded, we can scarcely feel pain or horror. We who belong to a generation that has seen men make soap and lampshades of human flesh, who have seen human beings "processed" in murder factories, we are the heavy-hearted. We cannot enter the Land of Canaan, where hearts will be light and laughter young and there will be no memory of man's terrible inhumanity to man.

We stand at the gates of the future, sure of our victory, but woe unto our memory if we lay down our arms upon the threshold or if we flag in the fight against Japan. Woe to our memory if it can be said by unhappy future generations that we defeated Hitler and Mussolini, only to lay down arms to the Hoovers, the Vandenbergs, the Wheelers, Hearsts, Knutsons, and McCormicks of America. If we allow Germany to be built up again as a bulwark against the Soviet Union, if we permit American cooperation to be transformed into American imperialism—woe to our memory if we allow the seeds of a third world war to be planted under our victorious feet!

We stand at the gates of the future. We can see the bright green of its prairies but we have not yet won it for our children. Tony, Reino, Casper, John, Stan—Hitler and Mussolini are dead. I swear upon your silent graves we shall not lay down arms until democracy is won! I swear we shall not rest until Tokyo has shared the fate of Berlin.

PICKET LINE IN OCTOBER

I lifted my eyes to the hills on the other side of the railroad tracks, painted high against the sky in rich autumn colors. The wind was soft, blowing a little of the red ore dust from the Northern Pacific freight cars clattering down the tracks to the elevators. Smoke rolled from the tall orange chimneys of the new blast furnace. Cars loaded with coke crawled slowly out of the yards of Interlake Iron. Huge black storage tanks squatted in the yards of American Tar and Chemical where fourteen men are out on strike today. And a flock of grey birds gurgled low in their throats as they swooped over the rumbling freight cars, headed south.

The guys covered the bench with a mackinaw to keep my white coat from getting soiled.

They grinned and said, "How's tricks?"

Over at Coolerator, a plant manufacturing refrigerators and normally employing a thousand men, the fellows are out on strike too. "They're a good gang," the guys say. "A bunch of 'em were out here on our picket line today. One of the guys says, 'Say, how come you stuck it out here at American Tar all through the war working a forty-hour week and averaging twenty-eight bucks a week in take home pay?' 'Because we were froze here. Couldn't get a release.'"

Eli Skorich pulls up a blade of dry grass and chews it thoughtfully. "I get less now than I did four years ago when you figure this withholding tax, cost of living and everything. People think workers were all making high wages during the war. Heck, I used to go to the bank to cash my check. Was ashamed to cash it at the store. Nobody knows me at the bank. Didn't want the guys to know what I was working for."

Bill Olson, president of the union, who has worked for the company for eighteen years, grins: "You ain't kiddin'. I cashed my two weeks' check—$62.50—at the bar and somebody says, 'Is that what you pull down a week, Bill?' 'Yeah,' I says. 'I'm ashamed to say that's two weeks' pay.'"

"People think workers got bonds, lots of cash saved," Sam Finnas, big, good-natured, laughs out loud. "You know what I do with a check when I get it? Right down to the grocery store I go an' there's your pay check gone. No more left. I'm better off to stay home, my wife says. That's what she says straight out. 'Sam,' she says, 'you stay home you don't dirty up clothes an' have to buy them all a' time. No use goin' down a' tar plant for lousy wage you get there.' My little girl she say, 'Daddy, don't go back to tar plant. You stink tar all a' time.' " He laughed out loud again. "She eight years old, my kid.

"Boy, this job sure raises heck with your clothes. Acid eats 'em. You get so much tar in 'em. Gotta use strong solutions. Three pairs a' shoes in no time. Look at my shirt. Fallin' to pieces."

Erick Johnson nods.

"Wear a pair a' mitt a week an' throw 'em down on the cement floor an' they sound like rock hit. Get full a tar an' harden in a week."

"It's doctor bills that take the guts out'a ya. That's what really hurts," Charlie Kilby says. "Had a few bonds but had to cash 'em in when I got sick."

"My kid brother had his appendix out," says Eli. "One hundred and five dollars for the doc, seventy-five dollars for the hospital. My dad got sick an' couldn't work an' my mother is ailin'. Boy!"

"What would I do with a raise if I had it? I'd buy me some good clothes, that's what I'd do. Right off. I'd buy me some self-respectin' clothes."

"Me?" says Bill, "I'd buy my wife some clothes."

"A refrigerator for one thing." Erick smiles. "I'd sure like a refrigerator."

"I'd pay up my debts," says Eli.

"I live in two-room house," says Sam. "Two-room houses too small for family. I'd like bigger house, more room, nicer to live. I tell you what. We lookin' for decent living wage, that's what we lookin' for. Bigger house, decent clothes, pay up doctor bill, no debts. Maybe icebox. Decent living."

The rumbling cars screeched at a standstill on the tracks and the wind blew red ore dust into our eyes. "Sure is a swell day, ain't it," says Eli looking up to the red and golden hills.

"Hope it stays this way for a coupl'a months yet," one of the fellow adds, wistfully.

OUR CAPTAIN—LIVES!
Dedicated to Franklin D. Roosevelt

They try to tell us that our captain sleeps.
They say he lies forever as he must
Empty and motionless, consumed in dust.
Our pilot's hands no longer at the wheel
Are folded, still and frozen, on his breast.
They say his restless spirit is at rest,
No longer do they speak his magic name.
The dead are dead...our captain sleeps, they say.
Now they are masters and they curl their lip.
He is not dead! Our captain does not sleep!
He walks forgotten on his floundering ship.

He is not dead. Our captain does not sleep.
Where once he stood erect and steered our course,
Challenged the ocean, jested at the wind,
His dark cape flowing and his face on fire,
The lurching ship, unsteady on its keel
Has changed its course, and toward the setting sun
Crude reckless hands now fumble at the wheel
That twists and turns with neither sense nor form,
The thunder rolls, the breakers pound and toss
And he...he walks forgotten in the storm.

Captain! Beloved Captain! Can you see
The ship you loved is headed for its doom?
Your course is changed! Your tender work undone!
While you whose voice was once so stern and proud
You sit forgotten in the gathering gloom.
Oh, Captain, tell your longing people why!
Speak, Captain, from the hearts of countless men
Where you live on, where you must never die!
Speak for your captain, you who hold him dear!
Or you shall meet the grisly face of fear.

And no one but the rocks shall hear your cries!
Speak, or your children atomized to dust!
Speak or the future shambles of your towns
Shall mock at you with empty, gaping eyes!

Where are you, breadline soldiers
Hunger marching men?
From Hoovervilles of 1929?
Have you forgotten jabs of bayonets
You veterans of the blood soaked picket line?
Have you so soon forgotten him who said
You have the right to eat, the right to live?
These men who tell you that your captain's dead
Prepare to feed you lies instead of bread!
Then speak! Speak up for him! Reject their lies!
Speak and your captain lives
Be silent and he dies!

Speak, and demand his blueprints be restored
The blueprints of that bright and shining world
Toward which he proudly piloted our ship.
Speak, and demand they sheath the naked sword
Where flags of every nation were unfurled!
Turn back the ship upon our captain's course!
Give us the future that we thought we won!
Give back our hope and turn us toward the sun!

Speak for your captain! Raise your voices high!
He is not dead! Our captain shall not die!

FAREWELL, SWEET WARRIOR
To My Husband, Henry Paull, Attorney for the People

The gulls are flying back home from the south. The ducks and the hell-divers are sunning themselves on the great unsalted sea that flows beside our house. Across the quiet water the long boats pass loaded with ore, and spring is creeping, green and tender on the hills. But you are dead. No more to share this boundless beauty. I sit with empty hands and contemplate my emptiness.

I sit today in emptiness and mourn you in the presence of your friends—the people, "the people" of the mines, of the factories, of the lumber camps, of little stores and humble shops, of scrub farms and faded offices everywhere throughout this wide good region of the Arrowhead.

If I could tell you how they mourned you, you would not believe me. Or you would weep with joy at the sweet and terrible majesty of a thing called "man." I would tell you how they came to pay their last respects to you—how they came in hundreds—men and women and children of all creeds, all colors, all nationalities, from all walks of life. I would tell you of the farm woman who apologized for her poor soiled clothes because she came directly from the barns and fields when she heard the terrible news. I would tell you of the Indian who stood with his face frozen in sorrow. I would tell you of the Negro woman who wept on your coffin and could not be comforted. I would tell you of the Catholics who counted their rosaries. I would tell you of the woman on Calvary Road holding a crippled child on crutches by the hand and weeping bitterly as your procession passed on to the grave. I would tell you the thing that touched me most—a shabby railroad worker, who stood bareheaded, with his hat upon his heart, as the long line of cars went by, as one would stand at the hearing of the national anthem. I would tell you this and you would say, "What have I done that I should merit this? Oh, what goodness, what sweetness, what gratitude is in the human race!"

Why do I call you "warrior"?—you who were so tender you could not even hate your enemies. Never has any man so hated injustice, ignorance, viciousness and greed, and yet often as I flayed you for your gentleness and tried to whip you into anger, you did not have it in you to hate the unjust, the ignorant, the vicious and the greedy. You hated vileness and fought it with relentless courage, but you could not hate the vile, made so by the circumstances of their lives.

Oh, how humble were your beginnings! A bedraggled newsboy, neglected child of struggling immigrants, a member of that vast army so little publicized, "Jews without money." Hopeful and pitiful people who came to the promised land to escape the persecution of the Czar. And the pity for them that was born in you as you trudged the dusty city streets to earn a few pennies for your mother grew into a great pity for all the "little people," no matter what their race, their color or their beginnings.

Beloved warrior! I remember the time you were called to Sisseton, South Dakota, by farmers whose farms were being foreclosed in the depths of the Depression, farms which had been tilled by their people for generations, farms cut through by the pioneers. You were sick, very sick, when you boarded the train. Your face was the color of ashes. But you answered the summons of men and women about to be dispossessed. And when you returned, I have never seen you, either before or since, so glowing with happiness. "Irene," you said, "we saved their farms. We moved them back into their homes. You should have seen those people. You should have seen them in that courtroom fighting for their land. It was they who really won that case, not I. Irene, I have never experienced such satisfaction and happiness in my entire life." So I turn to you today, farmers of Sisseton, and say, "Thank you, my friends, thank you for being of such splendid stuff that you gave him the happiest moment of his life."

I remember you in Munising, Michigan, when the lumber barons of Cleveland Cliffs and Henry Ford incited the people of Newberry against the lumberjacks so that they beat four humble men to death and left scores of them to crawl wounded and bloody into the town of Munising.

I remember how we went one tense midnight into the town of Munising, you, Sam Davis and I, and visited the wounded lying like injured dogs on the floor of strike headquarters. And how they asked me, "Why did they do this to us, sister. We only asked to live like men and not like pigs. We only protested against a wage of fourteen to thirty dollars a month, against drinking infested ditch water and sleeping on hay with bedbugs and lice crawling over our bodies. Why did women and children join the mob to beat us? We are the men who cleared the land upon which the town of Munising was built!"

And I remember the next day how a lynch mob gathered around us. Yes, I remember the feeling of being closed in by a mob gone mad with hysteria, how much it feels like being cornered defenseless by a crowd of the criminally insane. And how the prosecuting attorney and the sheriff led the mob. How these men stood mean and puny around you as you stood tall and white faced, and looking so much like our common ancestor, a man called "Jesus." And how they snarled, "We'll get you, Jew b——. We'll get you, you dirty kike. You're the one who defended communists down here four years ago. We didn't forget." We stood there, waiting, the mob indecisive, clasping their iron pipes and clubs in white knuckled fists. I leaned over and picked up a puppy from the arms of a little boy who was part of the mob. I stroked its head and calmed my nerves by the comfort of the dog's eyes which were so much warmer, so much more compassionate than the eyes of these, my fellow men. And somehow my presence broke their spirit. They were not prepared to lynch a woman, so they said later. And so you were spared.

I remember that terrible day in Ironwood when a crippled lumberjack hobbled into my hotel room to tell me, "Hank's been kidnapped." And the long centuries of waiting and suffering before I found you lying on a dirty bed in a cheap hotel in Hurley, your clothes torn and your face covered with blood. You told us then how you had defended yourself against your assailants—you with your giant strength, your powerful arms, your swift trained movements of an athlete. How they had dumped you, bleeding, in the dust of the highway. Oh, how many battles I could recall! Crandon! Laona! Markham! Minneapolis! But the scar you got in Ironwood was our badge of honor. Sometimes when you felt ill, that scar across your nose would glow fire and I would say, "Our badge of honor is glowing on your face." Yes, that was our ordeal, our baptism of fire that admitted us forever into the ranks of the working class.

Beloved warrior. Sometimes I would try to spare your health and I would snap at the people who came to you for help and used up your fading strength, and you would say gently and without reproach, "Irene, be patient with them."

My buddy has fallen beside me in the thick of battle. I stumble on, blinded with tears. My heart is broken, but there is not time for that. The hill must be taken. Objective: progress. Objective: the brotherhood of man. Objective: a good world where not a few, not the privileged, not the rich, but all the little people of this world can enjoy the warm rich bounty of their mother earth. I stumble on, repeating again and again the words we framed and hung upon our wall to guide our children:

> They are slaves who fear to speak
>   For the fallen and the weak;
> They are slaves who will not choose
>   Hatred, scoffing, and abuse,
> Rather than in silence shrink
>   From the truth they needs must think;
> They are slaves who dare not be
>   In the right with two or three.

This rugged shore you loved, these wailing gulls, these gaunt, immortal hills, this everlasting sea, bid you farewell! Farewell, sweet warrior! While I,—I murmur to the challenging night.

> Empty and dark do I raise my lantern
> but the people, the people shall fill it with oil,
> and they shall light it also.

OPERATION GEORGIA!

It's a hot sticky day in the Negro slums of Atlanta. The noonday sun beats down on your head and the heat gathers you in so you can't escape. You go in and out of the rotting, unpainted shacks, in and out of taverns, stop people on the streets. "Will you help put Henry Wallace and the Progressive Party on the ballot in Georgia—a new party—a new kind of party?" You hand out pamphlets—"Jim Crow Must Go."

It's tough going at first. Dark eyes regard you with suspicion. Dark faces brood quietly over the pamphlet, open it, close it. You think maybe they don't understand so you keep explaining, explaining. But they understand all right. The dark eyes meet yours and you can see they want to believe you. Sometimes the words in them are unspoken. Sometimes they come out with at tired shrug: "What's the use? Ain't no party for colored folks nohow. Ain't no use to sign nothin', I reckon."

And you recall for them the abolitionist movement of the pre-Civil War days—the formation of the new party under Lincoln. You paint with the ardor of your own conviction the continuity of that party and this—the continuity of hope and decency and of the battle for freedom from one generation to another.

The faces light up, slowly, warmly. The fingers, cramped over the pencil, write, and hand the pencil to a relative or a neighbor. "Sign. Sign." We've been in the neighborhood for three hours now and hardly have to explain anymore. "Ma'am!" you hear them calling from the rickety porch of a tenement. You fumble up the dark staircase. "Thank you so much for comin' up, Ma'am. My daughter here she ain't signed yet. The rest of us we done signed." Groups gather around us on the sidewalk. Children run up and ask for more pamphlets for their folks.

A group has gathered around us and we hold a political discussion right out there on the sidewalk. As we say goodbye one of them expresses the great warmth and hope that has spread through this community today, spread faster than little pamphlets that are moving from hand to hand. "Thank you, thank you. This is a great day in Georgia. This party is bringing a breath of hope to the South."

It's dinner time and we're starved. On this Operation Georgia you start out at nine a.m. and you work through until eight p.m. and you eat wherever you're lucky enough to find a place to eat.

"You can't serve us?" we ask the woman in the little Negro restaurant. "We're terribly hot and hungry."

"It's against the law, Ma'am. They could put me in jail."

"You couldn't serve us in the back room?"

"I'm sorry. There is no back room. The kitchen looks right out on the street."

Something is blaring in our ears. Something about white supremacy and the white primary. We turn irritably to the radio as if by glaring we could stop the rasping voice.

"It's Herman Talmadge," the Negro woman says, without smiling. We don't know what is in her mind. We look back at her customer who is eating out of a plate stacked with chicken and rice and we feel baffled and guilty, and the emptiness in us is deeper than hunger.

Now it's a mill section we're covering today—a white mill section in Atlanta. When I came down here from Minnesota, I had the typical Northerner's version of the Southern people. Surely they must be another variety of man to oppress their black brothers so cruelly. Surely there must be a sharp line of demarcation that separates these people from the people I have known.

The beloved name of Roosevelt opens the door to you in the mill villages and the doors don't slam in your face. The workers listen.

Wallace, the friend of Roosevelt—the only man carrying out the program of Roosevelt—the man who says the workers must be protected against another depression.

"Chivalry" and Bigotry

The woman who comes to the door is lean and bony. She's carrying a baby and there's too much humility in her face.

"I reckon I don't count for much. My husband an' my daddy always says votin' is a man's business."

"It's you who suffered in the Hoover days, you who saw your

children go hungry, you who should be most concerned that it does not happen again. Voting is your business. You do count. You count as much as any man."

Maybe it's because you're so defiantly sure of yourself. Her gentle eyes meet yours as if to say: "You really believe that, don't you? You really believe a woman counts!" She lays the baby down and reaches for the pencil.

In the next house the man is at home. He is long and lean and grizzled and is solemnly bent over his breakfast. You state your business and he looks up without haste. "Wouldn't drive a stranger from my door, Ma'am," he says with chivalry, "but I'm a white man and don't favor no n——r lovers."

You take him off the subject of the Negro question and remind him of the Hoover days—point out the danger of another depression—show him the similarity between the Roosevelt and Wallace programs. He hears you through.

"Are you aimin' to tell me a n——r is a good as I am?" he comments irrelevantly.

"What she is sayin' is right." His wife has been listening, bent sullenly over the apples she is peeling for a pie. "Wallace would make a better President than Truman any day."

Her husband keeps chewing, calmly. No use wasting time with him. You thank him and get ready to go, then turn to his wife, "Maybe you would sign, Ma'am."

Without a word she turns and leaves the room.

"I reckon she'll sign all right," says the husband, drawling out his words with an incongruous grin, "if she's fixin' to get run off the place."

You stop a young worker on his way home from the mill. He understands your business, listens, nods his head. "I can't write, Ma'am. You write my name in there for me." Then, his eyes flashing, he opens the palm of his hand and shows you a shallow flesh wound on the inside of his thumb. "I tore it on a cable this mornin'. Jest a little hurt like this an' y'know what? He fired me! The boss done fired me! I got a wife an' three kids an' that boss done fired me for gittin' this thumb tore a little on a cable. He can't do that, kin he, now, Ma'am? He can't git away firin' me fer a little thing like that?"

Sorry Leaders and a Mean Law

The scars of a broken union are fresh in this mill village. Some of the men are bitter against the union. They say the leaders did not try hard enough, that they deserted them and did not give them leadership. "I'm worst off now. I lost my job. I got run out'a my house. Won't never be a union in these parts no more nohow." The leaders who failed the workers in the Southern organizing drive bear a great responsibility for the fact that thousands of discouraged workers have turned to Herman Talmadge, seeking hope in his demagogy.

Only one worker did not blame the union leaders. He blamed the Taft-Hartley law. "They been gittin' mighty tough with us since that Taft-Hartley law. How? Well, they cusses us out, runs us out if we say anythin'. Treats us real mean. Got no job security. It's a mean law. Is Mr. Wallace agin' that law?"

The mill worker in the little white house is wiping dishes and laying them carefully on the shelf. The name of Wallace doesn't startle him. He smiles and welcomes you in. He wants to talk to someone. "I work down in the mill," he says in explanation of the apron around his neck. "My wife died about six months ago. She used to work at home and in the mill, too. Now I work at home and in the mill, too—jest like she did." He pauses and spits out a mouthful of tobacco juice. "Y'know, I never knowed all the work she had to do." He pauses again. "I'd sure go a lot easier on the women."

In the next house the millworker's wife listens politely and shakes her head. "I never votes. I never even votes for the deacon of the church. If a good man gets in, that's good. And if a bad man gets in it's not my fault. You see I voted for Hoover in 1928 and two years later I told the Lord that, if he'd forgive me, I'd never vote again."

Confusion from Fear and Uncertainty

In the white slum area around the Fulton Bag Manufacturing Company of Atlanta the reception was almost as friendly as our reception in the Negro slums. Such a general reception was the exception rather than the rule, but it gives the lie to the egg and tomato throwers who say they express the feelings of all the people of the South. In one humble house I was invited to share the dinner of the man, the woman and the crippled son. When I left, the whole family rose to show me the door and to shower their blessings upon Wallace, the Progressive Party and the "brotherhood of man."

On the broken-down porch of one of the miserable "homes" in this area sat a barefooted man, a shabby woman, and three tattered children. I humbly beg their pardon for the thought that almost kept me away from their door. "They look so poor," I had thought. "They must be demoralized and hard to talk to. I wonder if there's any use."

The family greeted me with the hospitality they would extend to a welcomed guest. The man apologized for his bare feet, explaining that he had such a bad case of pleurisy that he lost his job and has been unemployed for a long time and has no shoes. In that little impoverished family group I found so much native intelligence, so much clear understanding and human dignity, that when I left all of us felt a mutual regret that we would probably never meet again. The mother took a petition on her own initiative and said she would have it filled among her friends and neighbors.

But it's not easy going. There are doors slammed angrily in your face—mostly in the middle-class districts. There are insults hurled at you, but mostly by cranks. Even an occasional Klansman will stop and talk to you and explain that he doesn't really hate the Negro, but if FEPC [Fair Employment Practices Commission] becomes a law, the Negro will take his job. If segregation laws are broken down, who knows what horrors would ensue! He signs your petition to show he is not so bad and he walks away from you in confusion—for there is confusion. Confusion unlimited. Race hatred like a disease infecting the Southern people. Hatred springs from uncertainty and fear.

There is the bewildered groping of little people who are afraid—afraid of an uncertain future, afraid of plants closed down, afraid of war—beating their fists against the Negroes because they don't know their real enemy but know there must be an enemy some place. You see them in the thousands shouting and yelling at a Talmadge meeting—humble little men from the backwoods counties with their shabby women, their children on their laps. You hear Talmadge tell them their real enemy is civil rights "incubated in Moscow and brought to the South by Henry Agard Wallace." The band plays "Dixie!" and the long legged girls on the stage wave Confederate flags. But when the shouting is over and the mob spirit dies down, you find them walking, confused and bewildered, as we found so many of them on the streets of Atlanta, Macon and Savannah.

"Somebody's Got Us Plumb Bumfuzzled"

We stopped this worker in the main street of Savannah. He was a building laborer, waiting a day between jobs. "I'd like to he'p you, Ma'am, but I can't sign that. Mr. Wallace is for Russia, not for the United States."

With patience and simplicity, you try to set forth the present foreign policy of the United States and contrast it with the foreign policy of Roosevelt.

He looks at you, a long, deep look as if by searching your face carefully enough he can find the truth to guide him. He reaches for your pencil. "I want to do the right thang," he says with a slow smile as he signs the petition, "ef I knew the right thang."

Why do those words bring a lump to your throat? All day long lean workers and slow drawling farmers have told you apologetically, "Shore like to he'p you, Ma'am, but can't go for Mr. Wallace nohow." All of them, like this worker, want to do the right thing if they knew the right thing. Your sense of responsibility to the people is so deep and tender that your voice is unsteady when you say, "What I tell you is the truth. I wouldn't lie to you, Mister. I couldn't lie to you."

You're sitting in the little square in Savannah, shaded with palm trees, waiting for the hot noonday sun to cool off. And looking up, you see the same worker you just signed up an hour ago—the one who said he wanted to do the right thing.

"I was fixin' to ask you somethin', Ma'am. Is Mr. Wallace for Civil Rights?"

"Yes," you say, "he's for civil rights."

"For n——s too, Ma'am?"

"For everybody."

He would probably ask to have you take his name off the petition. But he just stands there, uncertainly, looking down. "Sit down. Please sit down." He sits down beside you on the bench.

And you paint a simple picture of the chicanery of the landlords, the bankers, the men of power and wealth who keep two races of man divided in order to profit from the misery of both. "When Mr. Talmadge shouts about civil rights, you forget, don't you, that his daddy said no working man is worth more that fifty cents a day and a pair of overalls? You forget about high prices, low wages, long hours." The worker is looking at you again with that long searching expression that brought a lump to your throat an hour ago. "Ma'am," he says, nodding his head and looking straight into your eyes, "I reckon somebody has got us plumb bumfuzzled up."

Great Day a' Coming

Yes, this is Operation Georgia. Way down in the deep South. Where a little army of sixty or so young men and women bring in between two and three thousand signatures a day. There are Negro boys and girls from all over the South who have come to help. There are the Southern white intellectuals like indefatigable Branson Price, and Southern mill workers like wonderful Annie Mae Leathers and her two sisters. They served one hundred days in the Atlanta jail for leading the mill workers' strike in '34. They were charged with inciting to insurrection, and they found conditions in jail better than conditions in the mills. They went to work in the cotton mills when they were ten years old for twelve cents a day.

There are young people who hitchhiked in here all the way from New York and San Francisco. Some of them sleep on army cots in party headquarters or manage elsewhere in some makeshift way. When you're stranded in Macon or Savannah and the money is slow in coming from Atlanta because there isn't any money, you go all day without eating or pool your resources for a cup of coffee. There's a big jagged hole in the window of headquarters at Atlanta where somebody hurled a stone, and a partially burned cross leans indifferently against a wall. One of the boys is taking it home with him as a souvenir.

Nobody feels sorry for you down here if you've had a tough day. Palmer Weber, who heads the Southern campaign, is a hard driving man who drives nobody harder than he drives himself. "If they slam

118

the door in your face in one house, go to the next house. If one guy won't sign, go to the next guy. If they won't let us speak in town, we'll speak in the country. If we don't get into one church, we go to another. If we can't speak at eleven, we come back again at three, but we keep on driving!"

You start out at nine a.m. with your petition and you check in at eight at night. And if you're lucky and happen to be in Atlanta when Sammy Heyward is there—he cancelled three weeks of lucrative engagements in New York as a first-rate Negro folk singer to come and canvass in Operation Georgia—you forget that you haven't had any supper and Sammy tunes up his guitar and all of you are singing, "Great day! Great day a' comin'! Great day! Gonna build this country strong!"

Humor and Great Courage

There's humor in Operation Georgia. There's the time a canvasser came to an old tumble-down shack without windows, leaning forlornly on a few rotten rafters. The floor had cracks wide enough for a cat to crawl through and there was no furniture except a broken chair and a stove. Straining his eyes in the dark, the canvasser saw a man, barefooted, dressed in rags, lying in burlap sacks on the floor. The canvasser stated his business and the man sat up stiffly and with high indignation among his gunny sacks. "Tell Mr. Wallace to go back to Russia," he said angrily. "Why don't somebody tell that man that under capitalism we have achieved the highest standard of living in the world."

Then there's the kid from Brooklyn who told us this one: "So the minute I mentions Wallace, what does he do? He turns an ice pick on me. So am I supposed to let him drive an ice pick through me? Not me! I slugs him one. Then I runs for dear life. Just as I'm runnin' out of the house what do I see. I see Mary walkin' along pigeon-toed like—just like she's takin' a little stroll on Forty-second Street. 'Hey, Al,' she says, nice and slow-like, 'how many signatures have you got?' 'Signatures, hell!' I says. 'You think this is Brooklyn? Run for your life!' "

I wish I could give you a picture of the courage of our people in the South. Of the simple courage of Larkin Marshall, the Negro candidate for the Senate. When the Klan burned a cross on his lawn he was asked by the press to make a statement and he said, "Just say I ain't goin' nowhere. Just tell 'em they can carry me out but they won't run me out."

"Time to get off our knees and stand on our feet," he told our canvassers' meeting at Macon. "This is no easy stamping ground. Got to fight every inch of the way. I been everywhere in this state. In the cities and in the cow counties. You got to have guts to make the folks know the truth and the truth will make you free."

I wish I could convey the admiration we felt for the Southern progressives who are way out in the vanguard of a still hostile and uncomprehending South. The courage of James Barfoot, candidate for governor, and his brave wife, Doris, who realize what it means to be challenging Herman Talmadge, who represents the most evil forces in America today. Barfoot believes he has a fighting chance in the finals because there is a great sentiment against Talmadge, because the county unit system does not operate in the final elections, because the successful Southern candidate generally feels his battle is over when he wins the primaries. He points out that there are one hundred and forty thousand registered Negro voters in Georgia compared to fifty thousand in North Carolina, and that eighteen-year-olds can vote. "If only the rest of the country would realize," says Barfoot, "the strategic importance of our struggle in the South to the whole struggle for democracy in America, they would rally to us with funds and with forces."

I recall Margaret Bourke White's photographs of the South in *You Have Seen Their Faces.*

Working from Atlanta to Savannah, in the slums, the mill villages, on the streets, speaking to at least two thousand people, I can say I have seen the faces of the people of the South. I have seen their faces in the back of the Jim Crow buses, in the Negro churches, seen the faces of the children. I have seen their faces gathered around the sound truck when James Barfoot spoke and Sammy Heyward sang "The Freedom Train." I have seen the thin faces of the white mill workers' wives, and the fear and insecurity in the faces of their husbands. I have seen the sweet faces of the young backwoods farmers and the hard courage in the faces of the Negro veterans. And I cannot help feeling that someday the South will be the loveliest part of America.

But to bring that day will take a courage and a self-sacrifice, a patience and an understanding that even we do not yet dream that we possess. That day will come, as Larkin Marshall says, when we bring the truth to the people—and the truth will make us free.

THE SONG OF A DEPORTEE

To Charlie Rowalt and Pete Warhol

Who is the alien in this land
You'd ship away to die?
How strange the day to hear you say
That "alien" is I!

Oh, earth I savored on my tongue
When all my world was new!
Oh, earth I kissed when I was young
I'm "alien" to you?

Deport the hand that plowed the land
And sowed the furrowed bed—
You can't deport the ripened wheat
You can't deport the bread.
Like pollen in the drifting wind
I'm rooted every place
My longing sleeps at every dusk
Upon the prairie's face.

A country is a naked thing
Of earth and sea and stone
Until its toiling men like me
Put flesh upon its bone.
I planted this triumphant bridge
It will defy the sea
When my defiance burns to dust—
You cannot exile me.
My flesh is in its tested steel
My nerves its iron beams
And every ship that leaves this port
Is loaded with my dreams.

Here's rock eroded by my sweat
And every dusty street

Remembers well the silent bell
Beneath my jobless feet.
Deport me but you still will hear
My pulse throb in your mills
My heartbreak still will walk these streets
My hope will climb these hills.
You can't deport me from the land
Of which I am a part
In every pounding rivet gun
You'll hear my beating heart.

I'll sigh among the landless men
Of all horizons shorn
I'll whisper in the withered stalks
Of all the ravished corn.
You'll hear the echo of my axe
In every lumber town
With every blow upon the forge
You'll hear my fist come down.

No matter where I drink my beer
Or where I eat my bread
On every harried picket line
You'll hear my measured tread.
In every whine of singing steel
You'll hear my angry moan;
You can't deport the living flesh
Upon a country's bone.

WALL STREET HONORS
THE UNKNOWN SOLDIER

With heads bent low and bowed with grief
Upon your grave we lay this wreath.

Well, things are looking up this spring,
The market's really taken wing;
We ought to see a handsome boom
With plenty of scratch and elbow room.

He gave the most a man can give,
He died that other men might live.

Man, what a haul in '17!
We took the fat an' we took the lean,
Just chicken feed...all said and done,
To what we took in '41!
U.S. Steel just hit the sky,
And Bethlehem went plenty high;
Republic Iron and Steel was soaring
And Standard Oil was really pouring!

Who knows, perhaps he had a wife
Who mourned the passing of his life.

American Sugar waxed fat and sleek,
Railway Steel Spring hit a peak;
American Can sold pretty dear
And New York banks hit a record year.

How happy the little wife must be
To know he died for liberty!

Net earnings on capital stock were bright,
And foreign trade reached an all-time height;

Wheat went over three bucks a shot,
But a dollar was all the farmer got!

How proud his mother must have been!
(This time we really muscle in!)

These babies know we have our price,
The Dutch East Indies would be nice,
The British held the field enough,
Their customers will like our stuff.

How proud to know the son she bore
Gave all he had to end all war!

Greenland's an important base,
And Turkey's a strategic place;
One thing cannot be overlooked:
If peace breaks out, our goose is cooked!
Our brand-new arms would go untested;
Good God! The dough we've got invested!
The crash would wipe us off the map.
With all these orders in our lap.

Without the hope of fame or booty,
This noble son has done his duty.

We've got to make our soldiers frisky,
Less chocolate sodas and more whisky;
To dominate the Chinese yen,
Is worth a couple million men.
We need more bodies if this will be
The Great American Century.

And so we honor you, the dead,
And lay this wreath upon your head;
With silent prayer…be with us yet.
Lest we forget…lest we forget.

OH, TO BE A BILLIONAIRE!

Gee, it must be slick to be a bloomin' billionaire,
With interests here and interests there, and interests everywhere;
And loads of workin' stiffs like me with lots of blood to spill,
For his sugar cane in Haiti and his rubber in Brazil.

Oh, John D. Rockefeller was a patriotic guy,
He said, "You lazy slackers, go on, sacrifice and die."
And I said, "But just one question, Mr. Rockefeller, why?"

"I've got oil wells in Romania,
And oil wells in Iraq,
And a soldier's life is cheaper
Than a single share of stock.
I've got oil wells out in China,
Where my coolies starve and toil,
And what's a million human lives
To a geyser gushing oil?"

It must be nice to own a little congressman or two,
And a bunch of commentators on the networks red and blue,
And an army of professors telling folks what to believe,
And to have the daily papers in the lining of your sleeve.
I suppose that I'd be tempted to pull off a couple tricks
If I owned a TV station, Channel Five, or Channel Six.

Oh, Mr. J. P. Morgan was a patriotic guy,
He said, "You lazy slackers, go on sacrifice and die."
And I said, "But just one question, Mr. J. P. Morgan, why?"

"I've got money in the factories
Of the western hemisphere;
I've got money in a thousand banks,
Three thousand miles from here.

I've got my dough invested
From Berlin to Timbuktu;
Your daddy died to save my loans,
So why in hell can't you?"

If I had a million coolies droppin' shekels in my till,
In the swamps of Puerto Rico or the forests of Brazil,
Maybe I would need policemen stationed near and stationed far,
With my front yard up in Greenland, and my back yard in Dakar.

Oh, Mr. René Dupont is a patriotic guy,
He said, "You lazy slackers, go on, sacrifice and die."
And I said, "But just one question, Mr. René Dupont, why?"

"I make money in munitions
And I sell to friend or foe,
If my bullets bring me billions,
I don't ask them where they go.
I'm not soft or sentimental,
Give me anybody's sons,
For I've got to have the fodder
If I'm gonna sell the guns."

If I owned a fleet of merchant ships, it sure would make me mad,
If some chiselin' ship came snoopin' 'round the coast of Trinidad,
And I'd yell "It's an invasion!" if some lousy ship would sneak
'Round the frozen shore of Iceland or the coast of Martinique.
And if sweating coolie labor dropped its shekels in my till,
Then maybe some Korean shore would be my Bunker Hill.

But I haven't any coolies, I'm the only guy who sweats,
And I haven't any Interests, but the interest on my debts;
It's a long way to Formosa from Winnetka, Illinois,
And a bumpy ocean voyage is a thing I won't enjoy.
I don't yearn for Indonesia, I can do without Iran,
And the Africans don't need me, I'm a strictly U.S. man.

I'd yearn for old Lake Michigan if I were dead and gone,
Pushing poppies on the pampas of the lonely Amazon.

I'm not mad at anybody, red or yellow, black or brown,
For a man is just a man, I say, when all the chips are down,
And if my hand could reach across the oceans and the air,
I'd say to every man on earth, "Hi, brother, put 'er there!"
So will somebody please tell me why my blood has got to spill,
For the sugar cane in Haiti or the rubber in Brazil?

OF LOVE AND SORROW
To Korea

I gaze with horror on your withered land,
Burnt bare as if by some unnatural drouth.
Sword still unsheathed, in my avenging hand,
I kiss the world upon its suffering mouth.

Motherhood—1951

The apple trees are budding into fruit,
Green bursts the grass beneath the sudden showers.
My son is sprouting like a fresh green shoot,
My daughter's blooming like a tall red flower.

I hear my sisters weeping night and day
Beside their saplings torn up by the root.
I see them fold the withered leaves away,
And tremble for my flower and my fruit.

A she wolf sinks her teeth into the foe
Who steals her young.
A tigress springs with devastating claws
When she is stung.
A leopardess stands guard with gleaming eyes,
Prepared to leap…
But I, the greatest mother of them all,
I only weep.

Oh, children, I am worthy of your scorn;
Where is my vaunted might?
Good mother earth who burdened me with love,
Give me the claws to fight!

"That's Jim"

It's August in Minnesota. But already tawny September is in the air. Watching the soft swaying of the vast, glistening cornfields, I felt no sense of urgency that my car had broken down and I was due in Blue Earth early that evening.

Standing beside my stalled car looking out upon the lush, fruitful prairie, I was taken aback when the clumsy truck loaded with scrap iron drew up to the shoulder of the road and came to a stop. A good-natured face peered out of the driver's seat.

"Trouble?" he asked.

"Yes," I nodded, "thanks. Can you give me a lift to the next town? I'll have to get a garageman to come out and look this heap over. She won't even budge."

"Sure, hop in." He threw open the door. "Swell weather, ain't it? Hell, all this stuff you hear about California, Florida. Give me good old Minnesota, any old day, that's what I always say. Give me good old Minnesota. Of course when she starts kickin' up a mean northeaster around January, I can't say I'd mind havin' enough green stuff to head for Miami till she blows over." He spat out the window. "This war keeps up and scrap iron pullin' in twenty to thirty bucks a ton. Who knows? Every dog has his day."

"You think it's worth the price?" I asked.

"What price?"

"War," I said.

A furrow deepened his good-natured face and gave him a bewildered air.

"I'm against war just like the next guy," he said, "but everybody's rakin' it in—the big boys—they're rollin' in it. The way I look at it, some has it and some hasn't. As long as it's layin' around, why shouldn't I cash in?"

A Model T Ford rumbled painfully up a country road.

"That's what I mean," the driver said with a jerk of his thumb toward the clattering jalopy. "Some has it and some ain't. I got a load a' bathtubs in from the State Home for the Feeble Minded last week. They're remodelin' the joint—high time. So they unloads these tubs on me an' I'm sellin' 'em for seven, eight bucks a piece. Yesterday an old farm woman comes into the yard. She got a dress on 'er like a sack an' these here thick stockins—you seen 'em—some kinda heavy cotton stuff, an' she starts lookin' over these tubs. She picks out one that ain't quite so crummy an' she asks me how much. I says eight bucks an' she says, 'Hmmm'—like that.

"Pretty soon she takes out a tape measure. You know, like you measure dresses an' stuff. She starts to measure this here bathtub. Then she measures herself. First the tub. Then herself. Sideways and lengthways, from her hips to her feet.

"I think the old dame's blew a fuse so I goes over to talk to a customer. Pretty soon I turns around. Where do you suppose this old lady is? She's sittin' in the bathtub, big as life. She's just sittin' there with the screwiest dreamy look on her face. I almost swallows my rear plate.

"When she sees I'm lookin' she gets out embarrassed like and she says, 'I was just tryin' this tub for size.' Mindja, tryin' a tub, can you beat that? 'I'm buyin' it,' she says. 'You see this here is the first honest to goodness bathtub I ever had. Summer time I'll have it in the yard near the hog pond. I won't have to drag water so far from the pump. I can heat it right there in the yard. An' winter time I can have the boys carry it into the kitchen. It's a mighty fine tub,' she says."

He spat out the window again. "Too deep for me," he said succinctly and was quiet.

Suddenly he put the breaks on and drew his truck to a dead stop.

"Holy Jesus!" he breathed, "just get a load a' that iron!"

He was looking out upon a sprawling farmyard, its unkempt appearance contrasting sharply with the neat farms we had passed for miles upon miles. It was so long since the house had been painted, its two front windows looked out upon the road like the sorrowful eyes of an old man. My host's eyes were attracted particularly to a tractor that was rusting to death in the center of the yard.

"Three tons of iron layin' around there loose or I'll eat my shirt. Three tons easy. Maybe four. Say." He turned to me with an appealing excitement. "It wouldn't set you back too much, would it, if I stopped here for a few minutes an' raked up this iron, eh? Won't take me long at all."

I said, "Sure, go ahead. Mind if I come along?"

The driver nodded, "Sure, come on. Show you how easy it is to make a buck these days."

We walked up the yard together and I followed him straight to the tractor which he proceeded to examine with interest and admiration as I've seen my father, a cattle buyer, examine a prize bull.

Suddenly we both turned and saw the farmer watching us. He was lean and withered and gnarled with arthritis. He didn't ask us what we wanted. He hardly seemed interested. Even though he looked at us, I had a strange feeling of not having made any contact with his consciousness. His dull grey eyes looked as if they had died in his face a long time ago.

"Mighty nice load a' scrap you got here in this yard." The driver grinned. "You can make yourself a nice piece of small change, mister. I'll take the whole works off your hands. Clean up your yard. This here tractor looks like it ain't been used in years."

"My son Jim used to run it," the farmer said flatly, "before he went to war."

"Yeah? Ain't good to let a piece a' machinery layin' around loose like this. First damn thing you know it's nothing but a hunk a' scrap. Too bad. I'll take it off your hands—lot a' scrap you got in that old plow layin' over there in the field too."

"Let 'er rot," the old man said.

"Let 'er rot!" the driver cried, with genuine amazement. "Why, mister, do you know what you're sayin'? There's a war on. You want to let this here honest to goodness iron rot in the field when our country's in a war? You know we need bullets to shoot gooks. You don't fight wars with BB guns. It takes bullets. And bullets take iron."

"Let 'er rot," the old man said. There was a tone of finality in the dead voice, but this did not faze the thick-skinned driver. I turned away sick with shame for him as I heard him pleading, "It ain't patriotic, mister."

In my eagerness to disassociate myself from any identification with him, I had walked almost to the farmhouse itself, and I stood at a closed-in pen face to face with an old, bearded goat who eyed me with a friendly curiosity but with the dignity of a patriarch.

And then I was aware of the woman's presence.

"It was Jim's goat," she said.

She too was lean and withered and though she showed no signs of the arthritis that was crippling her husband, she too had deep sunken eyes that a long time ago had died in her face.

"He was just a little shaver when we got him—used to try to follow Jim to school so we had to pen him in. Jim was mighty crazy about that goat."

I smiled because the picture of this bearded patriarch following a boy to school had a pleasant element of humor and because I thought I was expected to smile. But the woman was not smiling.

"You got a boy?" she asked flatly, without curiosity.

"Yes." I smiled again because I always smile when I think of him, his dark, chiseled head, his athletic body just blooming into manhood, his smile that brings back his father with a rush of bitter sweetness—memories of the boy from the moment he was born— I carry them all in my heart as mothers do, like an album that I turn over page by page, and look at, all to myself.

"How old?" she demanded.

"Fourteen in November."

"Pretty soon *he'll* be old enough to die." Though her eyes did not change or take on any warmth, something in her face looked at me with pity and identification.

The woman made me shudder. She was like a cold breath blowing over my boy.

Was there something in the way love leaped to my eyes when she asked me "You got a boy?" that broke the dam within her and let down the torrent of her words—words that had probably not flowed out of her for years? Was there something in my swift smile when she recalled to me my beloved child that made her know I would understand the boundless joy and abysmal sadness that a mother feels bringing her beautiful son to the brink of manhood in these frightening times?

"Come in," she said.

I followed her into the house. The house had a musty smell, like a cluttered attic. It had an even mustier appearance. The mementos of a boy cluttered the living room—from an overstuffed teddy bear with one eye, propped up against the mirror of the old-fashioned buffet, to a bicycle leaning against a wall. Pinned to the walls were a child's drawings in colored crayon on manila paper, one a lively drawing of a boy with a long tasseled cap riding down a snow bank on a sled, another an autumn aster. In one corner was a baseball bat, a catcher's mitt, a football helmet, a tricycle with two wheels missing.

Glancing over all the details of this tragic museum I got the gruesome feeling of seeing someone who refuses to bury the dead body of a loved one.

She took out the family album and with her lean, parched hands began to turn the pages, not with the sweetly melancholy smile that you see on the faces of those who recall the happy moments with departed loved ones. She was not smiling. There was no joy, no nostalgia, no sweet remembering as she turned the pages.

"That's Jim," she said.

I saw a husky baby in the arms of a strong, hearty woman of about forty. She was bursting with pride. I looked at my hostess and could not identify the hearty woman in the picture with the aged and withered woman at my side.

"I was forty-two when he was born an' Pa was fifty. We never thought we'd ever have a baby. He just come to us—like a miracle."

Countless snapshots showing Jim creeping, toddling, standing uncertainly against a chair, walking, being held by his mother, being held by his father all testified to the pride and joy that Jim had brought into this farmhouse.

She turned another page.

"That's Jim," she said.

She pointed to a picture of Jim growing up, graduating from the consolidated school. He had a warm, intelligent face, an eager smile and open, wide-eyed look of a boy who is full of love and wonder at the world.

"He got the best marks," she said, "the best marks in the school."

There was Jim running the tractor, Jim stroking the goat, Jim feeding slop to the hogs. There was Jim on his knees bent solemnly over a row of seedling corn—a hundred snapshots lovingly recording Jim.

She turned a page and both hands flattened against the heavy paper, pressing it down. She pointed to the one large picture in the center of the page.

"That's Jim," she said, and the way she sucked in her breath when she said it, I knew this was the prized picture of them all. It was Jim in cap and gown graduating from the University of Minnesota's School of Agriculture.

The words began to flow. "He went to the farm campus in St. Paul and he had all kinds of ideas how to make corn grow bigger. The stalks wouldn't be so tall. Stalks wouldn't need to grow half so tall, he said, but the corn would be bigger an' sweeter. He said the energy would go to the corn instead of the stalks. An' he had ideas how to keep rust off the wheat an' scabs off the apple trees.

"He used to sit on the tractor down there, singing to himself. I'd look out the window an' see him ridin' the tractor down the fields in the sun, singin' and thinkin' up new ideas how to make things grow better. He was always thinkin' up new things. Our farm was the show place. Farmers used to come around askin' him this an' that—he didn't believe in keepin' no learnin' to himself. The pigs he raised on his own special thought-up diet won first prize at the state fair year before he went away an' he called a county meetin' an told the farmers how to mix this feed so everybody could have good pigs. He'd stand there lookin' over a neighbor's fields growin' good, with pleasure, just like it was his own. When a farmer had a good crop, you'd think it was money in his own pocket the way he'd feel about it. Said he liked all life-givin' things—didn't matter who it gave life to—it was just a good thing to have more and more life-givin' things, better an' bigger harvests.

"When he come back from the war we had a big party. Farmers come from miles around, roasted a big pig, roasted corn an' spuds—everybody happy to see Jim back. So he could help fight rust and drought so everybody could live better. Pa had arthritis and couldn't do no more farm work an' the farm was beginnin' to go to pot. Then Jim come back from the war. That was a great day—a mighty great day—I guess that was the biggest day in all Yellow Medicine County."

"He came back?" I said.

"He come back and then they took him again. Reserves. They sent him to Korea soon as the war broke out. Air Force. He didn't wanna go. He didn't feel like war no more. He said he just couldn't kill another man. Said he just couldn't drop another bomb down on somebody's farm. Said there's no sense in this war, them folks over there never done us no harm, said there's lots a' things we don't know nothin' about and it ain't for us to go buttin' our noses in other people's business."

Her eyes stared past me.

"I remember the day he left. He had just plowed up the ground for Pa and hired a man to do the spring seedin'. He was standin' right there lookin' out the door an' everything smelled fresh—turned-over earth always has a special good smell in the spring. 'I'm not a killer,' he says, 'I'm a man who's got a talent for givin' life to things. I'm not a killer. I can't kill.' He keeps sayin' that over an' over. 'Ain't no sense in this war an' I don't wanna hurt nobody over there. If they was sendin' me to build up somethin', bring life to somethin', but I can't kill no more. I'm not a killer. I can't kill nothin', nobody.'

"An' the way he talked an' the way he looked I got a scared feelin' down to the roots of my hair an' creepin' over my flesh when he kept on a' talkin' an' a' lookin' like that 'cause it just wasn't the right kind of a look for a man a' goin' to the war."

Suddenly the door opened from the bedroom and a shock traveled down my spine from head to toe. A weird, disheveled creature stood in the doorway. Its mouth was open and its eyes dazed. It was probably a young man but madness had aged and altered it so much it seemed to have no age, no sex, and no humanity.

As I turned to it with horror frozen on my face, the woman closed the album softly and laid it on the shelf. Without following my eyes to the bedroom door, she said, "That's Jim."

136

LAY A FLOWER

Poem to Meridel Le Sueur on the occasion
of the death of her mother, Marian Le Sueur

Lay a flower upon her sleeping hair, my daughter,
For you have thanks to give her before you say farewell.
Do you walk with an air of easy freedom?
Then give her thanks
For it is she who hacked your freedom out of rock.
Do you walk as an equal at your husband's side?
Then remember her well
Who hurled defiance at her husband's scorn
And, with her little children in her arms, slashed new paths for
    you to travel
Derision beating like hail upon her face.

And you, my son, give thanks that you shall know because of her
A comradeship our fathers never knew
Because no man is comrade to a slave.

She was no smiling Madonna
The sweet and self-effacing portrait of a woman
Painted so many centuries, by countless men.
She was fierce as a bird is fierce that has to fly over high and
    lonely crags,
With angry claws she tore at prejudice and scorn
And swooped like a hawk on all who'd rob her children of their
    new won heights.

Lay a flower upon her sleeping hair, my daughter,
For all her heartache and her lonely pain,
For all her sweetness hammered to pointed steel
To better battle for your womanhood and mine.

Lay a flower upon her sleeping hair and cherish her
As you cherish the sea
And mountains that climb the sky.

high, through lacy forests of bamboo, by rivers so swift, I fa
line to marvel as the feet tramp by, "How beautiful are thy
I fall back into step beside the priests beating on their an
ums and chanting the Buddhist prayer, *Namo Myoho Renge*
d one o   r that at
pment fo   on a thirty
ousand ki   uschwitz

On the   ers visited
ounded c   n front o
emorial   e tomb be
oll with   wn victims
scribed o   me shall
repeated   mmunica

Scores   embers o
iroshima   with the
grims as   z. "These
ies," the   rm the
mbolic p   formed or

These p   y to count
e world, p   cide. "Ca
ite quick   he frontie
eed and   ur differe

"Nothin   we overs
hen we br   the childr
iroshima and of the survivors of mass extermination in
ncentration camps like Auschwitz before the peoples and

We march   and towns, t
d villages hu   out to us from
eets. Peasants   e their two ar
n benediction. Children follow us in droves and, linking
th us, march us to the neighboring village. A hand reaches o
u from a passing bus and eyes grip yours in a momen

SECTION FOUR
THERE WILL ALWAYS BE THE PEOPLE

TO BILL HEIKKILA, AMERICAN
Whom they tried to make a man without a country;
Given at his funeral in San Francisco, May 10, 1960

I am the wind
I am the northern wind that blows across the Arrowhead to you,
    Bill Heikkila
Across the land of ten thousand lakes
And the big sea waters.
I am the wind that whines in the open pits of Nashwauk and
    Hibbing and Coleraine
And blows upon the red dust of the Mesaba
I am the wind in the hoarse voices of the ships at Allouez,
    Duluth, Split Rock and Castle Danger
And all the ports of call of the Unsalted Sea.
You've heard me purring in the birches of the Big Fork, the Gun
    Flint and Echo Trails
Over the bunkhouses of the lumberjacks
I am the same wind that howled like a wounded wolf on the
    winter prairies.
I come to you bearing the perfume of the first spring crocus
The buds of lilacs
I come stroking the grey fur of the pussywillows.
I am the wind that breathes your father's name in the
    underground coal pits of Hanna, Wyoming
In the blast furnaces of the Monongehala
As I shall breathe your name forever in the Arrowhead
You live, Bill Heikkila, you live.
You live in the timbers of the mine shafts
You live in the rock between the furrows
You live in the stumps of cedar
And burnt over popple
On the road you cut to the Pale Face River.
The land nourishes men and men nourish the land
You have seeped to the roots of Minnesota
Like the melted snows of fifty-four winters.
I shall breathe your name, Bill Heikkila, among the jackpine
I shall mingle your dust with the red ore of the Mesaba

And where the long boats load at Allouez
And the fog horn warns them off the rocks of Castle Danger.

I am the wind that carried your shouts
I have spread them like pollen.
I am the wind that lifted your banners
I have scattered their seed
They shall blossom again on city streets
In another season.
You live, Bill Heikkila, you live
I am the Northern wind.

PETITION AND PRAYER IN WASHINGTON

At sundown, Sunday, November 20, 1960, before the White House in Washington, hundreds walked in prayer for the release of Morton Sobell. Six members of the clergy, including Reverend Kenneth Beck of St. Paul, Minnesota, the Reverend Milton Andrews of Seattle, Washington, and the Reverend Richard Gatchell of Palo Alto, California, read from the Psalms and from the Sermon on the Mount as the marchers shuffled silently through fallen leaves and passers-by stopped quietly to listen.

Although no rabbi was present at the prayer, Rabbi Jacob J. Weinstein of KAM Temple in Chicago and National Chairman of the Committee for Labor Israel, wired his regret that he could not be present, stating, "I remain steadfast in my conviction that Morton Sobell is innocent of the crimes charged against him…. I pray that our country may prove mature enough to accept differences of political opinion, even radical difference from majority views, as a healthy safeguard of the democratic process and that we may speedily free ourselves from the evil influence of those who believe that an objectionable idea can be answered by imprisoning its advocate."

The prayer climaxed an extraordinary two-day conference that indicated the growing change in the climate of public opinion. On the speakers' platform at the Saturday night banquet in Washington's beautiful Shoreham Hotel, Helen and Rose Sobell were flanked by such participants in the program as the Reverend John Paul Jones of Ashfield, Massachusetts, a national board member of the American Civil Liberties Union and consultant to the U.S. delegation when the United Nations Charter was formulated in San Francisco; Thomas I. Emerson, Professor of Law at the Yale Law School and former special assistant to the U.S. Attorney General during the Roosevelt administration; Burns Chalmers of the Washington American Friends Service Committee, all accompanied by their wives; and the chairman of the evening, Stephen Love, Chicago attorney and a prominent Catholic.

On exhibit in the green room were petitions signed by six hundred lawyers and educators and by twelve hundred clergymen, among them eighty-one rabbis. Throughout the banquet hall sat clergymen, many of them very young men, from many parts of the United States. The sponsorship of the meetings included the Reverend Martin Luther King, Jr.; Dr. Reinhold Niebuhr and Dr. John C. Bennett of Union Theological Seminary; Rabbi Jacob J. Weinstein; Norman Thomas; Rabbi Balfour Brickner of Washington; Roger Baldwin, Chairman of the International League for the Rights of Man.

Several rabbis had scheduled Friday evening sermons on the Sobell case as their theme for Thanksgiving. A delegation of ministers was to present the petition of twelve hundred clergymen to the President on Monday. It was a far cry from 1953.

As the marchers at the sundown prayers before the White House moved through crumbling piles of autumn leaves, the street lights whitening the bony branches of November trees, the woman beside me asked, "Do you remember the last time we were here?"

It was June 19, 1953. The slowly turning sun was shining on the green lawns and flower beds of the White House, shortening by every second the doomed lives of the Rosenbergs. The pickets marched, silent before the taunts and provocations shouted at them by the crowd gathering on the mall. Time was measured off by passing cars loaded with American Legionaires and men in uniform. They shouted racist and anti-Semitic curses and displayed signs announcing, "Four Hours to Go," "Three Hours to Go." A counter picket line of sick crackpots led by a gaunt, wild-eyed little woman from Virginia pranced like witches in some macabre nightmare, carrying homemade signs like "Ship all the dirty Jews back to Russia," "Two fried Rosenbergs coming up." Well dressed men smiled at them as they passed and patted them on the shoulders.

The booming voice of a policeman seven years ago split the pickets' ranks as he made way for an indignant, tight-lipped woman carrying a camera. "Make way," he shouted as the woman looked about her testily. "Go ahead, lady. It's your country. Take all the pictures you want. You got more right to be here than they got." The woman proceeded to photograph the beds of petunias on the

White House lawn.

In a last effort to be heard a few minutes before the sun went down that evening in 1953, Manny Block, the Rosenbergs' devoted lawyer, pounded on the White House gates. His eyes were black-ringed and wild. He looked like a man hunted by a pack of jackals as the gatekeeper pushed him back into the grasping arms of pursuing newspapermen. They snatched at him, and, as he leaped into a cab seeking a telephone to reach the deaf ears of the President, the pursuing pack leaped after him.

As the racist and anti-Semitic taunts then beat down upon us, it was a battle to keep our objectivity and our "long view." The Negro carrying the picket sign beside me had remarked bitterly, "When they frame a Negro, it's rape; when they frame a Jew, it's treason." I had a desolate feeling of isolation as if I had suddenly become a stranger in my own land. At eight o'clock applause and a cry of triumph from the crazy mob on the mall.

"No tears," a voice had exhorted us. "Don't give them the satisfaction." So tearless the picket signs went up as high as our arms could reach and tearless the signs came down for the last time. Helen Sobell spoke the final words of courage and consolation and the marchers dispersed on heavy feet to homes in Washington, New York, Philadelphia, Boston, Chicago, Detroit, Minneapolis, Los Angeles. And Helen, her soft eyes stark with agony, stood alone upon an unfamiliar street, in her own and unfamiliar land, and the great iron gates clanged shut upon her life.

But now, at this great conference in Washington one knew for a certainty that Helen Sobell was no longer alone. The six Protestant ministers who stood with their heads uncovered before the spreading tree in front of the White House reading the Hebrew Psalms more than offset the prancing shadows half a block away on the night of the sundown prayer. Rockwell and a group of his American Nazis gyrated rapidly in a narrow circle like Macbeth's witches brewing poison. Among their placards were these: "The Gas Chamber for Jew Spies and All Spies," "Kennedy Is in— Greenglass Is Out" and "Keep the Jew Traitor, Morton Sobell, in Jail."

Their presence was ominous, but the climate of our land had changed.

I had heard Stephen Love when he first entered the Sobell case years ago. But in this chairman of the Saturday night banquet there was an entirely different man. He had espoused this cause through the route of his intellect. I saw him now, an older man, deeply mellowed, who spoke with a profound identification with the sufferers in this drama.

There was a new dimension in depth as he expressed with tenderness his admiration and regard for "the Sobell women." His voice had a ring of emotion as he cried, "People say, 'even if he is guilty.' He's not guilty! Of that I am absolutely sure. I have been practicing law for forty-nine years. I've tried a great number of cases and I have read this two thousand eight hundred page record a dozen times and I'll tell you that I would argue this matter with anyone and convince anyone. It isn't only a question of Sobell's being incarcerated too long. It's a question of his being incarcerated at all!"

When a packet containing one hundred dollars was sent up to him during an appeal for funds, he looked at the audience and with a moving gesture said, "Look, here's a hundred dollars from a lady who couldn't come. Just a lady called 'Sylvia.' There are a lot of good people in this world, aren't there, really?" Spontaneously he asked the audience to join in a prayer. "I'm not a minister," he said, "I'm not a priest, although I'm a man of that faith, but as Thanksgiving approaches we ask you to put in the hearts of men the light to see that justice and right prevail. We thank you, God." And having delivered this simple prayer, he left the meeting to make a radio broadcast for Sobell while the crowd rose in ovation for him.

The Reverend John Paul Jones is a man of great dignity of bearing, tall, white-haired, with a trace of Harvard in his voice. After completing his formal speech on the note, "The release of Morton Sobell could be a work of healing and redemption for America," he spoke extemporaneously to relate an incident that occurred on the Sea Beach Subway Express from Brooklyn not long ago.

The subway stopped at Thirty-sixth Street and a woman, evidently a stranger to the city, found the door slammed shut in her face before she could get out at her station. With fierce determination she put her right hand through the door and pushed in an effort to force it open. As a minister of the gospel, he said, he felt it his duty to be of service so he rose and informed her that it was impossible to force open a subway door once the operator way in the center of the train someplace has pressed the button. "The woman," said the minister, "paid absolutely no attention to me and continued to tug at the door with all her might. Again I adjured her, 'My good woman, please believe me. I understand the subway system, and it is literally impossible to reopen this door.' But she put both her hands in the doors and pushed with all her strength. The doors flew open, the woman walked out, and the doors slammed shut again.

"Everyone laughed. Not at the woman. At me. I was technically right, of course. She couldn't open that door. It was technically impossible, but practically she did get out." The crowd roared its appreciation at this tribute to Helen Sobell's tenacity of purpose.

At the conference the following day Professor Emerson gave a careful, lawyer's presentation of the case, concluding that "injustice has been done to Morton Sobell." He named many prominent people who had reached a similar conclusion, including Bertrand Russell, who had sent a wire to the Conference expressing his belief in Sobell's innocence.

In answer to a question from the audience as to why, if the legal facts are so clear, lawyers and clergymen cannot storm the Justice Department with these facts, he replied, "The Morton Sobell case is not just a question of law. One can't depend too much upon the legal process. Because what can be done depends so much on the whole tone of the society in which we live."

The Reverend Milton Andrews, a young Methodist minister from Seattle, was chairman of the afternoon meeting. In taking up the collection he smiled, "I ask you to involve yourselves that you may be spared the paralysis of subversive inactivity."

Helen Sobell, beautiful as always in her self-possession and poise, read a letter from Morton: "I wish I had some feeling of the Washington meeting. It's all so distant...another planet, another person, another time. Here? Me? Now? Only because you say so. Sure I'm preparing myself for the day of liberation, and yet within my heart I cannot feel it as such. It is only with the intellect. This is not enough.

"Yet what can I do? To instill the spirit within my being after it has been beaten and eviscerated? Time after time? I'm afraid I can't. Not any more. From here on it will be purely of the mind. The mind will do my hoping for me...the heart will simply pump the blood into the body like it's supposed to. Yet this is not true. It only seems so. I don't despair. I still hope to come while Mark is but a child and you, my love, a young woman. This is firmly entrenched within every fibre of my living being and nothing can eradicate it...except death. Thus I really do hope with all. Only I dare not allow myself to believe this too much."

It would have encouraged Morton if he could have spoken to some of the people who attended the conference, Americans we have never been able to reach before. Here was a young public relations man who was invited to come by an acquaintance. It was his first contact with the case and he came, he said, simply to find out what it was all about:

"I wanted my girl friend to come with me but her mother didn't want her to because this case is controversial. When she said that, I was determined to come because where there's fear you can be sure there's going to be injustice. I hate injustice because I'm an American dating back to the fight against King George. You have to believe that injustice can be conquered. You have to keep believing. The minute you stop believing, you begin to die."

FOR ROSE SOBELL

Twelve springs have come and gone and passed me by
I am buried in winters
Up to my heart in snow
The air I breathe is raw
With little thaw
And I have been frostbitten in July.

They say that April paints the meadows green
Buttered with crocus from the flowering ground
How would I know
It is so long ago
Since I've seen April
I am winter-bound.

In spring the skylark has a joyous note?
I can't recall...perhaps the skylark has
I have not heard it for the scream of gulls
On the abandoned rock of Alcatraz.

I hear the sounds unheard by other ears
the fall of footsteps on a prison floor
the clink of keys
the clanging of a door
the solitary thought
the fall of tears
a moan of anguish breaking out of sleep
the sound of minutes ticking out the years.

I search the darkness like a jungle cat
I see by night
I hear sounds still unborn
I prod, I dig, I scratch, I claw the ground
I plant my seed in rivers and in rock

I climb, I run, on hands and knees I creep
I listen deeply to each stirring sound
Of conscience turning over in its sleep.

With every April I return again
and stand here shouting on the Temple stairs
Stop for a moment in your Easter prayers
I am the mother of all martyred men.

Take heart, my son, beneath the winter freeze
the river swells, the frost relents and breaks
seed dropped in crevices of rock have grown to trees
the delta flowers where the river ran....
If conscience sleeps it's not the sleep of death
I shall pursue that conscience till it wakes.

Take heart!
Our spring will come
I trust in Man.

WE WILL REMEMBER YOU, CUBA

Five bombs exploded that day in Havana and a tobacco warehouse went up in smoke. But newsboys were cheerfully hawking the newspaper *Revolución*. Fruit peddlers were singing out, *"Mandarinas! Naranjas!"* The queen of the carnival smiled from the front pages of the papers. Truckloads of singing *milicianos* and busloads of volunteers were returning from the canebrakes decked in plumes of waving cane. An electrical supply truck rolled by Vedado painted with handmade slogans: "Liberty With Bread and Bread Without Terror," "Fidel or Death," "This Is Not Guatemala!"

The bombs are forgotten. The Soviet tanker *Druzhba* has just discharged a quarter of a million barrels of oil in the port of Havana, a Czech ship has unloaded five hundred and eighty-three cartons of machetes, and the Russian sailors are cutting cane in Matanzas.

Volunteer teachers are headed for the Sierra Maestra. The *pescadores* are putting to sea their first fishing boats equipped with radio and refrigeration. A militia girl strides down El Prado, her gun swinging at her hip. "Oh, Susanna" blares brightly from the radio of Hotel Habana Libre while hammers and drills bang out houses and schools, hospitals and sport centers, and in the campos of the departed *latifundistas* where the grey plumes are on the cane, and in the tenderly tended fields of green tobacco, and where the new crops grow—rice and beans, tomatoes and corn, peanuts and soy beans, potatoes and malanga—white blossoms are already ripening on the cotton, and the poor are quietly inheriting the earth.

On February 12, 1961, school children of Havana placed a wreath on the statue of Abraham Lincoln in Fraternity Park. All Cuba mourned for Lumumba and a hand-lettered sign appeared on a flaming bush of red hibiscus in front of the clinic next to our hotel, "The workers of this clinic mourn and protest the murder of our brother Lumumba." This week an exhibit of Chinese contemporary art opens in Havana. On the Malecón by the sea a dove of peace will replace the rapacious eagle whose fierce talons grip the peak of the statue the United States erected to commemorate the *Maine*. On every newsstand, in every supermarket, in the Woolworth stores, and spread out along the sidewalk by Habana Libre you can buy Shakespeare, Homer, Cervantes, Whitman, Hemingway, Sartre, Tolstoy, or *El Capital* by Carlos Marx. And in the countryside, by the Jesús Menéndez Cooperative, a *campesino* clambers up a coconut tree, cracks open the fruit, and giving us a half shell of the fragrant milk, drinks a toast to the people of the United States.

I could tell you how many state farms have been organized since 1959, how many classrooms have been created, how many *caballerias* have been planted to the new crops of cotton and rice, but statistics are words without music. Others will recite them. I want to sing you a few snatches of song from the heart of Cuba.

"Vista Alegre" in Santiago de Cuba is where the *ricos* live. They live in air-conditioned mansions on the wide streets cooled with *ceibas* and the fronds of coconut palms and spreading mangos. Their well-kept gardens blaze with clusters of burnt-gold flamboyant and scarlet poinsettia, and over the walls the bougainvillea spills in breathtaking cascades of lustrous purple.

In the mud huts of Santiago by the grave of San Martí the *humildes* live. The poorest of the poor. Negroes. The long forgotten. They swarm in the hot dust of a Cuban Hooverville in shelters thrown together of pieces of tin, decaying boards, cardboard and cane. There are no sidewalks or streets and children play naked in the dirt among the tin cans and garbage. The floor of these shelters is the naked earth and cooking facilities are open fires. "Now it is dry, Señora, but oh when it rains! This is just one mudhole and it rains more inside the hut than out."

But half of the population of this slum has already departed. They have gone to live in the new housing project on the heights. Already more than half of the houses are completed. And so is the supermarket and the community center, the medical clinic and the school. Soon there will be a shoe factory to give the men work. And the *humildes* of the mudhole of Santiago de Cuba, not without laughter, have named their new neighborhood "Vista Alegre."

Where they are still waiting for their homes to be completed the women say:

"Ah, it will be good. Who among us have ever known hope like this? We had a hard life, Señora."

"We lived here half-crazy with fear. When the rebels were winning in the hills the police would come and take out our men and shoot them. They would torture our boys. They knew that our hearts were in the mountains."

"We had no place to work. We had to beg. Eat garbage."

Enrique Carbajal came forward to speak for them. He is strong and gentle. He is not old but he has lost half his teeth and his sunny black eyes are shadowed with remembered pain.

"Nobody thought of us. Nobody. Nobody. We were the forgotten. The politicians used to come here in election campaigns and promise everything. They threw us a few pesos to vote for them and never came back again." He turned to the man who had asked him a question about elections. "Elections now? We do not want elections. There is nobody to run against Fidel. Elections now would only invite our enemies to come out of their holes. What are elections, Señor? When you have what you want and your life is good, and your government is doing all it can for you and even beyond your wildest dreams, why do you need campaign speeches to make you promises? Our government is not making us promises. It is fulfilling them. 'Democracy,' Señor?" He made a gesture embracing all the ragged people around him, "Tell me what more democracy you can have in a land where people like us are given arms?"

In the new "Vista Alegre" of Santiago it is hard to believe that these are the same people who had lived in the mudhole. Neatly dressed, they walk with brisk assurance down the new cement sidewalks. Children play baseball. Old people chat in the yard of the community center. A fruit peddler is rolling his cart down the clean paved streets singing, *Mandarinas! Naranjas!*

A family greets us warmly from their front porch. They invite us in. A rubber doormat bears the English word "Welcome." A picture of Fidel is on one wall and on another the Virgin Mary. A bunch of artificial flowers gleams stiffly in a vase on the table.

"What do I like best about my house?" The mother exclaims, "Why the floor of course! Before we had only the earth!"

But the wiry little grandmother can't decide what she likes best.

She wants to show us everything at once. The sink. The stove. The electric lights. The toilet. The shower. The washtub outside with the built-in washboard. Then she clasps her hands in a gesture of prayer. *"Ai, contenta contenta contenta. Gracias,* Fidel. *Gracias, gracias.* May you always be as happy as we are now, Señora. May your children be happy. May your country be happy. May we all live and be happy. *Gracias* to the Señor in the heavens. *Gracias,* Fidel. *Gracias. Gracias."*

On a flat swamp bitterly wrested from the sea and to which the sea occasionally returns live the *pescadores* of Manzanillo. This reclaimed swamp is crisscrossed with stagnant ditches breeding mosquitoes in the green bilge water thick as mucous. Where the land is dry, naked children creep in the dust after the grunting pigs. The thatched huts are the sorriest *bohíos* in Cuba where families live hardly sheltered from the elements. These are Cuba's "peasants of the sea."

Like all the fishermen, Serafín Tomayo and Roberto Licca are lean, dried, eroded by wind and sun, men that the sea has bitten and salted. "We had to fill these swamps to live here. But sometimes the tide is high and we have to fill them again and we live in water. We used to go to sea with nothing in our stomachs and knowing we had left our families hungry. We could not go far in these little boats or the waves would capsize them. And you have to go far to get much fish. Now the government gives us good boats. It buys our fish and pays us well. When we are at sea we know the Cooperative will feed our families. The government has built schools and our little ones are already studying. It is building houses for us on the high land where the water cannot flood us. We will have a supermarket, a theatre. We already have a doctor. *Ai. Ai. Fenómeno! Fantástico!"*

And Elodia Barrios, a woman, cries, "The house they are building for me cannot be real. It is a dream. Yet I will be living in it soon. Señora, do you understand? If I had to swim the sea to get to this house, then I would swim the sea! Fidel is a god for us forgotten ones. We are crazy with joy!"

On the high land we were taken to see the model house that will be the new home of Elodia Barrios. No house was ever fashioned with more loving hands. Made from Cuban materials they tell you proudly and furnished with Cuban furniture made by Cuban hands. Light, modern, simple, using pressed sugar cane waste to produce effects of unusual originality and beauty. This model house is decorated in a delicate green and furnished with a modern couch in red with clean straight lines, two easy chairs, one black, one gold, two cane rockers in green, a coffee table of pressed sugar cane. The children's room is furnished with bunk beds and a modern desk for studying. The dining room is bright with casement windows opening on a graceful table and chairs, a sideboard and cupboard to match, all of a distinctly modern and Cuban design. When the *pescadores* move in in March, a social worker will teach them how to use the facilities for decent living. For there is no electricity or gas or plumbing in the swamps of Manzanillo. And when their houses are all completed, they will begin to build a new refrigerated warehouse like the *pescadores* of Guantanamo have built in the Cooperatives at Caimanera.

In the shadow of the American Naval Base white blooms are on the cotton of Guantanamo. We jog along a rough road into the Cooperativa Mata Abajo where forty *caballerias* are planted to cotton, peanuts, tomatoes, soy beans, bananas and onions. All Cuba rejoices in its diversified crops. They even hand you little coupons on the buses that bear the legend, "A one crop country is a doomed one." At Mata Abajo they tell us, "We are uniting all the cooperatives around here into one big state farm and we will have much machinery. We could have done much more if we had not had to send our tractors into the mountains to make trenches. Have you seen the Cooperativa de Pescadores at Caimanera?"

Julio Ortiz, a peasant of the sea, gave us unofficial welcome to the fisherman's cooperative of Guantanamo at Caimanera. He could not contain himself—there was so much to show us. He is tall and angular and lean, his freckled skin drawn tight on his fleshless frame. He is dark and dry bitten by salt like a net wetted and dried and wetted again, and there is only one tooth left in his head. He showed us the dock and the picturesque harbor of Guantanamo where *pescadores* were building boats with cabins equipped for the first time in their history with radios and refrigeration. "Ha ha ha," he laughed, "just today they called us by radio from Key Santa Cruz to tell us something is wrong with the motor of the boat and we sent out a mechanic!" This delighted him so that he laughed and slapped the young Indian student from Panama affectionately on the back. "What do you think of that, *muchacho?* And you know something else? We have schools for the children now even in the middle of the sea!"

Edelberto Quintano, the Cooperative's accountant who speaks English, showed us the brand new warehouse with the refrigeration plant with a capacity of one hundred and forty thousand pounds. "We have one hundred and eighty-five members in this Cooperative. We have almost completed the warehouse and then we will build houses. We have built a school for the children. We have free medical care. We have our own stores, nine of them. Not all our members are fishing. Some are building boats. We have four fifty-two-foot boats already out to sea. They can stay out fifteen to twenty days without worrying about spoilage because they are refrigerated. We have eight fifty-two-foot boats now in all and one seventy-five-foot. We are also making thirty-foot boats. Before the revolution the fisherman used to bring in twenty to twenty-five pounds of fish on a haul. Sometimes nothing. If there was too much fish on the market they got nothing for their trouble or they accepted what they could get. And there was always danger of spoilage. Now these big boats bring in up to five hundred pounds and no matter how much fish is brought, it is sold."

Julio Ortíz who was listening restlessly interrupted, punctuating his words with one long, lean finger. "Write this down," he cried. "Write down that the *pescadores* of Caimaneta were dying of hunger. Write down that if we got sick they cured us in the cemetery. Write that we were men without dignity and without hope. Now write down that we have everything a man needs. We are even forming a P.T.A." He laughed, "Ha ha ha. Come. I will show you something." He sprinted ahead of us, upstairs and down, into every corner of the new uncompleted building. "Blueprints?" he said in high good humor. "First we constructed it and then we said, 'Now send us the engineer to make the blueprint.'" He moved so briskly we could hardly follow his spry old legs over to the warehouse. But he would turn, grinning, and wait for us to catch up with him. Proudly as he showed us every corner of the plant, it was in the recreation room of the *pescadores* that the great meaning of the revolution overwhelmed him. "Look," he cried in Spanish, "look what we have—we, the *pescadores*—*biblioteca,* radio, television, *libros, musica, escuela."* Then suddenly whirling around and grinning at us with the single tooth and his eyes twinkling, he stepped back, cocked his head on one side and asked in English, "Sotisfied?"

We were still laughing, Julio Ortíz more heartily than any of us, as he led us to meet the young administrator of the Cooperative, Justo Núñez Martínez, thirty-one, who greeted us in his army uniform, his gun swinging at his side. "Welcome to a free country!" he cried and gripped our hands in a firm handshake. He used to work for the U.S. Naval Base at Guantanamo. "But when you ask me what I did before the revolution, the real answer is I fought for the revolution. You will find the rebel army even in the soup. We are of the same blood—workers, farmers, rebel army."

"Ai, ai!" cried Julio Ortíz, and he threw a long arm around the young man's shoulder, slapping him lovingly. On the wall above them, over the time cards of the *pescadores,* was the slogan, "Treachery to the Poor Is Treachery to Christ."

Everywhere from Oriente to Pinar del Río, from the Sierra Maestra to Matanzas, bursts of song from the heart of Cuba.

"We used to import turkeys for the holidays. Ha ha ha. Now we have enough to export. We used to import cattle. Now we export them to Venezuela."

"No, our chickens have open houses. Fidel does not want chickens in jails. We do not believe in jails even for chickens. Do you know someday there will be no more jails here?"

"We are building a school for every martyr. Then our twenty thousand will not really have died."

"That? No, that is not fruit. That is a field of cultivated roses. Cuba will have both—bread and roses."

"We're construction workers, Señora. Before the revolution we built houses for others but we lived in the slums. We couldn't earn one hundred dollars in a whole year. Now I am constructing my own home, building it with my own savings. I don't want the government to pay for it. There are others who are poorer."

"What is going on here is like a beam from a lighthouse that has no end."

"I wish you could see this two years from now. Then let them try to take it away from us."

"Carmelos de mello! Mandarinas! Naranjas!"

The crowing of a rooster on the bus from Manzanillo.

The brash clang of the Cathedral chimes of Santiago.

The feel of drying tobacco leaves, smooth as nylon.

The brothers Saiz were thirteen and fifteen when Batista's police assassinated them. They were rebels in the underground and the peasants of Pinar del Río protected them. The police would question a peasant and if he did not reply, they would burn down his *bohío*, and if he made a move to defend his home, they shot him.

There is a statue in the town of San Juan de Martínez. The young faces of the brothers Saiz look out upon the dusty square. But the real monument to them is the Cooperativa Hermanos Saiz blooming in the midst of miles of green tobacco painstakingly protected with cheesecloth tents to preserve the precious leaves from chewing insects.

In the midst of the lushest countryside on the island with here and there a thatched *bohío* blending with the tropical landscape, and in the pastures of green *pangola* the graceful white garza birds following the cattle, we suddenly came upon a development as modern, as startlingly new as the suburbs of Los Angeles, but fashioned with more individuality and concern for beauty. For each house is different, each color scheme varied and the houses do not march up and down the streets shoulder to shoulder to save money for the big contractors.

Night falls and the bus rolls on through the darkening Sierras. People board it. A woman is traveling with a rooster in a basket. It crows as a bonfire lights up a brooding hill. The kerosene lamps are lighted in the dark *bohíos*. People are standing. Chatting. Arguing. The bus somehow has suddenly come alive. A man is singing over and over to a little tune of his own, *"Viva la revolución, viva la revolución."* And suddenly from the very rear of the bus a voice cries passionately, "They call this communism! What do I care what they call it. For the first time I eat three meals a day. For the first time my children go to school. For the first time my wife has a doctor. For the first time I dare to speak my mind. Let them call it communism. What do I care? I call it *Libertad! Libertad!*"

This is Fort Moncada. This is where the revolution was born on the twenty-sixth of July. Five thousand children go to school here. And this sunny day they are at recess. Girls are marching briskly to their own band. Boys are playing baseball where once Batista reviewed his troops. Under a spreading bush of pink weigela a sign reads: "Careful. These gardens belong to the people."

Thirteen-year-old Enrico Rodriguez takes it upon himself to show us around. He is a manly boy and he speaks with the pride and authority of a man. "The revolution is the greatest fulfillment of Cuba." He takes us through the whole fort.

"Here is where the soldiers ate. Now it is our cafeteria. This was the soldiers' recreation room. Now it is a kindergarten. Here through this gate Fidel came in his car on the twenty-sixth of July. See these bullet holes? Here in the railing of this porch? That is where the soldiers fired at them. Here is where the police questioned the prisoners." The tall *maestro* writing on the blackboard does not turn around to look at us. He is writing in neat letters on the blackboard, "No voice is too weak to render tribute— Martí."

And Enrico passes quietly before the windowless cells. "And these were the torture chambers. They have scraped the blood from the floors. Soon they will knock out the walls and make windows and they will be medical rooms for the children."

We pause before the grey, eroded cells.

In Morro Castle in Santiago, whose ancient ramparts overlook the Caribbean, is a battered statue of Martí above the dungeon where centuries of martyrs have scratched their lonely agonies on the walls. It bears the legend: "To sacrifice your life is to live."

Gary González, the tall, lean passionate young member of Jóvenes Rebeldes, is standing at my side. His intense young face is thoughtful under his black beret and his hand is resting on his gun. Perhaps we are thinking the same thoughts as the frolicking children swarm over the fortress of Moncada and all around them the Sierra Maestra look down silently, lovingly, wrapped in sun and shadow.

I think of the young men who fought in those protecting

mountains. And those who are buried under the coffee trees and the flowering plants and the languid fronds of the wild bananas. And I think that here, in this fort, in that very room where the *maestro* is writing on the blackboard, "No voice is too weak to render tribute," sat Haydee Santamaría on the twenty-sixth of July. And the torturer came and pulling on a long white glove said, "Speak or I will give you your brother's left eye." And she heard the screams of Abel Santamaría and did not speak. And he came out with blood to the wrist of his white glove and said, "Speak or I will give you his other eye." And she said, "If my brother did not speak when you took his left eye, he would not have me speak out of fear that you might take his right." And the torturer said, "Very well then, I will take your fiance's manhood." And she heard the screams of Boris Santa Caloma and the torturer came with blood to his elbow and said, "Your fiance is no longer a man."

And I thought of Abel Santamaría and Boris Santa Caloma and all of the men and women down all the bloody centuries who did not speak so children one day would frolic in the forts of tyrants.

I turned to Gary González and said this aloud and Gary did not answer. Then he said tersely, "Yes, they gave their lives so we could live, and that's why we're ready to die to defend what they gave us."

There is a legend among the fisherman of Manzanillo that if you eat off the flesh of the lizeta fish, you will come back. We have eaten the lizeta and we will come back again some day to Manzanillo.

Adiós, Cuba. *Territorio libre de America.* Or let it be *hasta luego* to Habana and Oriente and Pinar del Río and Sierra Maestra. We belong to the crowded subways of Manhattan, to Detroit and Peoria, to the Golden Gate and the hot streets of Chicago. In the lush *caballerias* of cane and tobacco we yearn for the rustle of Iowa wheat. Ours is the bleak majesty of the Rocky Mountains. "Remember us!" you said as you waved farewell to us in Aguacate. "You have the free soil of Cuba on your shoes!"

Venceremos, Gary González! *Venceremos,* Julio Ortíz, Elodia Barrios, Loreto Mainelo, Enrico Rodriguez! *Venceremos,* Lumumba and all the betrayed *humildes* of this earth. We will remember you when we return to wrestle with the talons of the Great Colossus. We will remember you, Cuba. You will sing in our blood.

"Why Are You Marching?"

A hot midsummer sun scalds the sky some seventy kilometers north of Tokyo. We have been marching fourteen days. My sixty-six-year-old woman companion from America and I search the burning sky for clouds that might promise a cooling rain. Along the dusty road peasant women dressed in the baggy trousers of the fields stand by with pails of ice and thrust chunks of it into our hands as we march by.

"Thank you for your long toil!" they cry in Japanese. *"Banzai!* Peace!"

A peasant riding by in an old truck sees two Americans. He does not believe his eyes. He stops his truck and watches us as we pass by, drives on and stops again, gets out, and stands along the side of the road. When he is convinced that we are really Americans, a look of joy that is almost anguish contorts his face— an expression so compelling that I break away from the line of march and reach for his hand. He seizes my hand in both of his and will not let me go. He is saying something over and over in Japanese, some passionate hope that leaps across to me from all the barriers of language.

Yesterday it rained from morning till night. We were drenched to the skin and roads turned soft and we plowed some twenty-four kilometers through the mud. The last village meeting ended at half past seven with the reading of a resolution by the light of cigarette lighters. A Korean who was marching that day remarked to a companion, "All day these two American women have trudged with us through the mud and rain. Surely this is proof that there are Americans who love peace."

We are marching beside four Buddhists who have become our dearest friends. An old priest, a young priest, and two Buddhist nuns. They have marched with us every foot of the way in their baggy peasant trousers and their yellow capes thrown over one shoulder. They keep up a steady monotonous chant as they beat on their fan-shaped Dharma drums. Sometimes the women take off their great barrel hats and mop their shaven heads with a wet towel.

We march through valleys of rice so green, through mountains so high, through lacy forests of bamboo, by rivers so swift, I fall out of line to marvel as the feet tramp by, "How beautiful are thy tents, O Israel!"

I fall back into step beside the priests beating on their ancient drums and chanting the Buddhist prayer, *Namo Myoho Renge Kyo,* and one of them tells me through an interpreter that at this moment four Buddhists and Japanese Christians are on a thirty-five thousand kilometer pilgrimage from Hiroshima to Auschwitz.

On the evening of February 6, 1962, the four marchers visited the wounded city of Hiroshima and offered a prayer in front of the Memorial Tomb to the victims of the A-bomb. The tomb bears a scroll with the names of seventy-four thousand known victims and inscribed on it are the words, "Rest in Peace. This crime shall never be repeated."

Scores of A-bomb survivors, religionists and members of the Hiroshima Council against A & H Bombs prayed with the four pilgrims as they began their long walk to Auschwitz. "These two cities," they said, "Hiroshima and Auschwitz, form the most symbolic pair of tragedies that men have ever performed on the stage of history."

These pilgrims go from city to city, from country to country of the world, pleading the cause of peace, an end to genocide. "Can we unite quickly enough," they ask themselves, "across the frontiers of creed and race and political ideologies, forgetting our differences. We race against time."

"Nothing must be missed," they say, "nor can we overstress when we bring the sorrows of the A-bomb victims, the children of Hiroshima and of the survivors of mass extermination in Nazi concentration camps like Auschwitz before the peoples and the nations en route."

We march on through the hungering villages and towns, towns and villages hungering for peace. Hands reach out to us from the streets. Peasants rise up in the rice fields and raise their two arms as if in benediction. Children follow us in droves and, linking arms with us, march us to the neighboring village. A hand reaches out to you from a passing bus and eyes grip yours in a moment of profound communication.

In the steel town of Ono where the blast furnace is belching sheets of fire and smoke, we are greeted like a liberation army by what seems like the entire population of the town. There a man in working clothes watches us pass. His smile slowly turns to a grimace, and he weeps.

Photographers are pointing movie and television and still cameras at the Americans. Reporters trot along at our side. "Why are you marching?" they ask, writing swiftly in their notebooks. "Will you tell us please why you are marching?"

I reply, "I am marching because this soil is a symbol. Here on this earth was exploded the era of atomic war, the first scene of what may well be the last drama of Man's life." But my companion with the dry understatement of her Anglo-Saxon background says simply, "I am marching for peace."

I think of her simple words as the miles grind by. The Buddhist priests chanting their ancient prayers and I murmuring to myself, "How beautiful are thy tents, O Israel!" We are united in common memory, Hiroshima and Auschwitz.

In a village meeting after they served us tea and wished us godspeed, we link arms with the peasants and the villagers, and swaying from side to side, sing, "Never Again the Atom Bomb." I see that the man whose arm was linked with mine and the other with the priest's is an A-bomb victim, his face so horribly burned and mutilated that he looks like a monster. His features are smeared over his face and two teeth jut from the sides of his mouth like fangs. And I think this is the living memory of the Buddhist pilgrims.

And as I march—surely I have passed this way before. I have marched from country to country, from frontier to frontier. I have marched in flight from the burning crosses of the Crusaders. They have burned me at the stake in the name of Jesus. I have marched from the slashing swords of the Cossacks. They have slaughtered me at Kishenev. I have marched from Auschwitz to Buchenwald and from Buchenwald to Dachau. From the moment of consciousness of who I am and who are my people I have been marching. It is no coincidence I am here.

But this simple Anglo-Saxon woman who has no personal identification with horror and flight and persecution and genocide—she says, simply, "I march for peace." In her and in the tens of millions like her who have come and will come to this great understanding through the exercise of their logic, their common sense, their indignation and their compassion, there lies the final hope for peace.

"Mom, Why Did You Go?"

We walked silently through the hot Memphis night. The street lights of the Negro ghetto outlined the heavy blossoms of red crepe myrtle. The crickets were chirping wildly in the cropped honeysuckle. This was our first night of orientation at Lemoyne College, a Negro school. The grounds are quiet and well cared for, shaded with ancient mimosa. On the wall of the Administration Building is the legend "Behold how good and pleasant it is for brethren to dwell together in unity."

The Oxford, Ohio, orientation sessions had ended a week ago and the first volunteers of the Mississippi Summer Project had already fanned into the towns and hamlets of Mississippi.

We had been given fair warning all through this night's orientation.

"When you cross over the border into Mississippi, you are in mortal danger."

"They've been told you're communists, malcontents and sexual perverts, and anything they do to you is justified because you are coming to destroy their way of life."

"You might say this is a revolution and you're a band of revolutionaries and you can expect the fate of revolutionaries."

"Some of you will be dead before this summer is over."

Some of us were already dead: Jim Chaney, Andy Goodman, Mickey Schwerner.

"Now is the time to make up your mind if you want to go or stay. If you go, nobody will think less of you. There's work to be done for civil rights everywhere in the country. Please think it over. There is nothing to be ashamed of in turning back. Examine your motives."

The voices behind me were discussing motives as we walked down the quiet street under bending branches of red crepe myrtle. It was the voice of one of the ministers in our orientation group speaking to a college student from Stanford.

"How do we know what our motives are and what does it matter? A boy scout helps an old lady across the street. Maybe he has compassion for old ladies. Maybe he's trying to win a merit badge. Maybe he just wants to be seen. Probably all three. All motives are mixed. How does one ever know when one's motives are 'pure' and what does 'pure' mean anyway? All one can ask of a motive is that it produce a healthy social act."

"Sure I'm scared," the blonde girl from Seattle was saying to a young man from Pasadena. "I was scared most, though, when the fellow who came with me decided to turn back and go home. But look: I could as easily have been born a Negro or a poor white, couldn't I? But I wasn't. So I owe some responsibility to those who never had my advantages. What would you call it, guilt?"

"I don't know what you'd call it because sometimes I think I came for the wrong reasons. I feel empty. There's no purpose in anything. If there's nothing in a person's life worth dying for, there's nothing worth living for. I think this is something worth dying for, and that's why I feel it might give me something worth living for. Do you get what I mean?"

The girl's answer to this was muffled by the noisy clacking of crickets and the screech of a passing car, and, anyway, I had stopped listening. I had my own thoughts to cope with.

That letter from my daughter, which I could not even bear to read through twice. Bitterly, angrily, I had placed it in an envelope and sent it back to her.

"Come back and we won't say you chickened out. We'll just say you sobered up."

A silly, aging woman going off on some kind of emotional drunk—is that it?

"Are you trying to recapture the excitement of the Thirties? Why must you always go where the headlines are?"

No, not where the headlines are. I want to go where the passion is. Where the struggle is young and yet uncompromised and people believe that things can be changed. Where brother trusts brother because each has committed his life to the other and emotion is accepted at face value. Not diluted, sifted and psychoanalyzed.

The brilliant orientation speech by the Reverend Vincent Harding of Atlanta keeps running parallel to my own thoughts, like a bright, unmuddied river:

"I think we have to recognize that we are dealing with a

situation that is somewhat out of keeping with our American way of life at this point because we have now, especially in our generation, moved into the cool world in which men say there are no ideologies, there are no causes, anybody who gets excited about anything is kooky, anybody who thinks there's a cause to live and die for must be nuts, and so we are going to Mississippi for a cause in the midst of a society that doesn't believe in causes, except the saving of one's own skin. I think we'd better recognize that we're not going to be heroes."

As I walk down the street I wonder at all the many and diverse tributaries that feed the mainstream of one's motivation. Sometimes running deep underground. Sometimes flowing along the surface. Thousands of tributaries pouring from the every pore of one's experience, crossing each other, disappearing under the earth, surfacing suddenly.

I find myself remembering incidents from the early Forties. The bus driver on the home bound bus in Duluth, Minnesota, explaining to his passengers the reason for the high cost of living: "It's the Jews. The Jews are responsible for the high price of potatoes."

The state election campaign that year that Hitler was riding high. The nice young man who gave me a lift to work in his car and explained what was wrong with Minnesota politics: "It's the Jews. They're a cancer right in the heart of our state. We have to cut them out just like a cancer before it spreads."

The disease in Europe that was killing my people by the millions, spreading palpably in my own country, my own community—I could see it, touch it, feel it. In the face of an apathetic world: the more they killed us, the less sympathy it aroused.

The neighbor saying naively and without real malice, "But you Jews must have done something or Hitler wouldn't be killing so many of you."

I remember that September afternoon. A bright day, warm with the promise of Indian summer before the long northern winter. The balmy smell of pine smoke and the fresh and brilliant blue of Lake Superior.

Mothers are on their way home from shopping with their

children, for Monday is the first day of school. The bus is crowded but it has a pleasant and good-natured air of neighborliness and *gemutlichkeit.*

I am standing with my arms full of packages. Snow suits for the children. Tee shirts and overshoes. I am standing opposite a Negro mother and a small child whom I know. Both have been guests in my house. And a pleasant white woman with her small child. I am laughing and teasing both children. The bus is full of familiar faces of P.T.A. women whom I have worked with for the past four years. Several are officers with whom I have served on the P.T.A. board.

A seat becomes vacant across from the children and I sit down. There is a narrow space next to me, hardly enough for a person to sit comfortably, so I place my packages on it.

"Let me hold Timmy, Bernice," I say, and the Negro woman hands me the child and I place him on my lap.

I think how pleasant the day is, all blue and golden as the bus rolls past familiar landmarks of my native town. How lovely the people! How wonderful that the war is over at last! How nice that school is starting again!

A man boards the bus, and, giving me a strange and hostile look, sweeps the packages beside me to the floor, crowding himself painfully into the narrow space beside me. Too startled for anger, I move forward to the edge of my seat to accommodate him and push the packages toward me with my foot. I am still shocked by this hostile act when the man turns to the child and tweaks his hair.

"Hiya there, kinky," he snarls.

"This child's name is not 'kinky,' " I reply quietly. "And he's every bit as good as you are if not a good sight better."

The man cuts me with a cold, level look.

"It's plain to see from the nose on your face what you are," he replies.

"What a pity," I retort, still without excitement, "that you weren't in Germany when they disposed of Hitler and Goering and the rest of your friends. Then maybe the job wouldn't be left for us to do again some day."

The man's face reddens and his eyes burn with a cold blue flame.

"You dog!" he cries, spitting the word at me. "You louse! You crum! You rat! You robber! You thief! You murderer! You—"

I look at the man and watch the rising pitch of hatred directed at me. With every epithet the hatred gets hotter, more palpable, more menacing. I feel it scorching my skin. As it rises toward me I strike out at him, knocking off his hat. I am not striking at the man, but at the hatred that has been let loose at me, that threatens to consume me, that seems to menace my very life.

The P.T.A. women are all sitting quietly, watching without expression, their eyes shellacked over with the smooth glaze of uninvolvement. I feel for a moment as if this Negro child and I are the only people left in the whole world, alone, deserted and without resources.

My blow seems to have stemmed his hysteria, and he says coolly now, with a nod toward the white woman and her child, "You wouldn't hold *that* child in your arms. Oh, no, that child is an Aryan child. It belongs to the pure race."

I sit alone in this suddenly unfamiliar world, clutching the child closely to me, and I guess at the contempt behind the noncommittal glaze on the faces of the P.T.A. women I used to know so well. The bus still rolls by native landscapes suddenly grown strange and unfamiliar. The passengers are absolutely still as if waiting for something more to happen. Then a little Finnish working woman speaks up. She is old, worn and poorly dressed and speaks in a heavy Finnish accent. Leaning forward, she shakes her finger in the man's face.

"Is no pure race," she says. "All babies pure."

And suddenly another memory is washed ashore, bleached by time yet still bearing fragments of flesh and nerve.

I was very young and it was not long after the end of the First World War. And it happened not in Georgia or Mississippi but in Duluth, Minnesota, a cold, northernmost city on the border of Canada.

Three Negroes were lynched from the gooseneck street lamp on the corner of First Avenue West and First Street. They were traveling with a circus that came to town and they were supposed to have raped a prostitute called Irene. I remember hearing my mother read aloud in the *Evening Herald* a description of their last moments. One of the men had tossed his dice on the pavement and shrugged, "I won't be needing these any more."

"If I had been there I would have stopped them," I told my mother. Such a crime was done and the street lamp stood obscenely on the corrupted street and nobody tore it down and every time I passed it as I grew from childhood to adolescence and from adolescence to adulthood, I looked at it and felt corrupted too, and an old childish thought persisted, "If I were there I would have stopped them."

And now we were in our sleeping quarters in Memphis. It was a converted civil war hospital where the civil rights workers stayed during the two or three days of orientation before scattering over the state of Mississippi. The earlier orientation at Oxford was much longer but that was over now and the first contingent had already crossed the border with the bitter knowledge that three of their number were already buried some place in the mud or swamps of Neshoba County.

Insistently, urgently the phone rang and finally we answered it. It was a woman's voice.

"I am the mother of one of the boys in orientation with you," the voice said. "You sound like an older woman. Don't you have sons of your own? How would you feel to have your son going down maybe to get killed like those three boys? Why don't you send them all home? Why are you doing this?"

"What is your son's name? Do you want me to call him to the phone?"

"No! No!" the voice cried hysterically. "Don't call him to the phone! No! I don't want him to know I called. He would never forgive me. I just want you to send them all home."

Probably realizing herself the futility and stupidity of her call, she hung up.

The phone rang again.

"Mom?"

It was for me.

"Mom, I'm sorry about that letter. Please forgive me. But you can't blame me, Mom. I was so frantic when the boys were killed. I can't help it if I love you, can I? But even so I wouldn't have tried to stop you if I had been sure that what you are doing is what you really want—what you have to do. I had to be sure you were there for the right reasons."

I remembered the boy from Pasadena: "Maybe I came for the wrong reasons."

And supposing I were here for the wrong reasons? For something to sustain me? To fill the emptiness? Something worth dying for? How could I make her understand what my life of scarcely more that half a century has comprised? I who remember the lamplighter coming at twilight have seen men orbiting the earth. I who remember the Gypsies coming through in covered wagons. I will probably live to see men landing on the moon.

I who studied in sixth grade history about the terrors of the Inquisition and the witch hunts of Salem, secure in the thought that all such horrors are safely locked between the covers of a history book. I have known Buchenwald and Hiroshima. I who closed the chapter on the Civil War believing we had at last restored a deeply injured people to freedom and humanity. I am still witnessing their daily oppression, their systematic torment.

I have seen too much. The heart cannot encompass it. The mind rejects it. I am afraid I will give up, stop caring—that I will become like the millions of other zombies who see it happen yet shrug off their helplessness and uninvolvement.

In the ancient reception room of the old hospital converted into a drawing room the passionate face of the Negro doctor who bought this hospital and worked here and died here looks down in an expression of urgency and anguish. The boys are quietly writing letters home. A third, the young boy from Stanford, is picking out a tune on his new guitar. It is the melancholy strains of "Where Have All the Flowers Gone?"

I remember a poem. Who wrote it? I can't recall. An I.W.W. poet I believe it was, around the First World War. I cannot even quote it correctly. "Mourn not the dead, but mourn instead the apathetic throng, the cowed and meek...who see the world's great anguish and its wrong and dare not speak."

In my notebook I write a line I read somewhere. Where? That too, I can't remember. I don't know if I am quoting it verbatim, but it doesn't matter. "Life is action and passion. A man who does not share the action and passion of his time is in peril of being judged not to have lived."

My Grandfather's Ghost
in Hattiesburg

Little Grandfather, with skin as yellowed as the parchment of an old Torah and black eyes peering over my shoulder as I write, what are you doing here with me in Hattiesburg? It is a long way from your muddy ghetto bogged down in summer rains. Besides, you have been dead so many years. Why have you returned to walk beside me on this segregated street? The old news vendor who stopped me on my way to Freedom School this morning and said, "Thank you for being here, God is with you," had black skin but his eyes had the same tired hope I used to see in yours, and by some strange psychic transmutation I felt that he was you and I said, "But, Grandfather, I belong here."

The Jews of this Mississippi town are not happy that I am here. Too many of us civil rights workers are Jews, it seems. That's what the White Citizens Council says. "Jews and Negroes are undermining our white, Anglo-Saxon, Protestant society."

They have flooded this town of thirty-seven thousand with anti-Semitic literature. Jewish businessmen who thought they were Southerners pick the ugly leaflets off the porches of their California ranch-style homes. The neighborhood is serene and beautiful. Not a leaf is out of place on the graceful maples lining the well-paved streets. My compatriots look out of their windows. The moon is lovely on mimosa and shrubs of tailored cedar. But there is something cold out there in the beautiful muggy evening. Something very cold and very white.

My presence in the Negro ghetto disturbs them. The rabbi who was terribly beaten here two weeks ago—he disturbs them too. Until we came everything was calm, unruffled. They had been Southerners for generations; had they not blended well enough into the Southern landscape?

Of course if they would open some of the books in the public library they might find pages stamped with the legend, "Communism is Jewish." And a civil rights worker, on telling the arresting policeman that he was Jewish, was solemnly asked for his "naturalization papers." Then there was that Jewish businessman who called his best customer after the rabbi had been beaten here to ask why he had cancelled his account with him. "Haven't we always been friends? Haven't I always dealt fairly with you?"

"Did you approve of the rabbi coming down here?"

"Of course not. I'm a Southerner. I feel we can handle our own affairs. Let the Northerners clean up their own back yard."

"Did you approve of the beating he got down here?"

"No, that's where I differ with you. You can disagree with a man but that is no reason to beat his brains out."

"That is where I differ with you. We should have shot him dead."

And there was that Jew who wrote the letter to the paper to prove that he is the best of Southerners: "I was born and raised in Philadelphia, so you night call me a Yankee. But I have spent the last thirty years in the South and I am a Southerner through and through."

Laugh with me, Grandfather. Crinkle up your little face of yellow parchment and laugh, for I can see the incredulous shrug of your shoulders, the tragicomic twinkle in your eye. *"Shlimazel,* tell me! How can a Jew be a 'Yankee'? As long as there are ghettos anywhere—even if those ghettos are for Negroes and not for Jews at the moment—how can a Jew be anything but a *Yankele?"*

Since you insist on being here, little Grandfather, let me introduce George Harper, Chairman of the Mississippi Freedom Democratic Party of Forest County.

He is a tall, handsome man in his middle forties and runs his own small radio and television repair shop on Mobile Street in Hattiesburg. His father, a quiet man with great dignity, came down to visit him today from McComb. You would understand this father. He put all his love and all his labor into the education of this son, who was awarded a master's degree from Fisk University but ended up waiting on white men in their fancy country club.

George Harper has just registered to vote. It took a concentrated fight of eleven years to win the right to vote in the state where he and his father and his grandfather were born.

"I made an effort to register at least two to four times a year for ten years. They would say, 'We're not registering Negroes today. Come back later.' On one occasion I went to Mr. Cox's office and they were registering white people at the time and I asked the clerk if I could register and she said, 'Mr. Cox will have to register you.' 'May I see Mr. Cox?' 'He's not in.' 'When do you expect him back?' 'I don't know.' 'Then I'll wait.' So I sat down and waited.

"Finally Mr. Cox came out of the inner office, looked me over and snapped at the clerk, 'What does this boy want?' She said, 'He wants to register.' 'Well, we're not registering today and that's final.' 'Mr. Cox,' I said, 'when are you registering again?' 'I'll let you know.' 'How can you let me know since you have not asked my name or my address?' 'Get the hell out of here!' he yells.

"But I decided to worry him until I registered and I came daily for several weeks without results. Then he died and a Mr. Lind replaced him. It was then necessary to complete certain forms. I cannot count the times I completed these forms but each time I was told I didn't pass. 'Can you tell me, Mr. Lind, why I didn't pass?' 'No,' he would say, 'I can only tell you you didn't pass.'

"Finally after ten years, with forty-three other Negroes, I placed a Federal suit against him and the Fifth Circuit Court of Appeals ordered him to register us. I had been paying my poll tax religiously all these years. In my court appeal to permit me to vote in the primary that year I stated the order of the Fifth Circuit Court verbatim and the defense attorney asked me, 'Are you a lawyer?' I said no. He said, 'Have you a lawyer other than these government lawyers who have been representing you?' I said, 'They are not representing me. They are representing the United States government.'

"Was I concerned about reprisals? Yes, I was concerned then and I am concerned now. But I am more concerned about my two kids. How will they be treated in school and after they get out of school? What college can they go to? What jobs can they get? I've lived forty-six years in this environment and to a certain extent I'm hardened to it. However, I don't want my children to have to come over the same ground I've come over, to endure the same indignities I endured. I've lived my life—if you can call it living, but they haven't. They have their whole future before them, and I want it to be a better future than mine was."

He had to stop talking many times, gripped with pain from the ulcer that consumes him.

174

I thanked him for the many times he has fixed my tape recorder for me, for the trouble he has gone to to get me parts.

"I'm going to New Orleans for a few days, Mr. Harper. Sort of 'on furlough.' Is there anything I can bring you from there to express my appreciation for your kindness to me?"

He hesitated.

"Please tell me. You never accept money from me. It's not fair. I want to reciprocate."

"If it isn't too much trouble."

"No, I promise you. It's no trouble at all."

"Then perhaps you can find me a copy of *Robert's Rules of Order*."

Many ghosts walk this ghetto. Here, on Mobile Street, in Hattiesburg. They cut up a man here once, cut him in little pieces because he defended himself against a white man, and put the pieces of him in the windows of stores and service stations. The nose here. The ears there.

This street which I walk up and down each day, over it many a time they have dragged a man tied by the neck to the rear of a moving car—because he was black.

They tell me these things quietly, without emotion. They happened. They are facts of life.

Yesterday a Negro said to me, "You do not seem like a stranger here. You seem at home. It's very strange, but I'd swear that you belong here."

"Not strange. I do belong here. I am at home here because I feel somehow I have been here before."

So I tell him your story, Grandfather, because it is the story, more or less, of all ghettoized people.

On the outskirts of a Russian village some years before the revolution lived a Russian called Ivan. Between Ivan and Ben-Dovid, my grandfather, there had grown up since early childhood a strange friendship. A friendship between Jew and Gentile.

Ivan could speak Yiddish with a Peryaslov accent and around Ben-Dovid's home the family had become so accustomed to him that even the hard-bitten old grandmother would rattle off her troubles to him in Yiddish, forgetting he was a detested *goy*.

"*Er hot ein Yiddish harz* [he has a Jewish heart]," she would nod, approvingly, whenever she remembered, with a twinge of conscience, his hated origin.

On the nights of the seders, the Feast of Passover, commemorating the exodus of the Jews from the slavery of Egypt, Ivan had often sipped wine at the table of his friend, Ben-Dovid. The door of the house was open to him and whatever little there was to eat was shared with him.

The boys grew to manhood, married and went their own ways. Whenever they met in the market place or on a muddy street, they would greet each other with a warm embrace.

Life moved sluggishly in the little village. In the spring the air was sweet with the smell of cherry and apple blossoms. In the short hot summer, roving Gypsy bands camped for a night and you could hear their plaintive singing and see the flames of their campfires glowing in the open fields. In the fall the peasants passed through with their horse teams, wearily carrying their produce to market.

Then the long Russian winter settled in cold silence. Taxes were high. Forced military service took four years out of each man's life. Poverty lay upon the village, heavy as a stone. Sometimes a fugitive from the Tsar's vengeance would seek shelter with a villager for a night. Then a few trusted people would gather behind closed doors and drawn blinds with one standing guard against the Tsar's police, and listen to the stranger's talk of freedom. Yes, he was right. They were bitterly poor. Yes, they were oppressed by the Tsar, bled by the landlords. Yes, they were ignorant. No schools were provided.

Long after the stranger had left there were murmurings in the village. Men would dare to ask themselves, "Why does this man, the Tsar, oppress us?" And the murmurings would swell like a rising tide and sweep menacingly to the ears of the Tsar and make him uneasy on his throne.

Spring came one year after a bitter winter. The misery of the Russians knew no bounds. The Tsar, peering out of the windows of his Winter Palace, could almost see the dark anger of his people gathering like a storm.

With April came another eve of the Feast of Passover. Ben-Dovid had draped over his shoulders his white prayer shawl. The children sat solemnly at the table, their faces freshly washed. On the white tablecloth a glass of clear red wine had been poured

176

for the angel Elijah. "Open the door," said Ben-Dovid to his oldest child. "Let the angel come in and bless our house. Let him come in and drink his wine."

The child opened the door. But no angel swept past, unseen. A wild mob of villagers broke through the door. They tore through the house. They broke the few pieces of rough, cheap furniture. They ripped up pillows and scattered the feathers. They shattered the dishes. They tore the cloth from the table and the wine of the angel crashed to the floor. A wild mob of villagers—and their leader was Ivan.

"Ivan!" Ben-Dovid breathed. Anguish and unbelief were in his eyes. "Thou, Ivan, my friend!"

"Aye," said the Russian. And the blue eyes of Ivan filled with tears. "Thou are my friend. But the Tsar, our little father, decrees that it is the will of Christ that on this night of Passover we torment the Jews, thy people, and I come to thy house, Ben-Dovid, because thou art my friend, and thou wilt forgive me."

And from that time the grandmother said, "Can you trust a snake that you have given refuge in your bosom? That is the way that you can trust a Gentile."

Through struggle, manipulation and sheer untiring will, Ben-Dovid had succeeded in getting his oldest son admitted to the Russian schools under the quota allowed to Jews, and through more struggle, manipulation and unflagging will, his son had now been admitted to medical school in the city of Kiev. It was a thing to brag about in the synagogue, a thing to strut about. He, Ben-Dovid, who should have been a doctor himself, who had no inclination either for trade or for the Torah, he had a son who would be a doctor! What is closer to a man than his own son—it is almost like one's own self.

They rejoiced with him in the synagogue. Only Reb, the *Tzadik* (the deeply religious one) who had been stung so many times by Ben-Dovid's sharp, unanswerable jibes at the intricacies and contradictions of holy scripture, added a sour note.

"Your son will be a doctor. So it is good to be a doctor, but it would have been better if he had stayed in the village and studied the Torah. He could have been a good rabbi with his golden head."

"There are enough rabbis," snapped Ben-Dovid.

"Of good rabbis there are never enough."

"Good or bad, it is a matter of indifference to me. There are other things to be learned besides the Torah."

"You talk blasphemy."

"Those who cannot bear to hear the truth have only one argument—blasphemy. There are other things to be known—science, politics, art, literature. We huddle together in our Torah like we huddle in our ghetto, as if all the learning were in the Torah and all the world were in our village. But there is a world beyond the ghetto and there is learning beyond the Torah."

Moishe Bailik, who looked like Father Abraham in his flowing white hair and beard, Moishe who always blew the ram's horn on Yom Kippur, turned his majestic head toward Ben-Dovid.

"What would you have us do then, give up our Torah, lose our identity?"

"And even if we lost our identity, what would be the great loss in that?"

"You mean it would be acceptable to you that we died out as a people—that the Jews disappeared from the face of this earth?"

"So we die out as a people and live as individuals—so they cannot identify us to wage pogroms upon us and spill our blood on the pages of history of every generation."

Moishe Bailik rose to his full height. Like an avenging angel he rose with his black eyes flashing a bitter fire in the white snow of his bearded face. He seized Ben-Dovid by the shirt of his chest and held him while he cried:

"Yankele should die? Every vicious ignorant Gentile should live? Every Ivan, every Pyotr, every Anton, every drunken *muzhik,* every Cossack who cuts our flesh to strips and ravishes our wives and daughters, every barbarian who beats his own wife and his children—these pigs should live? Every German, every Italian, every Englishman, every Scot, every Frenchman, every Pole, every Russian should live? But Yankele who gave the world a conscience, Yankele who gave the world a God, Yankele who gave the world the Ten Commandments, Yankele should die?"

The old Jew spat, forgetting in his wrath that he was defiling the floor of the synagogue. He took Ben-Dovid by the shoulders and shook him fiercely.

"Yankele will live!" he cried, his voice almost breaking in a crescendo of tears, "Yankele will live!"

"Why are you shaking me?" Ben-Dovid asked, bitterly, shaking himself free of the old man's grasp. "Why are you shouting at me? Am I not Yankele?"

It was a silent Ben-Dovid who returned from a visit to his son in Kiev. He had left in such a sunburst of excitement. Neighbors dropping in to wish him a good trip, some carrying knishes wrapped in a white napkin, or that Friday night luxury, a piece of white bread.

"I have a cousin, a mechanic, who has a passport to work in a factory in Kiev, it seems he is a tool and die maker or something of that sort that is needed in Kiev—perhaps you will look him up for us and give him our regards."

"Tell your son Hershel a thousand blessings on him, that we miss him in Peryaslov. Such a golden one he is, such a good one! May he live to be such a doctor that people will kiss his hands. One hundred twenty years may he live."

"And Ben-Dovid, you are as absent-minded as a Torah scholar. Do not lose your passport to remain in Kiev over night. For a Jew caught in Kiev after sundown without a passport..."

And despite all the admonitions of his people beyond the Pale, in the excitement of his visit, in his dogged absent-mindedness, he had done exactly that. He had lost his passport.

So much pride, so much dignity he had walking through the streets of Kiev. "I, Ben-Dovid, a Jew, I shall be the father of a doctor." Such happiness as he had never known in Peryaslov he felt walking down the streets of Kiev. "I walk the streets of Kiev, the father of a doctor."

And then he found himself in a jail in Kiev. The gendarme struck his face and kicked him.

"Jew pig!" he spat.

The jailor kicked him.

"Christ killer—Jew! This will teach you to walk the streets of Kiev without a passport."

A drunken *muzhik* who shared his cell gave him a merciless beating.

"Jew...Jew...Jew..."

His son found him in jail, produced the passport his father had absently left on Hershel's desk, and Ben-Dovid started back to his village. His shoulders were bent like an old man's and there was no dignity in his walk.

It was only a week later that Ben-Dovid was riding his wagon to market to sell his meat. A jolt in the road pried loose a wheel of the wagon and it rolled across the road and over a bank. The horse and the wagon remained in the middle of the road while Ben-Dovid crept down the bank to recover the wagon wheel.

He heard a loud clatter of horses' hooves and a shouting on the road. As he crawled up the steep bank with the wheel in his arms, he saw a fine carriage driven by two fine horses stalled before his horse and wagon. The groom was beating his horse with his whip but the horse refused to budge from the center of the road. The carriage door flew open and a florid gentleman dressed in the finery of a landlord sprang out and, livid with fury, approached Ben-Dovid.

"Jew!" he shouted. "Is this your horse and your wagon that blocks my road?"

In reply Ben-Dovid took the horse's reins and tried to force him to move from the center of the road.

"Do you think I have all day to get to my destination?" the landlord cried, his face turning from red to vivid purple.

"I am doing my best," Ben-Dovid said softly.

"Pigs like you should not be allowed to block the roads of Russia! The Tsar should drive you all into the Black Sea! Move! I command you! Move!"

Sweat was pouring from the pale face of Ben-Dovid but he could not move his horse.

Enraged beyond reason, the landlord seized the whip from the hand of the groom and with all his might and all his fury, he struck it across Ben-Dovid's face. The pain blinded him. He was unaware the horse had moved and the wagon dragged to the side of the road. He was unaware of the landlord leaping back into the carriage and the clatter of horses' hooves as the disappearing carriage clacked along the road.

"Jew...Jew..."

"Oh, Mother of mine!" cried Malka, his wife, when she saw his face. "Oh, a black year on all of us, what has happened to you! Oh, woe unto us, what is that welt across your face? What evil has befallen you?"

"This is no welt across my face," Ben-Dovid said drily. "Look at it well. This is my Star of David."

They are singing in the ghetto church tonight.

It is not the kind of singing I heard in the white church I visited last week—that pale, diluted, that castrated singing.

It is not a singing out of a book. The sweat is standing on the faces of the singers. Pouring down their necks. It is a singing out of ghetto memory—of a man cut to pieces—of a man dragged by the neck down Mobile Street. It is a singing out of slavery and danger and the cry for a Moses to deliver them. I know this singing. I vibrate to it because it comes out of my own flesh and the sweat of it stands on my own face. I have heard it in the synagogue on Yom Kippur.

You walk with me tonight, little Grandfather, a silent ghost, down the segregated streets of Hattiesburg. On the other side of town the Jews live in neat ranch houses with honeysuckle vines and shrubs of tailored cedar. They are Southerners, but somehow they do not blend too well into the Southern landscape. Perhaps because part of their roots are here, yes here, on Mobile Street, wherever there are ghettos.

ONE MISSISSIPPI MORNING...

...Peter Werner left for McComb.

McComb is an area in southwestern Mississippi to which civil rights workers are not assigned. They volunteer. No white women are accepted.

I remembered our deep misgivings when we said goodbye to Curtice Hayes, young SNCC [Student Nonviolent Coordinating Committee] worker, when he left from the orientation at Memphis with the first small contingent the first week in July.

"It's the stronghold of the Klan," he said, "thousands of them armed with rifles and hand grenades. Five houses bombed the last eight weeks—five people killed but you never heard of them because they're Negroes."

He gave an incongruous little laugh.

"They tell us they aren't even going to wait until we get started. Going to get us first. I'm leaving tonight."

"You're leaving for McComb?"

"Of course. It's my home. Besides, if we can't work in southwestern Mississippi we may as well forget the whole summer project. Because it will say to the rest of the state, do like we did, use terror and you can stop it. And if Mississippi can stop it, so can Alabama and Arkansas and Georgia."

Curtice escaped with his life three weeks later when his sleeping quarters were bombed.

And this morning Peter Werner left for McComb.

The last time I saw Peter was one afternoon at Palmer's Crossing, a rural area near Hattiesburg.

Pete Seeger had come to town, his banjo hanging over one thin shoulder, his shirt soaked through with sweat and sticking to his lean body.

In Hattiesburg, sixty-three of us had been teaching in the freedom schools, going out into the Negro community urging people to register, setting up libraries and community centers. We were housed in the already overcrowded homes of Negro families who risked bombings and economic reprisals in having us there.

The little community center at Palmer's Crossing was bursting with Negro children and summer workers sitting crossed-legged on the floor. A young Catholic priest from Michigan was holding a little Negro girl in his arms, and on Peter Werner's lap sat a tiny child, so dark, it made a strange, surrealist contrast to his Nordic pallor. He held the child stiffly, on the edge of one knee, but his face was relaxed in one of his faint, rare smiles, and had a glow on it like pictures I recall of a blond Jesus.

"Are you really going to McComb, Peter?" I asked this morning.

"Yes," he snapped in his clipped voice, stuffing a few books into his plastic bag.

"Oh," I said, and then added, "good luck."

I had meant to tell Peter my feelings about him before we parted company, but I never did. His courteous restraint invited no dialogue. I was afraid his own feelings were too confused and unsorted and he would not invite me to stumble with him through his inner disorder.

Peter had walked into Hattiesburg with the rest of us some five or six weeks ago. He is tall, with blond curling hair, a square, Teutonic jaw, blue eyes—a perfect specimen of the "Aryan" race. He is from Flint, Michigan, and I understand some twelve years removed from Germany.

"Are you from Sweden?" my friend had asked him when we first met, avoiding the question "Are you German?"

"No!" he snapped, and turned away.

I gave him a swift and hostile glance. When he spoke his tones were clipped and curt, and every time he spoke I bristled. It was more than mere bristling, and I was shocked that I, a woman of mature years, with a son as old as Peter and a memory of two world wars, could hate a boy.

One day we went to court in Hattiesburg, Mississippi. It was the Municipal Court for the trial of misdemeanors. A blast of cold air hit our over-heated bodies from the air conditioning unit in the stark white wall. Peter Werner sat down, opened the book he was studying, *Electro-Magnetism* by Stratton, and began to read. Across his face, and dangerously near his eyes, a jagged red scar was just beginning to heal.

Bill Jones sat down beside us. Bill is a Negro, born and raised in

Alabama, who has been teaching for two years in New York. He is thirty-eight—and his life is in this freedom movement. Whatever he teaches—the Constitution, Negro history, French—he teaches with great patience and tenderness, as if each child represented to him his own childhood's threatened potential. Last night I met him coming home from school, a half dozen little boys clinging lovingly to him.

We spoke briefly and when I turned to go a little boy called back in a soft, Southern accent, "Be careful!" I was breaking security rules, walking alone at night. It was Bill's bitter disappointment that we were engaging in no demonstrative action this summer, testing no laws. "My children are getting tired of just being taught past history," he said a number of times, almost to himself. "They wonder when we're going to do something about enforcing the law. They've waited too long already."

On July 20, Peter, Bill and Susan Patterson, a white freedom school teacher from Seattle, were entering a drug store to buy school supplies in downtown Hattiesburg. It was the busiest corner of Main Street at two o'clock in the afternoon.

"Unaware of anything about to happen," Peter reported, "I was suddenly knocked to the ground by a series of blows to the ears, head and neck. Once down I was kicked in the face and kidneys. At no time did I lose consciousness and I clearly heard Susan's cries for help. Only when the police finally came and placed my assailant under arrest did I see his face for the first time."

Now the case was coming to trial and all of us had entered the courtroom together.

We were seated about ten minutes when the bailiff appeared, a gun swinging in the holster at his hip.

"You'll have to move to the other side," he said.

Bill Jones was with us as we all rose to do his bidding.

"You stay where you are!" the bailiff ordered.

"Is this a segregated courtroom?" Bill cried.

"You do like I tell you!" the bailiff snarled.

"I do so under protest!" Bill cried again.

Miserably, we rose to move away from him. We had agreed on a policy not to test the law during the tenure of the summer project, so we rose quietly and moved away from him. I looked back at Bill,

184

whose brow was creased in helpless torment and frustration. Our lines of communication had been broken. Four weeks of friendship and comradeship seemed suddenly cancelled out and a great white wall of alienation rose between us.

So we sat on opposite sides, seeing each other, yet apart, I wrestling with my shame and guilt; Bill wrestling, perhaps, with hatred.

In the last row on our side a half dozen white men and women, obviously of best Southern stock, sat like sculptured wax, not betraying by word or grimace their thoughts or feelings. On a side seat a poor white farmer studied the floor with faded eyes. His short sleeves exposed the lean brown sinews of his arms. His face had the look of ravaged land and rock.

The judge, a polio victim, swung himself slowly to the bench on metal crutches. He looked sick. And tired.

The court clerk, a bumbling little stereotype of middle age, opened proceedings with the reading of a long passage from the Bible, but he read so fast, with such a Southern slur of word and meaning, I could not understand the text.

There are times when life is measured not by time but by intensity. While we waited, I thought of Peter and how it seemed like four years, not four weeks since we first met here in Hattiesburg, all secretly wondering if we would return to our homes uninjured and alive.

I remembered how I grappled with the unreasonable feelings his presence evoked in me. I knew he too had laid his life on the line in coming here. I knew he too had need to redeem a guilt perhaps heavier than I could ever understand. Yet when he spoke, the voice of Goering raised pimples on my flesh and I heard the crackle of orders and the sound of the goose step.

It was one night after a small teachers' meeting. I had bristled at everything Peter said. He was to teach his specialty, mathematics and science. And when he said he would "test" his students, I retorted that these are not college courses directed toward a B.S. degree, that flexibility, not rigidity was in order. I resented everything he said. And the more I bristled, the more clipped his Prussian tones.

"It's no use," I said at last, rising to leave. "It's obvious we're at swords' points. Peter and I will never agree on method."

I did not say "on the German method," but it was bitterly implied.

The boy's head was bent in sullen misery over his open notebook. He could not fight me because I was his elder, and besides, he did not know for sure what he was fighting.

Walking home that night, I grappled with myself on a conscious level. "Germany is not only Hitler and Goebbels," I argued with myself. "Germany is Beethoven and the Ninth Symphony. Germany is Schubert's *Serenade*. Germany is Goethe and Bach. Germany is the lovely fairy tales of your childhood. It is Aunt Sadie reciting to you in German "Der Erlkoenig" almost half a century ago in an ice cold Minnesota room under a goatskin blanket, and you thrilling with a child's rapture to the sound, the drama, the rich warmth of the unknown and yet familiar language—for it is German from which Yiddish emerged, a winsome bastard unacknowledged by its father, a language that enriched you with a humor and an irony and a sorrow no other language could possibly express. You are equating the anti-Nazi underground with the storm troopers. Can't you see that Peter Werner is that other Germany? Consciously or not, he has come here to redeem that Germany. You are going to love Peter Werner before this summer is over, or fascism has forever stunted you as a human being."

I went to his classes when mine were over, listening to him from the half-open door. I watched him, so carefully educated to discipline and order, adapting to the confusion of a temporary and unavoidably slipshod pattern. I saw him laboring to pitch a tent when every trained nerve yearned to lay a stone foundation. In the same classroom I saw him tutoring some students in algebra and patiently reviewing with another student "two and two is four." At night I watched him teaching musical theory to two curious students, making carefully thought-out diagrams, pounding out simple notes on the church piano. Everything Peter had to give he was offering awkwardly of himself. But mostly I saw that he was offering love.

Then they told me Peter Werner had been beaten. And suddenly I saw him standing in the doorway of the C.O.F.O.

186

[Council of Federated Organizations] office with the ugly, bloody scars drying on his face, and impulsively I rushed toward him and kissed him. And with that kiss I began to heal a festering scar upon my own soul.

And now I sat in the segregated courtroom and looked at Bill. And he looked back at me, not loving me. His face was still twisted in an expression of pain and alienation. And I silently begged him, "Forgive me, Bill. Have mercy on me and my burden of social guilt which I am trying so desperately to redeem as I have forgiven and had mercy on Peter."

But now we all stiffened in our chairs as a swarthy man of middle age swaggered to the front of the courtroom and stood, legs apart, looking into the judge's face.

He had reached, the judge said, a painful decision. We strangers sitting in this courtroom had placed a terrible burden of responsibility both upon Mr. Hartfield, the defendant, and upon him, the judge. For it was an almost unbearable provocation, understandable to every Southerner, himself included, that inspired this act of violence. In the face of this flouting of Southern mores and manners, it placed an enormous burden of self-control upon the citizens of Hattiesburg. The act of Mr. Hartfield was deeply understandable to him as it is to any Southern citizen.

Profoundly as he sympathized with the feelings that motivated Mr. Hartfield, he is painfully forced to find him guilty as charged since he had obviously not acted in self defense or in response to any verbal taunts—that he attacked Peter almost two blocks from where Peter had allegedly elbowed him, that the testimonies of Mr. Hartfield and his only witness, a frail old news vender, were conflicting. And the judge addressed a lengthy dissertation to us, the civil rights workers sitting in the courtroom, a dissertation that was at once an ultimatum and a warning.

Painfully controlling his voice and feelings, he told us, "My friend, Mr. Silver, has called Mississippi 'The Closed Society.' We are not a closed society. We are a people committed to the principle of gradualism which you flout and outrage."

He warned us that should we appear in his courtroom again bearing wounds inflicted upon us by outraged Southerners, he would not deal kindly or sympathetically with us because our wounds would really have been inflicted by our own arrogant flouting of Southern society, that we would be held responsible for stirring passions to a point where natural outrage surpasses the limitations of control—and he fined Mr. Hartfield forty dollars, suspending twenty dollars.

"Can I say something, Judge?"

The judge looked down on the defendant like a kindly father upon a boy who has made an understandable error and whom he must punish unjustly.

"Of course, Mr. Hartfield."

"I want to say, Judge, that even if I don't have the same rights a Nigra does under the Constitution, I'm a free, white Mississippian and I always will be."

The judge nodded. "And you should be, Mr. Hartfield, you should be." He informed the defendant that his case could be appealed.

We all rose and filed out of the courtroom.

A friend muttered to me, "He has just told the goons if they want to beat us up, it will cost them twenty dollars."

I shrugged and nodded.

We walked out in a kind of uncertain single file. Bill alone, Peter alone, I alone.

Out on the hostile street we cast nervous looks about us. How does one get a colored cab?

But that night we were all together again, in the Negro ghetto, in the great summer crucible of Mississippi.

And this morning Peter Werner left for McComb. I do not believe the German accent will ever torment me again.

Nothing Can Happen to Papa's Heart

Papa and the rangy old trainman stood in the ancient depot at Duluth waiting for the Northern Pacific to come snorting in from Minneapolis.

"She's the last one, Jim," said Papa, with the characteristic twitch of his head. "I don't figure she'll last too long."

"Nope," said the trainman. "She won't last long, Moe. Wasn't more'n five or six passengers goin' down last trip. She won't last long, no sir."

They said no more, their ears trained to the familiar rumble of the tracks. The Northern Pacific was part of the very rhythm of their life and it wouldn't last long.

It was my last visit home. I hadn't been here for twenty years. I was taking this train ride to Minneapolis as a sentimental journey and Papa was seeing me off.

I took a window seat and looked out at Papa standing there as I had seen him stand a hundred times before. Almost imperceptibly aging, yet still at eight-two planted solidly on the ground, hard as an oak and timeless as a redwood.

As the train shook, chugged and then rocked firmly on the tracks, leaving Papa's sturdy figure far behind, I looked out the window at the familiar scene. Past the same little country towns—Pine City, Sandstone, Finland—past the same rivers and streams and ponds that made my native state the "land of the sky blue waters." Past miles upon miles of low shrubs and new growth of popple. Occasionally a scrawny jackpine. But something was wrong with the landscape. Someone had weeded out the big trees.

I noticed the quiet man sitting opposite me at the window. He looked like a working man, a special kind of working man. Once, many years ago, I had known thousands like him. But he looked unlighted, like a burnt out bulb.

"Excuse me, sir," I said, "are you a lumberjack?"

"I used to follow the woods," he said.

"Where are the big trees?" I asked. It was more a cry than a question.

He sighed. "Popple and jackpine, jackpine and popple. That's all that's left. Used to be the finest stands of Norway and white pine in the world right here in Minnesota. Best lumber you can get. All gone. Camps? All gone. Just a few shackers left. Scattered around International Falls—places like that. Lumberjacks? Ain't no more lumberjacks. Jumpin' jacks—that's all there is. Think they're doin' time if they stay in the woods more 'n a week running. Oldtimers used to do six months without breakin' for town. All died off now. Maybe a few left in the camps in Oregon and Washington but here the timber is gone an' the jacks are gone because jacks are men who follow the woods and where do you go when there ain't no woods to follow?"

Twenty years. Duluth looked like a ghost town. Skid row with its bars and pawnshops and honky-tonks was gone. Empty city blocks where it had been. Hundreds of lumberjacks and merchant seamen had kept those blocks alive. It was the only social life they had. That was when the long boats were carrying ore out of the Mesaba Iron Range to the Pittsburgh steel mills as if the red gold would last forever. Third largest port in the world it was in tonnage.

And we, when we were young, watched the aerial bridge swinging over the blue bay of Lake Superior dreaming of the St. Lawrence Waterway that would link us to the sea! The St. Lawrence Waterway is a reality now. But it came too late. Like the spring dream of a young man fulfilled in old age—bitter and frostbitten and devoid of passion.

After the 1937 strike there were over four thousand lumberjacks in the union. Sometimes I traveled with a business agent or the union president to the lumber camps along the Gunflint Trail or into the Big Fork country visiting the men, getting interviews for the union paper. They used to say, "There'll always be lumberjacks in Minnesota. They'll never get all the big trees. We got a long ways to go. Yep, we're here to stay. They can't drive us old timber beasts out of the woods, nope. Never."

This last visit home my brother took me to a museum in Hayward, Wisconsin, that was once the center of rich timber country. The museum was a lumber camp! It was a busy Sunday and tourists were swarming over it. There was the bunkhouse just as the men had left it when the last big tree fell to the cry of "Timber!"

Their tools were hanging neatly from nails on the walls. A few pairs of high boots were standing beside the musty bunks, as if waiting for their owners. A mackinaw hung on a nail.

Outside were the pump and a washtub full of water. In the enclosed meadow a big wagon loaded with lumber, high riggings, a huge log of Norway pine on display as big in diameter as a California redwood. A few horses were grazing lazily in the field. An old lumberjack moved about in his typical woodsman's clothes providing local color. And where the men used to sit hunched silently over their evening chuck around long unpainted wooden tables sat tourists, filling the room with clatter. It was a converted restaurant.

I sat down on a wooden bench where the jacks used to sit in the sun to sharpen their crosscut saws and I felt like the lumberjack I met on the rocking train—as if a big hunk of my life had become a museum piece. And I knew that Papa and the old trainman watching the Northern Pacific snorting in from Minneapolis on one of its last trips…I knew they must have been feeling something like that.

The Northern Pacific was also a part of my life. The long lonesome hoot of its whistle meant Papa was being carried away to the "country" where he spent most of each week, buying cattle like his father before him. It didn't matter what was going on in town—weddings, bar mitzvahs, birthday parties, a sick child—Papa had to make the train. If he was a little late he'd call the depot and they'd hold the train for him. Twitching his head like a powerful horse throwing back its mane, he would slap on his derby hat, grab his sheepskin coat against the burning cold, and take the hill in long strides.

He had a deep cleft in his cheek where a bull had gored him. There were only three times I remember that he hadn't caught the evening train. Each time a bull had gored him but he explained, "Bull didn't mean no harm. He was only playin'. Trouble with them bulls, they don't know their own strength." Papa didn't know his either. When a big teamster started mouthing off at a greenhorn, calling him "kike," Papa laid him with one blow. But he was gentle, unjudgmental, and the softest touch in ten counties.

A strange combination of orthodox Jew and pioneering

American, he seemed much more the latter to me, because he looked like a farmer and he talked like one, and he seemed much more at home on the prairies than he did in town. He was never so much at peace as when he sat at the reins of the old horse and buggy and we clap-clapped together over the country roads. It seemed then that the nervous tick and twitch of his eyes were not so bad. His face like his sunburned hands had the toughness and color of weathered leather so I was always startled when he pulled off his shirt to find his skin so fair.

Papa started buying cattle with his father when he was only fifteen. The farmers would hold their cattle for them, refusing to sell to other dealers. They were valued as "straight shooters," and Papa cannot remember a single instance of anti-Semitism directed either toward him or his father. Sometimes he would take me with him to the country. I was his oldest child and it didn't matter that I was a girl. As we made the rounds from farm to farm he would introduce me. "This is my kid," he'd say. "Ha ha. Likes to take train rides, so I brung her along," and the farmer would nod, "Well, well now, ain't she a nice little shaver," and Papa would boom, "She's a crackerjack!"

Papa was born in a barn on a hillside in the first snowfall of the season. My grandmother said she woke the next morning under a soft blanket of snow that drifted down through the cracks in the roof. Their first real house had no running water and one morning, when the weather was something like thirty-five below, Papa and his two young brothers went to fetch water in the barrels they carried on a sled. He was only fifteen and his brothers were younger and it was hard work getting the loaded barrels moving on the sled. They tipped it and spilled the water over him. In the fierce cold it froze at once. When he stumbled into the house he could hardly breathe for the layer of ice over his face. Crying out exhortations to the almighty, his mother grabbed an axe and broke the ice frozen to him. When he was warm again, and dry, the three boys started out again.

I don't know just when Papa gave in to Mama's nagging and stopped wearing the familiar derby hat, but I remember him always in fair weather or foul with the black derby on his head. "One day," he said, "I come into this general store in Fargo and Pete—he's a friend a' mine—he says, Moe, how would you like to buy two hundred fifty derbies? I says Pete, I'd sure like to help ya out, but I ain't got no use for no two hundred fifty derbies. He says, You can have 'em all for ten bucks. Nobody's wearin' 'em no more an' I can't get 'em off my hands. So I says, Well, if that's the case, sure, so I took them derbies an' put them in the closet at the Commercial Hotel, where I always stay when I'm in Fargo.

"Well, one day Gus Johnson he says to me, Moe, you know somethin'? Hans Lundquist, his daughter's gettin' married, so he comes to me an' he says, Gus, my daughter's gettin' married an' we figure like we ought to get up a little more formal like but none of us farmers got no formal duds at all. An' I says, Don't worry about that. My friend Moe he got two hundred fifty derbies stashed away in his closet at the Commercial Hotel. Hans says, The weddin's Sunday. You got no time to ask him. Gus says, I don't need to ask him nothin'. If Moe knew you needed them derbies he'd give 'em to you himself. So Gus he went an' gave Hans the derbies an', boy, them farmers really got themselves gussied up. It was one fancy weddin' with all them farmers dolled up in them derbies.

"Well, I never expected to get nothin' out of 'em. Last thing in my mind for Chrissake. But for two months after that every farm I come to to buy cattle farmer'd say, By the way, Moe, how much I owe you for that there derby I wore to Hans Lundquist's daughter's weddin'? I say, Nothin'. Don't owe me nothin' for Chrissake.

"Well, the farmer wouldn't say no more but when it came to strike a bargain for a cow he'd say, I would 'a asked sixty for this cow, Moe, but seein' as how I owe you for that derby, take it for fifty. An' that's the way it went right down the line. Must a' made five hundred bucks off them there derbies an' I swear to God I wasn't even tryin'."

Papa and his father were Lincoln Republicans. He voted Republican faithfully because his father did, but when the Depression left him and his brothers as well as most of the farmers of the entire countryside bankrupt he voted for Roosevelt. Still, my radicalism was a thorn in his side. Mostly for reasons of expedience, I'm sure, for he would never believe that his "kid" could do anything except from the purest motives. Yet he would nag me constantly.

"Get that monkey off your back! Why you runnin' round with all them jumpin' jacks? First thing you know you're gonna get yourself in a pile a' trouble."

He was a little deaf and he had a loud voice and there were times when I wanted to scream at him, "For the luvva Pete, shut up!" But he would insist with the monotony of a broken record, "What do you need all that foolishness for? Get that monkey off your back!" When my husband died and as McCarthyism began to come into full flower, Papa was even more insistent that this was the time to change my ways. When I took the kids and moved to Minneapolis, one of my compensations was not to have Papa nagging me.

And one day they passed the McCarran Act. I was then secretary of the Civil Rights Congress, which had been declared a communist front organization, and I could have been subject to five years in prison and a ten thousand dollar fine. I wanted to talk to somebody that day. Somebody very close to me. What if the worst should happen? Who would take care of my children? How could I protect the life insurance their father had left for their education? I wanted to talk to Papa but the thought of him bellowing in his loud voice, "Get that monkey off your back!" turned me off. "I'll sleep on it," I thought, "and maybe tomorrow I'll take a train home."

Papa made the decision for me. It was only seven o'clock the next morning when he called. He must have spent a sleepless night himself.

"Hi, kid," he said.

"Hi, Pop, how come you're calling me so early?"

"Nothin'—just wanted to see how you was, that's all."

"I was kind of thinking of taking the noon train home, Pop."

"Great. I'll meet you at the depot."

He was there at the old familiar depot as the Northern Pacific snorted in. We hardly spoke on the ride home. How are the kids? Fine. How's everything? Fine. How are you? Fine. When we got home he took my hat and coat and my bag and put them in the bedroom. Then he sat blinking at me quietly as I drank the tea with the strudel my kind stepmother proffered me. When I had set the cup aside he followed me into the living room. He followed me as

I moved restlessly from room to room. Finally, I went upstairs and sat down on the bed.

In a moment Papa was sitting there beside me.

"Anything on your mind, kid?" he asked.

"No, nothing special."

"Sure you got nothin' you want to talk about?"

"No, why should I have anything special?"

"Nothin'—just thinkin' maybe you got somethin' you wanna tell me."

"No—yes, I have, Papa. That's why I came. There's something I want to talk about very much but I hate to even start because right off the bat you'll start yelling, 'What did I tell you? Get that monkey off your back!'"

Papa looked shocked.

"No, oh no," he said, "I ain't gonna say nothin' like that. Noooo, I never kick a man when he's down. You're in the gutter, kid, an' I ain't kickin' you when I wouldn't even kick a stranger. I want to help you. You just tell me what."

"Oh, Papa," I almost wept. "Thanks, Papa. You understand now, don't you? You understand that, even if I wanted to, I couldn't get out of it now, don't you see? The only thing they'd ever accept is if I'd turn stool pigeon on my comrades."

Papa shrank.

"No," he cried. "No, no, you couldn't do that." He was blinking and tossing his head about as if a wasp had stung him.

I burst out laughing, not from mirth, but from a kind of unbearable joy.

"Papa," I said, "you don't know why I'm a radical. You think it's crazy. You've been after me for years to get that monkey off my back, and yet you would rather see me go to jail than to turn traitor to what I believe in and to the people who trust me. Don't you see, Papa, you're the reason I'm a radical in the first place. It's because I learned something from you just watching you, and I took something that you've always had, the most important thing there is—integrity."

He sat blinking at me with his one brown eye and one blue. He had only gone to the fifth grade in school and he didn't understand fancy words but he knew what I meant. He put his rough, sunburned hand on mine and we sat quietly for a moment without words.

About six months ago he called me long distance.

"You know somethin'?" he said. "The Northern Pacific is done for. They took the last train off last week. Good thing you come up when you did an' took that last ride. Buses taking over. People got their own cars. They ain't gonna run no more trains. They're talkin' about tearin' the depot down."

No more trains? Tear the depot down? I felt a surge of grief. It was like a death in the family.

I had another long-distance call last night.

It was my brother.

"Hey, Een?"

I knew something was wrong from the tone of his voice.

"Look, I can't do anything with Pop. He's going to this crummy doctor who doesn't know from borscht, and lately he's been losing weight, fading away. His pulse is low and keeps dropping. He sleeps too much and coughs a lot and his legs are swelling. The horse doctor thinks it's his heart but I don't trust him. Will you please call and get him to a heart specialist? I can't do a thing with him. He'll listen to you."

"Yes, I'll call. Right away. I'll call this minute."

Heart? Papa's heart? But that's ridiculous. Nothing could be wrong with Papa's heart. Papa's the midwestern landscape. Papa is the prairies. Papa is a herd of cattle feeding on the green hills. Papa is the clap-clap of the horse's hooves on a country road, the lumberjack sharpening his crosscut saw. He's a train whistle in the night, the long boats passing. Papa is the depot waiting for the evening train. Papa is the last of the big trees. He's immortal. He has to be. How can anything happen to Papa's heart?

With a trembling hand I dial the operator and ask for Papa's area code.

THE PEOPLE ARE A RIVER

You can never kill the people for there always will be more
Like the water in the ocean, like the sand upon the shore.
You can twist a flowing river, you can choke it with debris,
But a river, if it's flowing, it will always find the sea.
You can quench a million fires but we bear an inner light
Like the fireflies that blossom in the blackness of the night.
You can throw us back to savagery, but when your work is done,
Our wrath will cut a clearing through the jungle to the sun.
The wheels that make the world go round are guided by our hand.
There will always be the people. There will always be the land.

Above the crash of falling steel, of bombs and anguished cries
You can hear our pounding rivet gun build girders to the skies.
You can see us by the rivers loading cotton on the scows,
You can hear us at the bellows, forging iron into plows.
Though our cities be a shambles and our dead laid out in rows
We'll be standing at the throttle when the morning whistle blows:
We'll be oiling up the engines, we'll be watching on the ships.
The rhythm of tomorrow's song is waiting on our lips.

Though our silos may be blazing and our forests seared and torn,
We'll be singing down the prairies when the silk is on the corn,
We'll be haying in the meadow when the clover land is sweet.
When the time is for the harvest we'll be gathering the wheat.

eramics, lapidary, things like that." Making little pots? Poli
nes? What would she do with all those little polished ston
He steered her to the bulletin board. "Mom, look. He
ture by a Stanford professor on the influence of Shakespea
odern lite   A conce
amber n   ap vaude
tertainme   to lead s
e "I'm Fo   tle news
o called I   diting it
ne and co   be a whee
lot stuff,"   mented d
Jeremy   The mor
anged th   ered how
hbarrassed   were dr
tomobiles   icycle. "S
ry. I'm th   t afford a
t he susp   she'd stil
Then t   to the P
eeting lik   use they
ing to ch   "How do
pect fruit   heir kids
rnival at   they mad
arge mini   knowing
isn't a pe   dly wrun
other's neck. She was right of course. She always was. He
should be proud of her. But somehow he had wished he
Such things   om was involve
ery kind of bat   tolerate injusti
ust be awful not to be able to tolerate injustice. It must be
He remembered with particular poignancy the day she got
e o'clock one raw morning to demonstrate at San Qu
ainst the death penalty. He was a junior at high school. He

SECTION FIVE
KEEP ON BURNING

TO HANK

Beloved, this is your grave
This stone marks where you lie
I have planted upon it discarded shells
Blooming with barnacled flowerlets from the sea
I have planted upon it a white bird
                      a sea bird
I return you, my darling, to your mother.

Stay where you lie, my love
                 I beg you
Follow me no more.
I am hoarse from screaming for you into the vagrant wind
Of calling your name in scorching deserts
                      and drinking from a mirage
I am footsore from trailing your footsteps on the shadows
                       of mountains
Let there be an end at last
to finding you one brief moment in someone's smile
Another's touch
Or in the soft, dark depths of eyes
                      not yours.
I am a branch bent by the weight of the wind's longing
I am a fly strangled in gossamer spun by a spider
I am a wraith running barefooted in the snow
                    driven by storms.

Give me myself!
Stay where you lie, my love
You who loved me with so much mercy
Give me myself!

THE BLESSINGS OF SOLOMON

Since Solomon moved away from Newton Avenue, he had nothing to tie him to the living world but the Yiddish paper. He would wait for the mailman, standing at the picture window, straining his eyes toward Summit Boulevard.

The house he lived in was set back deep in the foliage, and the trained hand of the city's best landscape gardener had conspired with good fortune to rob him of even this meagre contact with the world. Even if he could have seen out upon the road, what was there to see on Summit Boulevard? The flash of cars—he could not even distinguish the faces of their drivers. The gleam of headlights at night. The musical honk of the fine automobiles. Sometimes the screech of a brake sudden as a scream. Yet, even so, little was better than nothing.

This house was the very latest in houses. Designed as if to spite him. In the back there was something they called a "patio." It looked out upon the impersonal silence of a wooded lot. Why couldn't this have been a front porch where he could sit and smoke the sweet cigarettes he rolled by hand and at least hear the world go by on Summit Boulevard? For the same reason he thought, with a touch of irony, that when you can afford mink, you do not wear Hudson seal, and when you can drive a Cadillac, it is a shame to be seen behind the wheel of a Buick, and when you have grown rich enough to live on Summit Boulevard, what fool would dream of spending his remaining years on Newton Avenue?

He recalled that it was the year Rose's husband, Ben, opened his fourth surplus store that he had taken leave of Newton Avenue. Taken leave forever of his friends, the delicatessen, the tailor shop, the fish market, the butcher shop, the synagogue. It was like taking leave of one's native village and going to spend your remaining days in a foreign land, among strangers where you would never hear your mother tongue, the sound of Yiddish, a language that melts in your mouth, a language salty as herring, warm as your mother's home-baked bread.

Mendel the tailor, his oldest friend, had tried to console him.

"Solomon," he said, "you are a man truly blessed. How many children are there nowadays who would put up with an old man? It's not like the olden times when they had respect for a father. Now they pack him off to an old people's home and they're rid of him. Do your children send you to the old people's home? God forbid!"

"God forbid!" nodded Solomon.

It was almost a year before he saw Mendel again. What maneuvering had gone into the arrangements for Mendel to visit him at Summit Boulevard! How long it had taken to summon up courage to approach his grandchildren for this favor! For the bus stop was two miles from this exclusive neighborhood. To come without a car one would have to stop at the drug store at the end of the busline and call the house and someone would drive out in a car to pick you up. It was hard to ask a favor of your children and grandchildren when after all you were a guest in their house. So he waited for an opportunity to approach the matter indirectly.

It came the day Sandra was holding forth over her shorty coat.

"I told you, Mom, not to buy stuff at bargain sales! This is no shorty coat."

"It is a shorty coat."

"It's not a shorty coat. It's a three-quarter coat. A shorty coat comes to here. Like this. It's smart looking. This hangs down—look how far it hangs. It's tacky. And you can't return it because you got it on sale. Honest, I'm so tee'd off I could give it to the Goodwill."

"You can cut it down," Rose suggested.

"Cut it down? Who's going to cut it down?"

Solomon saw his opportunity and interposed gently, "There's a tailor—you know him—Mendel on Newton Avenue near the shoemaker? He's a good tailor—hands like gold. He makes coats for even stylish ladies. He can cut it down for you and it will look like a new coat."

Rose brightened and looked at her father with a gleam of interest.

"You mean I'm going to go traipsing way across town to some old tailor on Newton Avenue?" shrilled Sandra.

"No, no," rushed in Solomon, "God forbid. Why should you go there? He will be glad to come here and take the measurements. Business is not so rushing with him. Maybe he can close up the shop for an afternoon."

"Sometimes a tailor can do a better job than a dressmaker," Rose persisted, "especially a coat. That's their business. Coats, suits."

The old man nodded, his eyes planted eagerly on Sandra's face.

"I will not go to some shmo of a tailor," she summarized, "and that's that. I'll take it to the alteration department at Lingaman's."

"It will cost you more than the whole coat," Rose grumbled.

"Let it cost," Sandra shot back. "Next time you won't do me any favors buying me bargains."

Solomon was defeated, but the next time he employed a direct approach.

"Dovidel," he ventured, "you're going some place Wednesday?"

"What's going on Wednesday, Gramps?" asked David.

"Nothing. I thought maybe you'd be home about two o'clock?"

"Why, what's doing?"

"What do you want, Pa?" asked Rose.

"Mendel the tailor, you remember him. He has a little shop on Newton Avenue by the shoemaker? He would like to come and visit me maybe Wednesday. But there is nobody of course to drive him here from the bus."

"Swell idea!" David cried warmly. "You haven't got any friends your own age here. I sure would do it, Gramps, but I'm going to a ball game. Sandy can hang around here Wednesday and pick the old man up."

"What do you mean *I* can hang around?" Sandra whined, flashing her brother a murderous look. Then she turned to her grandfather and kissed him lightly on the forehead. "I'm sorry, Grandpa. I'd do it but I've got an appointment at the beauty parlor at half past two."

"What do you do, live there?" asked David. "You had an appointment at the beauty parlor four days ago. I drove you there myself."

"Is it any of your business?"

"It wouldn't kill you to do the old man a favor."

"Listen to that! It wouldn't kill *me!* What about you? Why don't you skip your ball game if you're so big-hearted? How come I'm the mean one?"

"Shut up!" cried Rose. "I never saw two kids who could harp at each other so much all the time. It makes a person sick. In other houses it's a pleasure the way brothers and sisters get along, but here it's harp, harp, harp, nothing but harp." She turned irritably to her father. "It's gotta be Wednesday?"

"Wednesday, Thursday, it doesn't matter."

"Well, let him come Thursday. But one o'clock sharp. I'll pick him up and bring him here before I go to my bridge club. Then I can drive him to the bus when I get back. But let him be at the bus stop one o'clock sharp. I can't wait around."

"One o'clock sharp," the old man nodded.

For days Solomon rehearsed in his mind the conversations he would have with Mendel. A thousand things there were to talk about. If only he could remember them. Besides the headlines in the Yiddish paper, there were the anecdotes, and the thoughts about life that occurred to him from time to time. But they melted like snow in his mind because there was no one to hear them. Like youth and age. He must tell Mendel how it occurred to him as he stood looking out toward Summit Boulevard just the other day that youth looks out upon life from one wide open door, and age from a thousand bolted windows. This he must tell Mendel before it too melts away. Not that it is important. But a man likes to exchange his thoughts.

There was so much happening in the world. You had to talk to somebody. What about Nasser, for instance? And what will come of all this business with sputniks and bomb tests and what not? But with the family you couldn't exchange a word. As if it was not their world. Ben—what could you say to Ben? He knew about nothing but surplus stores. Rose had her bridge clubs. Sandra was interested in God knows what, and David—that was truly the most baffling thing of all.

When David was fifteen, Solomon, rummaging in the attic among his books, came upon the boy setting up a chemistry experiment. He looked startled and shamefaced at the sight of his grandfather. Misunderstanding his embarrassment, Solomon reassured him: "You do not have to be afraid that your grandfather does not understand what you are doing. In English I am ignorant, but in Yiddish I am an educated man. In the old country they called me 'the philosopher.' I know little of science but my interest is great."

David was sheepish. "Don't tell anybody about this, will you, Grandpa?"

"Who should I tell?" shrugged the old man.

"The folks know I'm pretty good at this stuff. If they think I'm too interested they'll get on my neck to try out for one of those science prizes. They're already bothering me about it."

"So what is so terrible? Maybe you would win one?"

"That's just it, you don't understand, Gramps. You win a thing like that, it gets around. The kids think you're a brain."

"A brain? What's a brain?"

"Brains." David tapped his head. "You know, brains."

"That's bad—brains?" puzzled the old man. "What can be wrong with having brains?"

"Oh, you don't understand. I can't explain it. They think you're nuts—different. It's just funny, that's all."

Solomon spread his hands in bewilderment.

"A funny thing the world has come to, a Jewish boy should be afraid of having brains," he was muttering to himself as he clumped cautiously down the attic stairs.

He was deeply disappointed these days to find that David was neglecting his studies, running around like an idiot to ball games. He did not dare open his mouth about it to the family. He would discuss it with Mendel.

Solomon pondered many times in his life how you wait and wait for some particular event. You exhaust endless days in waiting and anticipation. And suddenly it happens, and just as suddenly it is over and you are looking back upon it, pondering the nature of time and the brevity of life.

He had wished away a week of his life, living for nothing but Mendel's coming, and at last the waiting was over and Mendel was here!

Mendel came dressed in the shiny broadcloth suit he wore only on the high holidays. He sat on the edge of the satin chair, afraid to touch its pale arms with his hands or his elbows.

"And how is business?" asked Solomon.

"One lives," Mendel replied absently, a trapped look on his face, as if he were smothering in the room's lush opulence. "This is certainly a fine house," he added, politely. "A house like this must cost a man a fortune."

"How's Leah and the grandchildren?"

"All well, thank God," Mendel replied, still absently. "The taxes alone on a house like this a poor man could live on for half a year."

"And Sam Elman, he is better?"

"What better? From such a sickness, who recovers? God lives and the people suffer." He looked down at his feet. White rugs. Deep as an inch of snow. He wondered with a sudden stop of his breath if he had stepped on the freshly tarred street on Newton Avenue.

"Maybe you would like a smoke, Mendel?"

Mendel declined with alarm.

More questions, briefly answered.

"Come, let us go sit in the kitchen," cried Solomon.

"Aha!" cried Mendel, rising quickly with a grateful smile, "that is really a good idea!" But before moving from the spot, he carefully examined the soles of his shoes.

"We could sit outside," sighed Solomon, "but to spite us it's drizzling. Such a weather we have. Two seasons. Winter and July."

"The kitchen is very good," said Mendel, still smiling. "What could be better than a kitchen? It will be like old times."

His smile vanished as Solomon led him into the kitchen—a cold marriage of stainless steel and dazzling porcelain. "Like an operating room," thought Mendel, with a shudder, his eyes casting about for the kitchen table.

"There is a button somewhere," said Solomon. "You press a button and a table comes out of the wall." He pressed the wrong button and an ironing board leaped out at Mendel. He sprang back, trembling. Solomon pressed another button and a shelf began revolving.

"So who needs a table?" said Mendel, trying to put his distracted host at ease.

"Some place there is a button," said Solomon, doggedly.

He finally found it and they sat down together at the narrow little utility table of gleaming white formica. It scarcely resembled a kitchen table. They felt awkward and ill at ease.

Solomon rose. He wanted to serve his friend a glass of tea. He fumbled about the shelves and realized he didn't know where to look for anything. It was the maid's day off.

"Forget the tea," said Mendel, sympathetically. "Who's thirsty?"

But one doesn't entertain a guest and serve him nothing. He found some fresh peaches in the refrigerator. They ate them in silence, slowly, almost as if to postpone the need for a conversation. Then Mendel looked on with discomfiture as Solomon thrashed about for some place to dispose of the peelings and the peach stones. Where was the garbage pail? In some hole in the wall no doubt and only God knows where they have hidden the button. Defeated, he rolled the refuse into a scrap of Yiddish paper and stuffed it into his pocket.

At last Rose came home from her bridge game to drive Mendel to the station.

When it came time to part, they did not meet each other's eyes. They stood bleakly a moment, like two gnarled trees, numbed by the biting frost of December.

Then Mendel said in their beloved Yiddish. "Nu, be well."

"Go well," said Solomon.

"May we live, please God, to meet again."

Solomon shrugged. "The Lord is merciful. The greatest compensation in this life is that He does not compel a man to live forever."

It was another Friday night. A Sabbath eve. The family had all gone their separate ways and Solomon was musing to himself. He remembered with nostalgia that about this time of night the Sabbath service would be over in the synagogue and familiar friends would be gathering on the stone stairs to exchange a story, a bit of gossip, or a serious comment on the day's headlines. Then they would walk together slowly through the perfumed evening, sweet with pine and rustling apple blossoms. "But Mendel is right," he thought, "how many children are there nowadays who would put up with an old father? They'd pack him off to an old people's home and be rid of him. After all, he had his own ways."

Ben wanted him to stop smoking. Smoking causes cancer, he said, hardening of the arteries. So you live a little longer, so what? But of course his cigarette cough was another matter. It could get on a person's nerves, and dropping ashes on the rugs is also bad. To make matters worse he had a way of spitting into little pieces of newspaper, rolling them up in balls and forgetting to drop them into the wastebasket. Rose found one last week lying on her fine satin sofa and she exploded with unexpected bitterness: "There's kleenex! There's wastebaskets! This isn't Ma's house that you can go around dropping things, never picking up after yourself. If you had helped Ma a little more maybe she'd be living today. You old country men always expecting a woman to wait on you. So helpless you couldn't even wash a dish or boil water. You'd starve to death if there wasn't a woman around to take care of you!"

True, true, there are better ways now. A man helps his wife, thought Solomon. In the kitchen a man is no longer helpless like a left arm.

But after the outburst Rose was sorry.

"Pa," she said, "you need some fresh tobacco? David is going to the store. He'll bring you some tobacco."

And that evening he overheard her on the telephone talking to his son, Irving.

"Irv," she said, "it wouldn't hurt you to come over and take Pa for a ride once in a while or drop in for a game of pinochle or something. So you're busy, who isn't? After all, he was a good father. He did the best he could. A man can't sit all day like a dummy talking to the wall. After all, Ben's only a son-in-law. Say, he's pretty good as it is. After all, it's not his father. Never mind you're busy, Irv. He's not going to live forever. After he's gone it'll be too late to say you're sorry. You hear me, Irv?"

"She has a big mouth but also a big heart," thought Solomon sadly.

He did not want to overhear Rose's telephone conversations but her voice was loud and carried to the patio. Yesterday he heard her talking.

"Listen," she was saying, "he's not so young. He's seventy-one, God bless him. I should look so good at his age. What should I do with an old father—send him to the old people's home? But what are you going to do? They've got their own ways. It's an aggravation but you've got to put up with it. What do you mean old age pension? You think it's the money? How could I let an old man like that stay alone in a room some place? He can't even boil water for himself. And what if he should slip on the ice or something, what would people say? They get on your nerves, sure, but what are you going to do. Sick, what sick? A little of this, a little of that. He can't do much walking but I should feel so good at seventy-one. So you have a few aches and pains. Say, when you get old, what do you expect? An appetite he's got, thank God."

And thinking deeply this lonely Sabbath night, a brilliant thought sprang into Solomon's brain, like a butterfly bursting from the grey cocoon of pain that bound his soul, as if God Himself had planted it there out of His understanding and boundless mercy.

What is wrong with the old people's home?

Why have I been so fearful of the old people's home, he thought. Didn't the wise rabbi say never look upon tomorrow with yesterday's eyes? An old people's home was not a poorhouse. It was not like the olden times. Why should it be so dreaded? There I would find other people like myself. My own generation. Somebody to talk with. To exchange thoughts. To discuss the day's news. To walk with a little. To trade a joke. Here I am a dry, black stalk in a freshly planted vineyard. There how happily I could live out my years! They say Simon Frisch is in the old people's home. And Hyman Segal. Simon I haven't seen in three years. A *shlimazel* he always was. But he could tell a story to split your sides. Hyman, it's true, was a bit of a *noodnik*, but even a *noodnik* is better than nobody.

For the first time since he left Newton Avenue, he was a living man, capable of hope and joy and growth. He hummed a tune as he rummaged in his room among his few possessions. This he would take with him to the Home. This he would throw away. This perhaps David would like to have as a keepsake.

Tomorrow afternoon when she was alone, he'd talk to Rose. If he could convince her that this was what he wanted, she would be happy to please him. If she could see that he really wanted to go to the old people's home, that this would be a great joy to him and that he looked upon it with anticipation, she would not deny him this happiness. The money it would cost he was sure would be no problem. They could raise the money among the children. And then when it was all settled, think of the pleasure it would be for

Rose not to have him on her hands. And Ben. After all, only a son-in-law.

He approached her the next afternoon as she was preparing to leave for her Saturday shopping.

"Raisel, my dear," he said, using the familiar Yiddish.

"Yeah, Pa," she tossed off carelessly as she painted her lips in front of the mirrored wall.

"I've been thinking, Raisel, what is so bad about the old people's home?"

"What old people's home?"

"I mean an old people's home is a good idea. It's not like the old days. People don't look at it the same way."

"Old people's home? What old people's home?" snapped Rose. "What are you bothering my head with an old people's home?"

"I mean, Raisel, you can sit with people your own age. You have somebody to talk to. This is nice. A very nice thing."

"Well, so it's nice, so what?"

"So I mean, Raisel, I would like very much to go to the old people's home. This is what I would like very much. If you please."

Rose turned on him, her face pale.

"Pa, are you crazy? What would people say? That Rose Friedman sent her old father to the old people's home? What kind of a crazy business is this?"

"Let them say. What do you care what they say. I have friends there. Simon Hirsch—"

"Simon Hirsch!" cried Rose. "For months they talked about Joe Hirsch—they're still talking about him for sending his father there. It was a shame. It disgraced him!"

"People have different ideas now. Things change. It is no disgrace. This is what I want, Raisel. This is what I want very much. Believe me, this would make me very happy."

"Make you happy! What about me? You want to make a fool out of me all over town? An old people's home—imagine that! I wouldn't be able to look people in the face, for God's sake!"

"But I want—"

"You want! You don't know what you want! You've got a beautiful home in the best part of town. Everybody waits on you. A maid even brings in your Yiddish paper. And you want to make a fool out of me. You're in your second childhood!"

Solomon's silently gesticulating hands dropped to his sides.

"Some people just aren't satisfied no matter what you do for them," Rose cried, almost in tears. "Old people's home!" She seized her purse and jacket. There was the clackety clack of her high heels on the stone patio as she headed for the garage to get her car. Then a loud snorting of the high-powered motor as the sleek beast burst out of the garage with a roar and rolled down the street to join the endless caravan of cars flashing faceless along the dark ribbon of Summit Boulevard.

Freedom Is a Lonely Hill

Naomi caught her breath as her son Jeremy drew his Porsche up to the grounds of Indian Summer, a lush retirement home in the green lap of the redwoods. He jumped out of the car and opened the door for her. She stepped out onto the beautifully sculptured grounds carved out of the forest. Ancient trees guarded the compact apartments built without loss of an inch of space. The cement pathways passed between colonnades of trees, and here and there stone benches waited invitingly in the California sun. Everything spelled care, dignity and affluence.

Naomi looked around her. "Must cost an arm and a leg to live here," she said.

"Oh, Mom," Jeremy tossed off her first objection cavalierly. "You're not considering what you get here. Absolutely everything. Have you ever seen such a fantastic setting?"

"Yes, beautiful. But it must cost an arm and a leg."

"I wish you would forget cost," Jeremy frowned. "I told you from the start I could swing it. Come on, Mom, let me show you the place."

Naomi walked gingerly down the deep carpeted corridors to the library and reading room where Jeremy was directing her. It reminded her of a rich men's club in London or maybe Boston. And it was quiet, infinitely quiet.

"Beautiful, eh, Mom?"

"Yes, could be the lobby of a Hotel Hilton. The rich really know how to grow old gracefully, don't they?"

"There you go again, Mom. Feeling guilty. Like maybe you'll have it a little better than somebody else. It's time you stopped thinking about the whole world and started thinking about yourself. I want you to have the best there is. You're entitled to it."

"Why? I'm no more entitled than anybody else."

"I can't worry about anybody else. You're my mother."

He hurried ahead of her. "Mom, I want you to look at this library. Really look. No trash. A lot of retired professors from Stanford live here. And up to date. Look at this, Mom. Latest book, *Passages*. You can see they keep the library up."

"Yes, the books are good," Naomi said, glancing over the shelves.

"What did I tell you, Mom? Now look at the magazine rack. *U.S. News & World Report, Time, Saturday Review of Literature, National Geographic, The Smithsonian, New York Times, Atlan—*"

"Jerry, I see. I can read."

And suddenly a crazy memory invaded the reality of the moment. It was Jeremy at three and herself at thirty and she was trying to get him to try an outdoor toilet at a resort. The child simply would not sit down in the yawning hole. She took him to a neighbor's outhouse.

"Look, Jerry, curtains on the window. Isn't it pretty?"

"Oh, yes," said the child, clinging to her.

"Then sit down."

"No."

"Look, baby." There was sweat on her forehead. If this kid didn't go soon he'd be sick and their vacation would be over. "Look how nicely painted it is. A pretty blue. Isn't it a pretty blue?"

"Oh, yes, real pretty."

"Then sit down, eh, honey?"

"No."

"Mom. Oh, Mom. Hey, are you still with me?"

Naomi blinked. "Did you say something, Jerry?"

"Yes, I wanted to show you the dining room." He hurried her in the opposite direction. "First take a look at this menu for the coming week. You'd never have to cook another meal in your life. The finest French cooking couldn't be more gourmet. And the desserts. Chocolate rum cake flambé, baked Alaska—with your sweet tooth you'd have a ball."

"I'd have a ball getting fat. Can you imagine how fat I'd get eating like this three times a day?"

"Oh, Mom, what does it matter if you get fat?"

"What does it matter?" Naomi silently paraphrased the question. "Who cares how an old woman looks?"

"I know what you're worried about, Mom. Isolation. But there's a little bus that comes up here once a day. And you have access to two colleges. You can take all the classes you want. And look here,

Mom. The crafts room. You know, ceramics, lapidary, things like that."

Making little pots? Polishing stones? What would she do with all those little polished stones?

He steered her to the bulletin board. "Mom, look. Here's a lecture by a Stanford professor on the influence of Shakespeare on modern literature. Right up your alley. And look. A concert of chamber music. Mozart and Brahms. No cheap vaudeville entertainment here, Mom. Nobody comes up here to lead songs like "I'm Forever Blowing Bubbles." They have a little newspaper too called *Indian Summer*. If I know you, you'll be editing it in no time and coordinating programs and all that. You'll be a wheel."

"Hot stuff," Naomi commented dryly.

Jeremy looked at her quizzically: Same old Mom. The more she changed the more she was the same. He remembered how she embarrassed him as a kid when all the mothers were driving automobiles and Mom was pedalling away on a bicycle. "Sorry, Jerry. I'm the only breadwinner in this family. We can't afford a car." But he suspected that even if they could afford a car, she'd still ride a bicycle.

Then there was the time when she charged into the P.T.A. meeting like a wrestler at a ballet, raising hell because they were going to charge too much for the summer carnival. "How do you expect fruit pickers and cannery workers to send their kids to a carnival at one dollar a shot!" She had argued until they made the charge minimal, but he writhed in embarrassment, knowing there wasn't a person in the room who wouldn't have gladly wrung his mother's neck. She was right of course. She always was. He knew he should be proud of her. But somehow he had wished he had a mother he didn't have to be so proud of.

Such things were only petty skirmishes. Mom was involved in every kind of battle. All the time. She couldn't tolerate injustice. It must be awful not to be able to tolerate injustice. It must be like being allergic to almost everything.

He remembered with particular poignancy the day she got up at five o'clock one raw morning to demonstrate at San Quentin against the death penalty. He was a junior at high school. He heard her moving about and got up irritably, slipped on his bathrobe and came into the kitchen. It was still pitch dark and raining great sheets of water driven by a high wind.

"Mom, go back to bed, please. Nobody will be there."

"I'm going because I promised. I assume other people keep promises too."

He shrugged. He had long ago learned the futility of arguing with her on a matter of conscience.

"Can I fix your breakfast? One egg or two?"

"Thanks. Make it two. I don't know where you can eat around there."

As he poured her coffee, he noticed the lines of fatigue in her face. Why couldn't she sleep on a Saturday after working a grueling week. He wanted to force her to go back to bed but he dismissed such a futile thought.

"Mom, here's your raincoat. Please put this sweater under it. You know how cold it gets picketing. Put the hood over your head and here's a scarf. Tie it around your neck. No, tighter, Mom. Here, let me do it. If you don't get it tight enough the rain will get in at the neck and soak you clean through."

"Thanks, hon. You're a good boy." She kissed him.

When she was ready to go she turned to him, looking like a pixie in the pointed hood. She gave him a wry grin of self mockery and said, " 'The times are out of joint. Oh, curséd spite, that I was ever born to set them right.' Hamlet." And with that she walked out into the pouring morning.

"Hey, Mom!" He ran out into the rain after her. "You forgot your umbrella!"

"Go back," she scolded, "you'll catch a cold, you fool kid!"

It was still dark. He watched her cross the street and stood watching until a bus came by and picked her up. The bus would take her to a central meeting point and from there, thank goodness, she'll be in a car, he thought.

When the bus had swallowed up the slight figure standing in the wind and rain, he turned away shivering. He had gotten soaked in just that moment running after her.

No use trying to go back to sleep. He felt rotten. And damn angry with her for making him feel this way. Like it was he and not she who should be going to that demonstration. But he didn't feel the way she did. It wasn't fair to expect him to. He didn't feel he was born to right the wrongs of the world. They were infinite. He wasn't cut out to be a lonely iconoclast, a Don Quixote tilting at windmills, a tormented Jeremiah. So why did he have to feel so guilty all the time. Well, he was going to be successful in this world. Damn successful. And one of the reasons he wanted to be successful was that he could take care of her in her old age and protect her against poverty because he loved her.

His mother was still staring at the bulletin board when he took her arm and hustled her out-of-doors. "Mom, I want you to see the highlight of this place. The convalescent home. That's why I would feel so comfortable if I knew you were here and I would never have to worry about you again. If you really get sick, this convalescent home is just about the most modern and best equipped in California. And when you have to go there you take some of your own furniture along to make you feel at home. That's how sensitive these people are. When the doctor said your blood pressure is so high you could get a stroke, my blood chilled. I thought of you alone there miles away from me, maybe lying on the floor helpless and no one even knowing, maybe for days. Here a nurse looks in on you every day. A doctor is always on the grounds. If you feel bad, you just have to take your phone off the hook and somebody comes running in. And you'd be only ten minutes away from me and you could see the kids so much more often too. God, I'd feel good to know you were in good hands!"

"Do you realize that coming here would make me completely dependent on you?"

"Mom, how can you think in such terms? I'm not a stranger. I'm your son!" His sensitive face looked troubled. "I'm afraid I'm giving you the hard sell, Mom. I'm afraid I'm thinking primarily of my own peace of mind." She looked at the handsome, self-confident and successful man who was her son, and incongruously she saw a nine-year-old boy.

It was the year his father died. They were living in Montana and Jeremy was trying to help her out by removing the screen windows one fall day. It was a man's job, and coming home from work that evening she saw the boy shuffling uncertainly across the yard carrying a screen window three times his size. He stumbled and fell, his head tearing through the screen. He looked up at her, horrified, his face bleeding from countless scratches. Tears of pain stung his eyes. But she knew the pain was not for the shock and the bleeding scratches. The pain was for the hard-earned money he knew it would cost his mother to replace what he had ruined trying so hard to help her.

Remembering this picture, Naomi brushed it away with her hand as if it were something palpable. Why must such memories plague one an entire lifetime, memories no longer pertinent to present realities. If only there were some kind of selective amnesia to blot them out once and for all. Why, after all these years, must she look at the man and feel over and over again the heartbreak of the boy?

He opened the car door for her. "Mom, you took care of me. Let me take care of you now. Think it over, will you?" She got into the car and they said no more as it hummed smoothly along the sunny freeway.

She leaned back and again a memory blurred the reality of the moment.

She was a little girl in a community of immigrants called "Little Jerusalem." Baba and Zayda Sinkowski lived with them. They were her grandparents. Mama was kind to them but she couldn't conceal the fact that the house was crowded and they were in the way. The old people were always quarreling. Usually Baba started it because she was afraid that they were wearing out their welcome. Zayda would drop cigarette butts on the floor. He reeked of tobacco. He would pull a Yiddish newspaper out from under a raw fish to read it and not even notice the fish was on the floor. He spilled hot tea on the varnished table. He was a very sloppy old man. So they quarreled and quarreled and Zayda's eyes had a dead, haunted look like an animal who is cornered and knows in its gut there is no hope of escape.

And one day the old couple moved into a little flat of their own. Three tiny rooms in a basement. But they were cozy and Baba plastered colored paper on the bathroom window so you couldn't see through. Naomi had never seen Baba so happy. She fluttered about the flat as if it were a mansion, plumping pillows on the second-hand sofa, making gefilte fish in the kitchen, singing in her

218

toneless voice. And she and Zayda never quarreled now. His eyes brightened as if cataracts had been removed from them.

"Let me teach you Hebrew," he begged his granddaughter. "Study with me. You have a head like gold. The boys are clumps. Who can teach them anything? All they know is baseball. Study with me."

So Naomi studied with him, every day after school. The voice once harsh like the bark of a cornered animal was gentle. He was infinitely patient. He would kiss her forehead. "One hundred twenty years may you live, my child. A head like gold."

And how fast Baba walked! She took the hills in giant strides. In a half run as if she simply could not remember that her nine children were grown or dead and there was nothing to run for. Naomi remembered how her mother had once chided her. "Naomi, walk like a girl, for heaven's sake. Look how you stride! You walk just like your grandmother!" And she had chanted back to Mama a line from a poem, "God, give me hills to climb and strength to climb them!"

"Someday," Mama had prophesied dryly, "you'll be asking only for strength to climb them."

And all of a sudden they were back in Mama's house again. It seemed as if they had hardly settled themselves into the little flat when Baba had a stroke. From then on she remembered Baba creeping along, feeling the walls with her hands for support. Or leaning on a chair, silently looking out of the window. And the bitter quarrels began again. For now Baba was laden with even heavier guilt. Now they were not only non-paying boarders, but she was a physical burden. She was always apologizing. She seemed to be apologizing just for being alive. And Zayda. His eyes had died again. His voice again took on the harsh bark of a cornered animal. And he didn't ask to teach her anymore.

Jeremy's voice came crashing into her reverie.

"They're intelligent people living there, Mom. Three hundred fifty of them to choose from."

Naomi mused aloud. "Once I went on a cruise. The *Nordic Prince,* remember? Beautiful ship. Like a floating hotel. Seven hundred fifty people aboard. And would you believe I couldn't find a single person I had any rapport with? Oh, yes, there were two women, members of the John Birch Society. When we stayed off the subject of politics, they were really quite nice."

Jeremy's face darkened.

"That's what worries me. You get bored easily. You need change. You're restless."

Naomi didn't hear him. "Most beautiful ship. Seven hundred fifty people. And I was miserable."

He drew his car up to her driveway.

"Thanks, hon, will you come in for a cup of coffee?"

"No thanks, Mom. Got to get back. Think it over, will you?

"I will."

"You'll love the trails into the redwoods especially, Mom. And it's flat country. That's the beauty of it. You can walk for miles without having to tackle a hill and get winded. Well, gotta run. Bye, Mama."

She loved him when he called her "Mama" and she hugged and kissed him.

"Promise me you'll think about it."

"I promise."

Jeremy called her four days later.

"Mom, great news! I found out there's a possibility of your getting in within the year if you apply right away. They're expecting an opening. Old man with cancer not expected to last, poor guy. Just say the word and I'll put down the one thousand dollar deposit. You have to go through a lot of red tape like a physical, a psychological evaluation, but I'm sure they'd be impressed with your vigor and your contemporary outlook and all that."

"I'm so glad they'd be impressed."

"Mom, I don't like your tone of voice. Are you getting cold feet?"

"Jerry, hasn't it occurred to you that I wouldn't fit into a setting like that? That I've always been a free spirit? A non-conformist? A radical? All my life I've broken rules, challenged society. I've been a gadfly, always out there where the action is."

"Mom, you don't seem to realize that times change. You change. You're not the person you were. Your health isn't what it was then. You're kidding yourself."

"I don't like to kid myself."

"I know you don't but that's just what you're doing." His voice suddenly got high and strident, almost a falsetto. "Mom, I just can't bear to think of you in a nursing home with senile old people and everything smelling of urine and a nurse pushing some lousy food at you. I can't bear it! I just can't!"

"Jerry, maybe it will never happen."

"What won't?"

"Chances are I'll never get a stroke. Nobody said it was inevitable. Chances are I'll never have to be in a nursing home. Maybe we're just imagining the worst. Maybe I'll just go on until I drop right in the middle of the action."

"Sounds to me as if you've made up your mind."

"Jerry, it's my fault. I triggered your anxiety. When he told me I could get a stroke, I panicked. I never thought a thing like that could happen to me. I always had this feeling that I'm invincible. And suddenly I saw myself helpless. I got scared. I thought of my grandmother crawling along the walls and I lost my courage for a moment. I completely lost my courage. I wanted to be taken care of."

"You have a right to be taken care of."

"No. Not yet. Not yet."

"Mom, you're not thinking of security. I want to secure you against the worst even if it never happens. Call it 'insurance.' I want to insure you. I want you to have security. Oh, Mom, I want it so bad!"

"Think of my life, Jerry. Isn't there something that always took precedence over security?"

"For Pete's sake, Mom, what can take precedence over security?"

"Freedom."

"Freedom! What's freedom without security? Answer me that. You're not facing reality. You're talking in abstractions. Tell me, Mom, since you're so smart, what in hell is freedom?"

"Freedom is a lonely hill."

Jeremy hung up, the frustration in his voice edged with tears.

Naomi sat down by the window and tried to compose herself. She had hurt and disappointed him. How many times had she hurt and disappointed him and in how many ways! Again she brushed away the image of the nine-year-old boy with her hand as if it were something palpable. He was a man now. Not a boy. And he could cope with hurt and disappointment as a man copes. But she had to cope in her own way too. She had to hold her life in her own hands.

"I'm sorry, son," she murmured under her breath, and the line from the half-forgotten poem she had chanted at Mama more than half a century ago came tripping back into her memory on the nimble feet of her childhood.

"God, give me hills to climb and strength to climb them."

"Someday you'll be asking only for strength to climb them."

"No, Mama, you were wrong. I'm an old woman now and you were wrong. God, give me hills."

EVERYBODY'S STUDYING US
The Ironies of Aging in the Pepsi Generation
Excerpts

Everybody's Studying Us

We are living in the Age of the Image. We have exchanged substance for image. It is not necessary for a politician to be an honest man. All he need do is project an image of honesty. Sincerity? Who can recognize it? All we can go by is the "image," carefully studied, packaged and delivered. This is the heyday of the advertising man and the pollster.

We, the old, it seems, are projecting upon society a most unpalatable image of age. It frightens little children, offends the young, and terrifies the middle-aged. After all, we are the vanguard, and when we fall in our tracks it is the middle-aged, inexorably moving up, who will be standing in our place. It is so terrifying to them that they are bustling about trying to provide a pleasant image to conceal our nakedness.

So everybody's studying us. At the cost of three hundred and thirty-five thousand dollars they have just come up with a brand new image for us, researched, packaged and delivered by the Harris poll. And the Harris poll, dear friends, is sacrosanct. According to this poll, only fifteen percent of us haven't enough money to live on comfortably; only twelve percent of us are lonely; only twenty-one percent are concerned about poor health; only twenty-three percent worry about being victims of crime; transportation is no problem; only seven percent feel we're not needed.

Isn't that beautiful? We're a well heeled, well fed, well protected, mobile, well adjusted lot. Don't let anybody tell you we live on the lowest income of any other section of the population. Or that we are prime victims of crime. Or that we're lonely, heaven forbid, although the majority of us are single widows. Or that failing eyesight, slower reflexes or poverty have forced most of us to give up driving; and buses have become targets for hit-and-run muggers. Or that inflation has eaten away our savings or taxes undermined the foundations of our homes.

We may not exactly have it made, but Lord be praised, we have an image! A neat, presentable, respectable middle-class image, scrubbed with Ivory soap, deodorized with Ban, and perfumed with Chanel No. 5. Hail to the image! And if we're hungry, we can always eat it. It's concocted like cotton candy from sugar and hot air.

Age Is Not a Disease. It Is a Season.

Age is not a disease. It is not an affliction. It is a season. Could we stop the inexorable movement of the earth around the sun? Spring melts into summer, summer into autumn, autumn into winter, and then the snow falls.

A slick magazine for the aging is titled euphemistically, *Second Spring*. Are they kidding? Nature does not allow a year the gratuity of an extra season. Nor does it permit a person a second spring. And would we want it? Ask the old if they would really want a second spring with its winds blowing hot and cold, its sudden squalls, its wild rivers, its tempestuous rains with thunder and lightning, its quick freezes and quicker thaws. Who having lived it once would prefer it again to the good warmth of an Indian summer, the smell of wood smoke, the lakes lying quiet in the autumn sun, and an air of waiting, as if the whole world were pausing for a moment in reflection.

When my mother was dying at forty-nine, she said bitterly, "I feel as if the sun has gone down in the middle of the day. This cancels out everything."

I am sorry she died with such a bitter summary of her life. Because she could not have lived out the full cycle of her seasons, she felt that what she had already lived was "cancelled out."

Each season is whole and perfect in itself and one season does not cancel another out. There is also no sharp boundary line dividing one season from another. The flow of time is imperceptible. It is indicative of our mad culture that one season should be so overrated and another fraught with so much fear and dread. It is our disharmony with nature that makes us look back hungrily to youth, hang on desperately to middle age, and dream up distorted fantasies of "Second Spring."

Age is not a disease. It is not an affliction. It is a season. And when the snows of winter melt, another generation's spring is born.

All Aboard for Senior Liberation

No one can estimate the harm done Black people by Amos and

Andy, Stepan Fetchit, the minstrel shows, the Rastus jokes, and all such "good natured" putdowns. The lampooning of club women and their activities in the Thirties, the dumb blonde stereotype, the insulting epithets have done women more harm than studies and polls "proving" their inferiority. There is an insidious power in ridicule that conditions people to see the object as a pathetic loser and a clown, and without even thinking, the first reaction, quick as a reflex, is consummate contempt.

This is the age of consciousness raising. Never again will anyone dare to put on a minstrel show or any other such insult to Black people. The Blacks themselves have taken a militant lead in affirming their personhood. In doing so they have engendered in all of us a new respect and a new understanding. More and more they are being regarded simply as people, no better and no worse, and the stereotypes are crashing one by one like broken glass.

Women have not been quite that successful but they are getting there. Their liberation was long overdue. The speaker who once came to a woman's club feeling anything he said would pass in such an undiscriminating group, must now be on his toes. Women are a sharp, informed and critical audience. Any politician or professor appearing before a group of women knows now that he had better do his homework. And at long last many men are beginning to recognize the contempt implied in such references to women as "tomatoes," "broads," "old bags," or "cupcakes," ridiculing the very nature of the female body.

The raising of consciousness in relation to the old has just begun. But watch TV awhile and note that it still seems to be very funny to show a dotty old woman who doesn't know if she's headed for Boston or San Diego. Or a senile old man who falls asleep in the middle of a sentence. Age is simply hilarious. It's hard to understand how society can ridicule a stage in life that no one has ever escaped except through premature death. Is it whistling in the dark? Laughing at the bogeyman? I don't know. I only know that we're long overdue for another kind of consciousness raising. Senior Liberation.

Grandmas, When You Say "No," Don't Feel Guilty

I was enlightened but not surprised when I read a batch of statistics on child abuse to find that next to mothers the most frequent offenders are—don't faint—grandmothers! Dear, gentle, long suffering, self-sacrificing, little old grandmothers! I can just see the typical child-beating grandmother. She looked forward all her life to the day when she could go into a room and shut the door on all responsibilities to other people. Her hands are arthritic. She has a bad hip. Her nerves are as raw as uninsulated wires. And one day her divorced daughter dumps a family of young kids in her lap and says, "Take care of them. I have to go to work." If the anger of grandmothers could be measured by thermometer, it would shatter the glass and scatter the mercury.

A grandmother who does volunteer work which she takes as seriously as a paid job was asked to baby-sit for a week. After much agonizing about her duty, she told her son she couldn't do it. It depressed her to be so isolated in the suburbs where she had no contact with friends and where she couldn't do her work. Her son asked blandly, "What work?" Another grandmother feels obligated to give up any plans she has for Saturday night or Sunday afternoon when her son decides to dump his kids on her. "They're *her* grandchildren. Why shouldn't she just love to baby-sit?"

It has been assumed for centuries that children must liberate themselves from parents no matter how wrenching to the parents. This is solid folk wisdom as well as sophisticated psychology. But nobody has yet begun to recognize that it is just as essential for parents to liberate themselves from children. In every human relationship, limits have to be set. And to this day it is assumed that there are no limits to the sacrifice that parents, particularly mothers, owe their children. It is the good old concept that we must be good to everybody but ourselves, and, of course, mothers are Christian martyrs for which they are to be rewarded each Mother's Day with nauseous sentiments and a box of candy.

Songs We'd Rather Forget

I doubt if any male reader would be caught dead on Market Street wearing a straw bowler and white spats. Nor would a woman with all her marbles stroll down Wilshire Boulevard in a spangled shift above her knees and a Greta Garbo Empress Eugenie hat. Yet these were very stylish in the Twenties. Then will somebody please tell me why every time one goes to a social for seniors we are treated to a song leader who directs us in such hoary relics as "Let Me Call You Sweetheart," "Let the Rest of the World Go By," "I'm Forever Blowing Bubbles," and "I Want a Girl Just Like the Girl Who Married Dear Old Dad." Last social I attended, when the cheery songster burst forth with "I'll Be Loving You Always," I muttered bitterly to a friend, "A fine song to sing to a bunch of widows."

The rationale for dragging these musical zombies into our midst is that it will make us happy, poor old dears, just dying with nostalgia for the good old days between World War I and the crash of '29. It is assumed we stopped living somewhere around that time. But these chestnuts don't make us happy. To many of us they bring memories of dead husbands, dead wives, vanished sweethearts. Why do they take us out of contemporary society, stamp, file and computerize us into the 1920's? "That's the way it's got to be," shrugged one social director when I asked that question. "It can't be helped. They don't know any other songs. What do you want them to sing—rock and roll?" Well, we may be old but we're not senile. We can read. What's wrong with teaching us a few new songs? And what's wrong with folk songs that are immortal, appeal to all ages, and don't deliberately date us? Or gospel music? Or contemporary country music? Or peace, labor and civil rights songs? All we need are some song sheets and a person who believes we are still alive and breathing.

After sixty-five we don't fall into one amorphous category called "the elderly." There is just as much variety in our tastes as when we were twenty-five. The kind of cultural pap you throw at us to appeal to the lowest common denominator is an insult to our intelligence. Must we sit through act after act of cheap amateur vaudeville, pitiful "poetry," and songs that strip us of our contemporary status? Give us something really good and we will enjoy it. If it is a little above our cultural level, all the better. We will grow through it. But stop talking down to us. A ninety-two-year-old woman once said to me, "The worst thing about being old is how they patronize us."

"I Hate to Be Called a Senior Citizen"

I've heard that over and over. I've said it over and over. "Elderly?" "Retired?" "A rose by any other name," etc. What we really hate is *being* a senior citizen in a society that does not value us. It has the connotation of being shelved, retired, passive, powerless, even senile. I remember going unwillingly to my first "senior citizen" gathering. It didn't reassure me. A group of quiet old women outnumbering five to one a group of quiet old men. A young woman from one of the colleges was in charge of the meeting. She was what I believe is an "ex-tern" doing her field work in helping old people. She discussed volunteer work we could do. There was no discussion. Then we drank coffee and ate carrot cake with plastic forks and it was a very sad and very dull experience.

I went to another group and the highly motivated paid worker in charge pounced on me to enlist me in teaching old women to crochet. It wasn't until I joined a group oriented toward action that I found myself accepting both the term "senior citizen" and the status it describes. I recognized that what I obtained when I was young was still the rule of life now that I am old.... I regard the aged as an oppressed group. I see no cure for the oppression but what Frederick Douglass called "the thunder and lightning of struggle." Struggle is the law of life and, when one ceases to struggle in one way or another, he folds his hands and waits for oblivion.

Yet the particular struggle which we must wage for our simple dignity should not even be necessary. I heard a young Indian remark the other day in reference to some problem, "We'll call upon our elders." I turned the words over in my mind. "Our elders." There was honesty in the words. Respect. No effort to be cute or to give them a euphemism. It was the value placed upon the concept "our elders" that made them as beautiful as any words I've heard in any language.

The Secret Is to Keep on Burning

We must not concur in our obsolescence. To those who have tried us, judged us and sentenced us to this fate, we must say, "I refuse to accept the verdict!"

The man stripped of his work in a working world is still a man. A woman bereft of important relationships is still a woman.

The trick is to retain our curiosity even about our own behavior: our hunger to know, our wonder, and our capacity for indignation.

The secret is to keep on burning.

When our children were small and afraid to go alone into a dark room, do you remember how we'd take them by the hand and throwing open the door, cry, "See? There's nothing really to be afraid of! It was only shadows!" And we'd switch on the light! Gone were their fears and fantasies before the clean sweep of electric power.

Now as they follow us haltingly and fearfully into the unknown quantity of age, let us be able to turn to them and cry, "There's nothing really to be afraid of! Look! It's light!" And let them be able to answer in sudden wonder, "Mother, Father, it's light because you're burning!"

"Survival Is a Form of Resistance"—Meridel Le Sueur

There's a book on the market titled provocatively *Why Survive?*
Why be born?
"Why a duck?" as the Marx Brothers used to say.
Every creature of every species from the time the butterfly wriggles out of its cocoon, or the chick cracks its egg, and the baby utters its first cry, all struggle from that moment on for survival. There are so many obstacles to survival whether it be the lowliest insect on this planet or the finest specimen of the human race, that to live out the full quota of your years is like thumbing your nose at fate. "Ha! You thought you had me stymied but I made it!"

Is there a greater meaning than just that—survival? You tell *me*. I saw a rerun of an old movie, *Lost Horizon,* in which a group of people were trapped in an earthly paradise called Shangri-La. No one ever got hurt or hurt another in this utopia. No snow ever fell, for it was eternal spring. No one grew old there and no one died. Yet a few of the "inmates" of this paradise risked almost certain death to escape from it.

It's strange that man has always been able to conceive of hell and make it interesting, even believable, because, after all, it so resembles life on earth. But no one has ever been able to dream up an acceptable concept of paradise. Because without struggle, without contradictions, yes, without evil, life is not even conceivable. So regardless of what we may verbalize as our goal, it's just as primitive in the end as the goal of the butterfly or the chick—survival! Only we, the single living species conscious of itself, can shake its fist at fate and cry, "You thought you had me licked but I made it!"

Hear, O Our Children!

We are not a special interest group. We are simply your mothers, fathers and grandparents. We are not asking you for a handout. We ran the world until you came along. Operated the factories. Tilled the soil. Bore the children. Taught them. Tended the sick. Built freeways and railroads, dug subways. We are simply the generation or two that preceded you. When we are gone you will move up to the vanguard and another generation will wonder what to do with you short of pushing you off a cliff.

We are asking you, our children and grandchildren, for nothing that is not due us. At the cost of great sacrifice and many casualties we built the labor unions and the farm unions; won the eight hour day; eliminated child labor; won Social Security and the concept that health care is a human right, not an act of someone's charity.

Millions of us fought all our lives for a peaceful world. We did not achieve it. Do not indict us for our failure. We leave it to you to wage that struggle not in millions but in tens of millions.

When we ask for a chance to live our old age in comfort, creativity and usefulness, we ask it not for ourselves only, but for you. We are not a special interest group. We are your parents and grandparents. We are your roots. You are our continuity. What we gain is your inheritance.

MY WINTER LOVER

Even with my unpracticed eyes I can see that something is wrong with the X-ray on the easel. In one curve of the serpentine coils of the colon there is a bulge—a large, ugly outgrowth.

"A tumor," the doctor says. But the dark compassion in his eyes betrays him.

My eyes confront his with a probing question. I feel his struggle as he answers in a husky voice, "It's cancer."

Cancer. How many times I have wondered how I would react in just such a situation. How would I feel?

I don't feel anything.

At the telephone booth a few minutes later my best friend hears the verdict and cries, "Take a cab home, quick!"

I take a bus home. What's the hurry? A cab would get me home too soon. Like flying from one continent to another instead of moving slowly and thoughtfully by ship.

The bus takes almost an hour and I need at least an hour's thinking before I get home. I have to get some kind of reaction from myself. So far I haven't reacted at all. I shed a few tears in the doctor's office because I thought they were expected of me. I didn't feel them. Pretty soon I'd better start feeling something. Maybe by the time I get home the numbness will have worn off and I'll be feeling—something.

The bus ride is over and here I am. And still I have not properly reacted to the verdict, "You have cancer."

In fact, in place of numbness I feel a strange exhilaration as if some caged thing within me is stretching its wings for taking flight. This is not a proper reaction, I tell myself. This is totally unacceptable. And yet this is how it is. Who has a right to tell me what feeling I have is acceptable or not? And who can order his feelings to obey society's rules of emotional etiquette?

In my living room is a picture window overlooking a broad panorama of the ocean. The sun is sparkling on it today and the horizon, usually blurred in fog, stretches clear to the islands of the Farrallones—and beyond, far beyond, perhaps to China. The waves are gently stroking the shore, like cats lapping milk. This is the kind of sea they must have seen—the hawk-eyed *conquistadores* when they named this sea "Pacific."

I stretch out on the chaise lounge in front of the picture window where I can worship her whom I have worshipped all my life—the sea, my mother.

I don't know when I have felt so perfectly serene.

And suddenly I feel his presence. I know he is here. He has entered so softly, so lovingly, and there he sits. In the green chair facing me he sits and watches me. Fondly, I think. Quizzically, perhaps. But there is no irony in his smile.

"You're here!" I cry, sitting up straight on the lounge. "My winter lover! At last you're here!"

"Lover?" he shrugs. "It's said that one cannot love death until one has exhausted life."

"Or until life has exhausted you," I correct him.

"You're not exhausted."

"The fact is you've come for me. There's no need to split hairs."

"I've only come to witness," he says.

I ignore his statement. "Please come here. Sit down beside me. I want you. Why are you sitting so far away?"

"Patience," he says.

"But I have no patience! I have never had patience. If you will not come here to me then I will come to you—" and I rise to make a move toward him.

A warning hand motions me back.

"Restrictions!" I cry out, and like a sulking child hurl myself back on the lounge. "With everyone under the sun there are restrictions—fences, moats, stay out signs, stop signs. I thought from you I could finally get unconditional acceptance, nothing to hold me at arm's length, nothing to judge me, to fend me off—"

"You will get your unconditional acceptance."

"When?"

"When you are ready."

"You mean to tell me I'm not ready?"

He does not even trouble to answer.

"You have heard me cry out to you time and again and yet you tell me I'm not ready!"

"Oh, yes, I have heard you cry, and when I stopped to listen, your cries had suddenly changed to laughter. You see, it's no secret to me that you have a love affair with *him.*"

"With him? That bastard?" I bristle at his wry, indulgent smile. "Love affair! I detest him!"

"Methinks the lady doth protest too much."

"Well, yes. But you are speaking of the past. I do admit it has been so. I do admit I have been madly involved with him. You must agree he is a lusty lover. Sometimes his beauty is terrifying. How can anyone help responding to one so passionate and compelling? But you don't know how vicious he can be, how unpredictable and sadistic! You don't know how many times when he was embracing me with promises of eternal bliss he suddenly turned on me and struck me a blow that sent me sprawling. I could hardly make it to my feet again."

"Yes, I've seen you. But did you stay sprawling on the ground?"

I stare at him in disbelief. "Stay sprawling! Are you serious? Do you think I'd let him just lay me out like that without giving him as good as I got? I sprang up and clawed his face! I grabbed him by the throat and wrestled him! I let him know, believe me. I wasn't the kind of woman he could just kick around like that and get away with it. Why are you laughing?"

"No reason. I just wondered. And how did that little love spat usually end up?"

"Love spat! I hated him! There was no love in me when I went for his throat!"

"But something did happen. You did not go on endlessly fighting."

I am silent a moment.

"It was he. He was always the one who made it up. He would regret his treatment of me. He would be contrite and do something particularly nice. In fact he said he liked bratty, peppery women who gave him a good fight and I would end up in his arms again and that's the way it would always be—"

"And that's the way it will be again."

"No, you don't understand. I'm not young anymore. I am sick of his passionate kisses and his blows. Every time he knocks me down it takes longer to get on my feet. Sometimes I just stand there staggering and don't even try to fight him back. Don't you see! I am tired. I want peace. Don't you believe that passion can stale? That one can come to hate a fickle and sadistic lover and get sick of his games and want no part of him?"

"Yes, I understand that well enough. Many people go eagerly with me every day because of that. But not you. You are not ready."

"You refuse to understand me. It's you I love, not him!"

"And I say the sap is still flowing strongly under the bark."

"There is no sap flowing. It is frozen as firm as resin in December."

"It will thaw in April. If I am your winter lover, this is not my season."

I leap from the lounge to confront him. "You! You dare to speak to me of seasons! You who snatched my mother and husband away in the midsummer of their lives! You who cut down my sister and brother before they had bloomed enough to drop their seed!"

"Your brother and sister came to me, if you remember. I did not come to them."

He leans a bit forward in the chair as if to get a keener look at me. And now there is irony in his smile.

"You say you love me and yet you have just demonstrated the violence of your hatred for me."

I shrug. "Have you ever known violent love to be free of hatred?"

But he counters me. "And the violent hatred you profess for *him*—have you ever known it to be free of love?"

"Very well. So you have both hurt me deeply. Perhaps if there were a better choice, I would not love you at all. But as it happens, there's not. You're my only alternative to him. And how long can I endure his cruelty?" And all at once I turn to him, pleading, "My beloved, believe me. I forgive you everything you've ever taken from me. I will never attack you again. I have never seen you so closely before. Never felt you so near. And there is such promise in you— of peace, of an end to anguish."

He looks at me with a strange, ruminating sorrow.

"I could not take you even if it were my deepest desire to do so. For you have not had your day in court."

"My day in court!"

"You see, I am not the hand that pulls the trigger or that drives the knife. I do not plant the germ that spreads infection. I do not lead the pilot off his course or guide the hand of the captain who runs his ship aground the rocks. I am neither judge nor jury nor prosecutor nor executioner. I am simply the bailiff who hears the verdict and leads the condemned away. I did not want your brother and sister to plead guilty and be their own judge and jury and executioner. I would have spoken for your mother and husband had I the power or the right to stand before the bar. For it is a cruel court with much miscarriage of justice and verdicts untimely and unfair. But it is not I who pronounces judgment."

I have turned away from him and am looking at the sun that has taken the shape of a great red lantern, sinking slowly.

"The day is almost over," I brood. "See how the sun is drowning in the sea."

He nods. "But in the morning it will be reborn."

"Strange," I say sorrowfully, "you have only come to witness. And I thought you came because you loved me."

"You would not want my love even if I were free to give it."

"We have already been through this argument," I say, turning to him again, contradiction on my lips, when the phone rings.

It is my daughter.

"Mom?"

"Yes?"

"I just heard. Aune told me."

"Yes."

"When is the surgery?"

"Wednesday morning."

"When are you going to the hospital?"

"Tomorrow morning."

"Mom. Do you want me to come over right away? I don't want you to be alone."

"I'm not really alone. Don't come. Please. I need a lot of time for thinking."

"Mom?"

"Yes?"

"Sometimes whether one really wants to live is the thing that makes the difference."

"I know."

No begging. No crying. No pleading. Please, Mom. Live for my sake, for our sakes. Please want to. Please choose to. We need you. Nothing like that. Thank you, daughter.

"Mom, I know your ambivalence."

"Yes, I know it too. That's why I have to think. That's what I'm thinking about this very moment."

"*L'haim*, Mom."

L'haim! To life! My name is "Life." *Haia*—the Hebrew word for life. L'haim!

And suddenly I am aware that he is leaving, moving quietly toward the door.

"That telephone call made all the difference, didn't it?"

"Yes, it did."

"Then the time has come for me to say *au revoir.*"

I reach for him as he opens the door. He eludes my grasp.

"No, not yet. Stay just a moment. Please. I need a moment to shift my gears."

"I have time."

"Promise me something. It is not too much to ask."

"Ask then, and perhaps I'll promise."

"Please be there beside me Wednesday when they cut me open. He will be there too. I have already invited him. When I got that telephone call I invited him. But I beg you to be there too."

"I shall be there, of course. I have already been invited."

I still try vaguely to detain him. "I am so disturbed in my soul. A moment ago I felt so free, so sure. As if I were soon to stretch my wings to fly away from a prison cell. Or as if I were turning home at last from a shifting caravanserai. A Bedouin moving restlessly from pasture to pasture, always uncertain of tomorrow, I was turning home. And now I feel earth-bound again and sure of nothing at all. My wings have folded and yet the earth is good and smells of spring rain and fresh manure and I want to fill my lungs with the sweetness of summer grass."

"I know."

I reach out to touch him but the door is closed and he is gone.

Wednesday morning they shove me into the operating room. In five minutes I will be laid open and they will know how much of my vitals the cancer has devoured. And they are both here—my two beloveds—Life at my right, Death at my left. I feel no fear, no anxiety. Instead, an ecstatic blend of ennui and recklessness. A feeling that it doesn't matter who will take me for his bride. Whoever it shall be—so be it. And smiling, I fall asleep.

When I awaken in the hospital room, staggering out of the anaesthetic, they are with me—the two people in the vast world dearest to me, my daughter and my son. They are leaning over me, their faces floating. How beautiful they are! I did not know that faces could be so beautiful—like lotus flowers.

"Mom, you're going to live! The cancer was a slow growing one. The surgeon said he got it all. The pathologist said the prognosis is life."

I watch them floating over me—the beautiful flower faces of my children.

"I haven't been such a bad mother, have I?" It is a plea for grace, for absolution.

"You've been a courageous mother!"

Even in the drunken twilight of the anaesthetic I am laughing at the irony of that word, "courageous." I who had wanted to go away with my lover, leave you forever. Desert you. Deny you. Never to hold out a helping hand to you again or to your children, nor give you solace in the loneliness of your own pastures. You call me courageous and I have the arrogance to plead, "I haven't been such a bad mother, have I?"

And suddenly I am aware that he is here, here at my bedside, watching me.

"You do not need their absolution," he murmurs softly. "Your own choice has absolved you."

And I hear him moving toward the door. Softly, silently he moves. I want to reach out a loving hand to him but not to detain him—to say some word—yet I cannot say it. He is no longer here. I thought I heard him speak. Just before the door closed. I thought I heard him say, "My darling—*au revoir.*"

ACCEPTANCE SPEECH
Joseph Shachnow Prize from Jewish Currents

Although I, a sixty-eight-year-old woman, am accepting this award, it really belongs in fact to an eight-year-old girl who made a vital choice sixty years ago in a little city in northern Minnesota. It was a choice that sealed her Jewish identity and brought her inevitably into the pages of *Jewish Currents.*

This eight-year-old girl was in the third grade, listening to the teacher lecture on current events. She was discussing the wave of immigration from southern European countries. This was a great misfortune to our country, the teacher said, that this wave of immigration should come from southern European countries, which spewed up the undesirable immigrants, while the desirable ones from northern Europe came in such small numbers.

I, this eight-year-old girl, walked out of that classroom in a state of shock. I can still remember my thoughts over a span of sixty years. The teacher said southern European immigrants are undesirables, a blight to our country. My people are from southern Europe. Therefore my people are undesirables and a blight. A seed of self-hatred was sown upon virgin soil. Would it sprout that fateful moment or would it die a-borning? The choice I made would determine the whole course of my life.

All the way home I struggled with myself. Teachers were not mortals. They were holy. Their word was law. They knew everything. They were so far from the realm of ordinary humanity that we could not even imagine them tending to the same bodily functions that plagued our mortal bodies. A far, far cry from our day of striking teachers physically, sassing them, defying them. One didn't even contradict a teacher in those days. She was sacrosanct. She carried in her the authority of all recorded knowledge. Therefore she must be right and my people must indeed be undesirables, and I the offspring of a national blight.

My footsteps slowed as I approached my home. Who were these undesirables, I asked myself, getting down to cases. And I began to count them over in my mind as a Catholic counts the beads of his rosary. Baba and Zayda Zlatovski, Baba and Zayda

Levine, Mama and Papa, Uncle Loy, Auntie Sarah, Yankele, my little brother—was he a blight? On and on went my list and my litany, and suddenly, as I opened the gate to my house, I cried out in a burst of passionate defiance, "It's a lie! The teacher is a liar!" It was the most critical insight of my whole life. I had made a choice. From then on I would accept no authority until I had tested it in the crucible of my own experience.

But it was not enough to know a truth in your own flesh. You had to communicate it. From then until the sixth grade I shaped my insight into a profound conviction. And then I wrote a poem and gave it to my teacher. I described the experience of a Jewish child. The injustices heaped upon me. The venalities. The lies. The whole familiar fabric of anti-Semitism. And I ended it on this note: Jesus, whom you worship as the son of God, was not of your tribe, but of mine. Not your people, but my people gave birth to him. Even the features of his face were not your features, but mine. If he was as ever loving and as long suffering as you say he was and for which you worship him, how must he feel when he sees you tormenting and degrading us? How he must weep for us, his people, comforted by Mary, his Jewish mother!

The teacher, a stiff-necked frostbitten spinster, as grim in personality as a New England winter, as bleak as Plymouth Rock upon which her ancestors had descended from the Mayflower, read the poem in tight-lipped silence. Then she took it and plastered it to the blackboard with scotch tape. "Nobody leaves this room," she said, "until you've read this poem." She gave over the last period to this ritual, each child going to the board, reading, and returning to his seat.

She could have shortened the ordeal by reading it aloud herself or having me read it to the class, but perhaps she felt it would be better imprinted on their minds if each one read it for himself. Sometimes I think perhaps that was the most effective thing I ever wrote. I like to think that in the year of the vulture those children, now adults, faced with the evil reality of genocide, remembered that poem in the sixth grade class and said to someone, if only to himself, "I object!"

GRANDMA'S BATTLE CRY

It's blowing in the wind again. It's drifting in the rain
Before the dead have moldered yet or wounded healed their pain.
I am so old, my grandsons, that I remember when
I marched to hail the armistice, and I was barely ten.
That was the war against all war, to save democracy
Praise God, they said, we've won the peace for all eternity.

I marched again when some years passed and marched and
    marched and then
There was the war to end all war and so I marched again.
I marched in Minneapolis and Chicago and Duluth
In San Francisco and New York I marched to shout the truth.
I marched in Hiroshima and I knelt before a stash
Of tens of million bones of people atomized to ash.
And with the distant rumble of new regiments of men
I read the warning on the tomb, "This must not be again."

I marched to staunch Korea's blood; I marched for Vietnam.
I marched to stop the napalm and I marched to stop the bomb.
I've marched and marched, O Lord, I'm sure I've done my due.
I've marched since I was barely ten and now I'm seventy-two.

I should be lying in the sun or dreaming in the grass
But how when generals everywhere are polishing their brass?
Entranced with dreams of four star roles, so help me, Lord,
    they're glad!
It's said that whom the gods destroy they first must render mad.
Their burning eyes see No-Man's Land and armies poised for
    action
And you, my warm and loving sons, you're merely an abstraction.

It's geopolitics again, and oh with what finesse
The players push their pawns about, these masterminds of chess!
How cunningly they plot each move, how logically they spar!

240

And checkmate one another like the masters that they are.
How stimulating, how intense, a world to lose or gain,
Except for one dismaying fact…the players are insane.
Composed, dispassionate they play, this game that madness
    spawns
And I can't even look away. My grandsons are the pawns.

Some people keep on fighting when they've lost an arm or leg.
Some still keep up the struggle when they're fragile as an egg.
I've heard men rasping, "I object!" with voices turned to gravel.
I've seen a woman raise a fist who couldn't lift a gavel.
And even with a broken heart one still can make a stand
So lead, my grandsons, lead the way, reach back and take my
    hand.
We'll march again, confound them all, don't quibble at my age!
I'll shield you with my brittle bones! I'll nourish you with rage!

ABOUT IRENE PAULL

Irene Paull's life spanned a most volatile time in human history. Power and greed brought unspeakable murder and destruction to our world in the twentieth century, and, at the same time, aspirations for peace and freedom encircled the earth. It is our firm belief that all people must be seen in the places where they live and the events of their times. We offer this abbreviated biography and a sampling of the historical events occurring during Irene's lifespan. For a more in-depth understanding, we encourage the reader to study history. We do not presume to speak for Irene. We believe that her writing and her body of work speak most eloquently.

Irene Paull was born April 18, 1908 in Duluth, Minnesota. She was the first child of Maurice Levine and Eva (Zlatkovski) Levine. Irene would be followed by her siblings, Yank, Stanley, Etta, and Byron. Her large, extended family, with roots in the Russian village of Peryaslov, and the rural, early industrial character of Duluth and Lake Superior were the backdrop of her childhood. Her childhood was also marked by the experience of anti-Semitism, revelations of Darwinism, and the terror of a Duluth mob lynching three African American youth.

After finishing high school in 1925, Irene attended college but left before graduating to move to Chicago.

1908-1930
Fire at Triangle Shirtwaist Company. 146 workers trapped behind locked doors were burned or crushed to death or died leaping from windows. 100,000 marched in protest in New York City.
Margaret Sanger arrested and jailed for writing first book about birth control.
Woodrow Wilson elected President.
Textile workers strike in Lawrence, Massachusetts, organized by I.W.W.

World War I.

Joe Hill, I.W.W. organizer and songwriter, executed by a firing squad.

Russian Revolution.

Nationwide general strike in support of shipyard workers in Seattle.

Palmer Raids.

Prohibition (Eighteenth Amendment).

Women's Suffrage (Nineteenth Amendment).

Warren Harding elected President.

President Harding died. Vice President Calvin Coolidge assumed Presidency.

Sacco and Vanzetti executed.

Nazis won seats in Germany's Parliament.

Herbert Hoover elected President.

Irene's first poetry published.

Stock Market crash.

The Thirties

Irene met Hank Paull when she was sixteen. He visited her in Chicago, and he proposed to her several times. "I gave him such a terrible time. I wasn't ready for him at sixteen. I didn't even know how babies were born. I made him wait five long years before I married him, because I didn't want to marry. I wanted to see the world. I wanted to experience everything. I wanted to be a writer. I used to be so mad because boys could ride the rails and girls couldn't. And here was Hank, breathing down my neck. I kept meeting other guys and breaking up. He couldn't stand it. He was a one-woman man." They were married in Chicago in 1929 and returned to Duluth for a wedding with family and friends. He pursued his law career and Irene worked in his office.

The Great Depression brought many hardships. Homelessness and hunger were rampant. Roosevelt's New Deal helped to quell rising discontent. Rural electrification, coops, W.P.A., C.C.C. gave work to people.

Hank defended labor leaders and political activists. Irene and Sam Davis started the *Timber Worker* newspaper, which later became

Midwest Labor. She wrote a column under the pen name, "Calamity Jane." Irene wrote passionately about the workers, the Spanish Civil War, fascism, and racism in the United States. Woody Guthrie and Pete Seeger traveled through Duluth, staying with Irene and Hank.

Irene's mother died late in Irene's first pregnancy. Irene and Hank's first child, Bonnie, was born on August 22, 1933. Irene's father remarried. Irene's sister Etta died in 1937. Irene and Hank's second child, Michael, was born November 13, 1938.

1930-1940
Floyd B. Olson, Farmer-Labor Party candidate, elected governor of Minnesota.

Unemployment on the rise in Germany; Nazis won more elections.

Mahatma Gandhi started campaign of civil disobedience against British rule in India.

Japan invaded Manchuria.

Scottsboro Cases.

The Veterans' Bonus Army March on Washington, D.C.

Franklin Delano Roosevelt elected President.

Hitler became Chancellor of Germany.

Prohibition repealed.

Truck Drivers' Strike in Minneapolis.

Social Security Act passed in Congress.

Munich. Hitler appeased.

Congress of Industrial Organizations (C.I.O.) formed.

Jews fled Europe. Britain and other countries, including U.S., restricted immigration of Jews.

Governor Olson died. Lieutenant Governor Elmer Benson assumed office.

Franco overthrew democratically elected government in Spain.

U.S. Senate declared embargo on Loyalist Spain. Congressman John T. Bernard, of the Eighth District of Minnesota, was the only one in Congress to vote against the embargo.

Spain fell to Franco.

Memorial Day Massacre at Republic Steel Strike in Chicago. Police shot and killed ten picketers.

Nazis marched into Poland.

The Forties

World War II continued through 1945. In Europe, Nazis rounded up Jews and put them in concentration camps and systematically exterminated six million Jews and one million others (dissidents, homosexuals, Gypsies, communists)—the Holocaust. Pearl Harbor, Battle of Britain, Manhattan Project, atomic bomb, United Nations, Yalta, Hiroshima and Nagasaki—a time of terrible destruction.

Irene continued writing for *Midwest Labor*, and her writings were published in a collection entitled *We're the People*.

Irene's brother Stanley died in 1942.

Hank Paull died suddenly from a heart attack in 1947. The streets of Duluth were filled with working people to honor this great labor lawyer. Irene talked of great loneliness the rest of her life; she never found anyone to replace Hank. "I've never seen anyone to equal him in character. I lived with this man for seventeen whole long/short years, and I paid the price in pain and loneliness when he died. In spite of everything, the price was right. I'd pay it again." In 1948, Irene, Bonnie and Michael moved to Minneapolis.

1940-1950

Smith Act passed.

Germany invaded Norway, Denmark, the Netherlands, France, Belgium, and U.S.S.R.

Battle of Britain.

Pearl Harbor.

Executive Order 9066 gave Army power to arrest Japanese Americans without warrants or hearings. They were sent to detention camps for the duration of the war, losing all property and possessions.

Reports of Nazi wholesale murder of Jews appeared in popular media.

Battle of Midway.

Invasion of Normandy.

Stalin, Roosevelt and Churchill met at Yalta.

Allied saturation bombing of Dresden.

Manhattan Project; Los Alamos, New Mexico; development of
atomic bomb.

Mussolini captured and shot.

End of war in Europe. Germany surrendered.

Concentration camps liberated. Horrors of the Holocaust exposed
to world.

U.S. bombed Tokyo.

President Roosevelt died. Vice President Harry S. Truman assumed
Presidency.

Atomic bomb dropped on Hiroshima. Three days later another
dropped on Nagasaki.

War ended in Pacific.

United Nations founded.

U.S. sent aid to Saudi Arabia in exchange for oil rights.

Millions of U.S. workers on strike.

Civil war in China.

India won independence from Britain.

Gandhi assassinated.

Jews declare state of Israel in Palestine.

N.A.T.O. signed.

Progressive Party founded in Philadelphia. Henry Wallace entered
presidential race. Irene traveled to Georgia to canvas for Henry
Wallace's campaign.

Hubert Humphrey elected to U.S. Senate.

The Fifties

After the war, women were strongly encouraged to leave their jobs
and go home and let men have the jobs.

The Cold War, Iron Curtain, second Red Scare, anti-Red
hysteria, H.U.A.C., McCarthy hearings, anti-Bomb protests,
deportations of foreign born, Smith Act trials, U.S. post-war
incursions into other countries (either covertly or overtly) under
the auspices of stopping the "Red Threat," escalating military
budget, nuclear testing. U.S. and U.S.S.R. stationed nuclear
missiles in Europe. Space industry began. TV and movie industry
targeted by McCarthy. Auto industry boomed. Rosenberg and
Sobell trials.

Irene said she lived in constant fear of her children being taken away during this anti-communist fervor, especially if she were sent to prison, yet it didn't stop her work. She wrote plays and poems, organized meetings, and worked on Rosenberg and Sobell support committees. Passionately involved in the defense of Julius and Ethel Rosenberg, Irene went to Washington, D.C., in 1953 to petition to stop the execution and was present at the vigil when the Rosenbergs were pronounced dead. She would write to Meridel Le Sueur years later, "So many people whose lives will never be the same again because of that day in 1953. It's as if a part of your vital organs were cut out and buried with those two beautiful, innocent, young Jews and another part will suffer pain all your life with the traumatized children."

Financial and political pressures increased for Irene in these years as it did for many. She decided to leave Minneapolis and to break with the Communist Party. Irene and Michael moved to San Francisco in the mid-1950s. Upon hearing Khrushchev's report in 1956 on the crimes of Stalin, she wrote, "It was one of the most horrible experiences that ever happened to me, equal in importance to the death of my husband. I no longer had a faith. I no longer believed in Utopia." In 1959, she wrote to her friend, Alma Foley, "I am anxious to get active in political work again. Seems like for a while I was numb. I couldn't do a thing.... Now I want to do something."

1950-1960
McCarran-Walter Act.
Korean War started. Ended in 1953.
W.E.B. Dubois spoke in St. Paul.
Irene worked for Civil Rights Congress, fighting discrimination against African Americans.
Dwight Eisenhower elected President.
French defeated in Vietnam in Battle of Dien Bien Phu. French left. Eisenhower sent U.S. advisors.
Supreme Court upheld *Brown vs. Board of Education*, outlawing school discrimination and segregation.
Rosa Parks refused to move to the back of the bus, starting Montgomery, Alabama bus boycott.

After C.I.O. purged of progressive element, A.F.L./C.I.O. formed.

Suez Crisis. Egyptian president Nasser nationalized Suez Canal. Britain and France invaded. World pressure forced them to withdraw troops.

Khrushchev revelations about Stalin atrocities.

Soviet troops marched into Hungary.

Sputnik I launched by U.S.S.R. It was the first satellite to orbit Earth. Beginning of space race.

Eisenhower sent U.S. troops to Lebanon.

Cuban revolution.

The Sixties

The Cuban revolution, the escalating war in Vietnam, the civil rights movement, the War on Poverty, assassinations of President Kennedy, Martin Luther King, and Bobby Kennedy, H.U.A.C. hearings, anti-war movement, women's movement.

Irene continued to write, especially for *Jewish Currents*, where she published much of her work. She wrote to Meridel Le Sueur in 1961, "Am writing practically every day. I bless you every moment for teaching me how to keep a notebook. Do you know that I actually didn't know how? Only until I read yours did I learn how. Oh, pal, why couldn't we have gotten together twenty years ago? If you had taught me then how much history of Minnesota I could have preserved.... I only remember them as one remembers music without remembering the words. I feel as if I have lost the richest part of my life by not recording them, but at least I have a few good years left and I'm glad that I have learned now so these years can be not only endurable but richer. It is only I regret so losing so much of the historic years in which Hank and I were in such an enviable position. The greatest contribution I could have made was to record it. If only somebody had made me see that then."

Another letter: "I am not satisfied with anything I write. But I know that that too is a form of conceit. Who am I that I should have been blessed with a bigger talent than I have? I'm lucky enough the Lord gave me this little half pint's worth. And I'm truly grateful for it, although there are so many times when I feel like the waiter when I gave him a small tip, 'Thanks for nothing.'"

Another letter: "No, Meridel, I am not ill. I am in better health and spirits than I have ever been. Cuba gave me a reason for being. I have never felt like this about anything since Spain.... I couldn't stop shouting. Neither could the others. The words came out of us like charges of machine gun fire. Sometimes when I think about Cuba, and remember things that happened and things that were said, I cry, and part of why I cry is the joy of knowing that the old passion is not dead, that I am still capable of feeling as keenly as I ever felt in my life, that age and events had not desensitized me as I thought they had. But more than that, the youth, with the light in their eyes that was in our eyes when we were fighting for Spain."

Letter to Meridel: "I wish I had some of the quality of flowing like a river, calmly following its predestined course, oblivious to time."

Irene's four grandchildren were born: Bonnie's children, Paul and Gabrielle, and Michael's children, Barrie and Jeff.

1960-1970
John F. Kennedy elected President.
Sit-ins at lunch counters all over the South.
Women for Peace organized.
U.S.S.R. cosmonaut, Yuri Gagarin, first person to achieve orbital space flight.
Congress of Racial Equality organized freedom rides.
Irene traveled to Cuba as a journalist.
S.N.C.C. formed.
Irene traveled to peace march in Japan, visiting Hiroshima, Nagasaki, and other cities.
Medgar Evers killed in Mississippi.
March on Washington organized by civil rights organizations.
President Kennedy assassinated. Vice President Lyndon Johnson assumed Presidency.
Irene subpoenaed before H.U.A.C. She said, "It's obvious you called me here for the purpose of harassing me and holding me

up to ridicule." Then she sat down and said no more.

James Chaney, Andrew Goodman, and Michael Schwerner killed in Mississippi.

Mississippi Summer Project. Irene spent summer in Hattiesburg, Mississippi, working on voter registration.

Congress passed Voting Rights Act.

U.S. troops sent to Vietnam.

Malcolm X assassinated.

Martin Luther King, Jr., assassinated.

Riots in Watts, Chicago, Detroit, Newark.

Robert Kennedy assassinated.

Police rioted at Democratic National Convention in Chicago.

Richard Nixon elected President.

Tet Offensive in Vietnam.

Anti-war marches across the country.

Soviet army invaded Czechoslovakia.

U.S. astronaut, Neil Armstrong, walked on the moon.

Stonewall Rebellion signals gay rights movement.

Black Panthers, Fred Hampton and Mark Clark, killed.

The Seventies and Early Eighties

Accelerated bombing and mining of Vietnam, U.S. corporations targeted for producing inhumane weapons, anti-war movement grew, campuses and streets erupted in protests and marches and death, war atrocities exposed, Native Americans asserted their rights to sovereignty and self-determination, Chicano farmworkers organized unions and boycotts, women's movement grew, food coops and other alternative projects thrived, women's right to choose safe abortions legalized, senior rights movement, U.S. support of Latin American regimes protested, Nicaraguan revolution, beginning of massive budget cuts in social programs.

Irene worked against the war and kept fighting for human rights. She was editor of *Senior Power*, a newsletter for The California Association of Older Americans, and worked on the California Legislative Council (an activist organization). She wrote, "It's amazing that those who were active in their youth and remain active in their old age never seem to age. I never think of these people as old any more than I think of myself as old. They generate so much energy and excitement because they're still involved in the mainstream of life." Irene's articles were published in a book entitled, *Everybody's Studying Us*. Her writings have also been included in several collections.

Letter to Meridel Le Sueur: "I am deeply touched that you have collected the whatnots I have written for deadlines over the years. Meridel, what a person you are! That you would so tenderly collect such trivia. Remember when I told you that you are the Earth itself, accepting everything upon it? Flowers and trees and toads and rats and insects and hummingbirds and flowing rivers?"

Another letter: "Thank you, Meridel, for all that lovely work, keeping, saving, collecting all the while I was burning and throwing things away. And for putting the idea in their heads to collect my stuff. I always wished I had it all in one place so I could give it as a bequest to my grandchildren. The little presses are really rolling all over the country, like a counter-culture to the establishment. Because the establishment press isn't looking for literature, it's looking for horses to circus.... I guess the people *are* a river.... It is very hard to deal with the past."

1970-1981
Escalating bombing raids in North Vietnam and Cambodia.
Two students killed at Jackson State in Mississippi and four students killed at Kent State in Ohio.
Nationwide student strike against the war.
American Indian Movement occupied Wounded Knee, South Dakota.
Watergate cover-up exposed.
Nixon resigned. Vice President Gerald Ford became President and pardoned Nixon.
Vietnam War ended.
Jimmy Carter elected President.
Irene's father died.
Ronald Reagan elected President.
Irene died August 12, 1981, in San Francisco. She is buried in Duluth, Minnesota.
Memorial for Irene Paull in San Francisco, October 11, 1981.

Bibliography by Section

I Duluth

"To Die Among Strangers," *Jewish Currents*, November, 1972,
pp. 12-17.

"The Wrath of Deborah," *Jewish Currents*, November, 1959,
pp. 12-16.

"The War Against the Gentiles," *Jewish Currents*, June, 1966,
pp. 11-18.

"Duluth 'Kasrilevka,'" *Jewish Currents*, October, 1958, pp. 19-22.
Also, *The People Together: A Century Speaks, 1858-1958*, edited
by Meridel Le Sueur, Minneapolis: People's Centennial Book
Committee of Minnesota, 1958, pp. 40-41.

II We're the People

All selections are from the book, *We're the People; also Ballads by the
Workers*, by Irene Paull, Duluth: Midwest Labor, 1941(?).

III Love and Sorrow

"Mama's Boy," *Jewish Currents*, June, 1964, pp. 4-9.

"Song of the Warsaw Ghetto," *Jewish Currents*, April, 1966, p. 7.

"At the Gates of the Future (ca. 1945). Reprinted posthumously
in *Työmies Eteenpäin*, September 24, 1981, 36:22, p. 9.

"Picket Line in October," (publication unknown), October 28,
1945.

"Our Captain—Lives!" *Minnesota Labor*, April 11, 1947, p. 5.

"Farewell, Sweet Warrior," memorial pamphlet. Also, *The Worker*,
(date unknown). Also as "Henry Paull: Attorney for the
People," *North Country Anvil*, October, 1972, pp. 22-23.

"Operation Georgia!", *The Worker*, September 26, 1948, pp. 1 and 4.

"The Song of a Deportee," *Minnesota Labor* (publication date
unknown).

"Wall Street Honors the Unknown Soldier," *Minnesota Sings for
Peace!*, Minneapolis: Minnesotans for Peace, 1951, pp. 28-29.

"Oh, to Be a Billionaire," *Minnesota Sings for Peace!*, Minneapolis:
Minnesotans for Peace, 1951, pp. 10-12.

"Of Love and Sorrow," publication information unknown.

"'That's Jim,'" *Masses & Mainstream,* October, 1952, 5:10, pp. 28-33.

"Lay a Flower" appeared in Meridel Le Sueur's book, *Crusaders,* New York: The Blue Heron Press, Inc., 1955; republished in St. Paul: The Minnesota Historical Society Press, 1984.

IV THERE WILL ALWAYS BE THE PEOPLE

"To Bill Heikkila, American," *Poets of Today: A New American Anthology,* edited by Walter Lowenfels, New York: International Publishers, 1964, pp. 103-104.

"Petition and Prayer in Washington," *Jewish Currents,* January, 1961, pp. 9-13.

"For Rose Sobell," *Jewish Currents,* September, 1962, pp. 16-17.

"We Will Remember You, Cuba," *Mainstream,* May, 1961, 14:5, pp. 36-44.

"'Why Are You Marching?'" *Jewish Currents,* October, 1962, pp. 7-9.

"'Mom, Why Did You Go?'" *Jewish Currents,* May, 1965, pp. 16-20.

"My Grandfather's Ghost in Hattiesburg," *Jewish Currents,* January, 1966, pp. 13-19.

"One Mississippi Morning...," *Jewish Currents,* February, 1965, pp. 16-20.

"Nothing Can Happen to Papa's Heart," *Jewish Currents,* December, 1970, pp. 12-17.

"The People Are a River," *North Country Anvil,* October, 1972, p. 74. (Poem has also appeared in various forms since the 1940s in several publications.)

V KEEP ON BURNING

"To Hank," November 28, 1973, dated by author, unpublished.

"The Blessings of Solomon," *Jewish Currents,* May, 1960, pp. 22-27, 40-41. Also, *The Midnight Sun: Stories and Poems on Old Age,* edited by Stephanie Jones and Suzanne Korey, San Francisco: Jungle Books, 1978, pp. 13-23.

"Freedom Is a Lonely Hill," *Jewish Currents*, March, 1979, pp. 12-16. Also, *Every Woman Has a Story*, edited and published by Gayla Ellis, Minneapolis, 1982, pp. 161-168.

Everybody's Studying Us: The Ironies of Aging in the Pepsi Generation, commentaries by Irene Paull, cartoons by Bülbül, San Francisco: The California Association of Older Americans, 1976.

"My Winter Lover," *Jewish Currents*, June, 1975, pp. 22-26.

"Acceptance Speech: Receipt of Joseph Shachnow Prize from *Jewish Currents*," excerpt, *Jewish Currents*, June, 1977, pp. 8-11.

"Grandma's Battle Cry," *Senior Power*, March-April, 1980, p. 2. Musical adaptation, © 1980 Irene Paull and Barbara Tilsen. Also, *Every Woman Has a Story*, edited and published by Gayla Ellis, Minneapolis, 1982, pp. 202-203.

Writings, oral interview tapes and materials are at the Minnesota Historical Society archives in St. Paul, Minnesota. Irene published extensively in *Midwest Labor* (Duluth), *Minnesota Labor* (Minneapolis), and *Jewish Currents* (New York).

OTHER BOOKS FROM MIDWEST VILLAGES & VOICES

Rush Hour, by Kevin FitzPatrick, 1996.

Payments Due: Onstage, Offstage, by Carol Connolly, 1995.

Winter Prairie Woman, by Meridel Le Sueur, 1991.

Caravan, by Ethna McKiernan, 1989.

The Necklace, by Florence Chard Dacey, 1988.

Down on the Corner, by Kevin FitzPatrick, 1987.

Heart, Home & Hard Hats, by Sue Doro, 1986.

Payments Due, by Carol Connolly, 1985.

Every Woman Has a Story, edited by Gayla Ellis, 1982.